WAYNE STINNETT

RISING FORCE

A JESSE MCDERMITT NOVEL

Caribbean Adventure Series

Volume 13

DOWN ISLAND PRESS, LLC

2018

Published by DOWN ISLAND PRESS, 2018
Lady's Island, SC

Library of Congress cataloging-in-publication Data
Stinnett, Wayne
Rising Force/Wayne Stinnett
p. cm. - (A Jesse McDermitt novel)
ISBN-10: 1-7322360-2-8
ISBN-13: 978-1-7322360-2-8
Down Island Press, LLC

Graphics by Wicked Good Book Covers
Edited by Larks & Katydids
Final Proofreading by Donna Rich
Interior Design by Ampersand Book Interiors Book Design

FOREWORD

Well, I finally did it. Since writing the first novel in the Jesse McDermitt series, I've wanted to move Jesse to sail. But, the crusty old curmudgeon wouldn't budge from his over-powered fishing toy. I even tried to blow it up. He just bought another one. In this story, I forced Jesse over the deep end, aboard a ketch, delving into a different lifestyle than the rigid one he's lived all his life. Since the breakup of the Caribbean Counterterrorism Command, Jesse has been like a ship without a rudder; wandering aimlessly with no direction in life. In this story, Jesse will be trying things that, to this point, his usual stoic moral compass would not allow. But, rest assured, a new mission in life is coming soon. I hope you enjoy it.

As with all my other books, my wife has provided great support with this effort. Thanks, Greta, for always being there for me to bounce ideas around.

I call the people who first read my work beta readers, for lack of a better name. But they are much more than that. Collectively, these individuals hold a wealth of knowledge, which they freely give. Without their input, much of the little, but realistic details of my work, would never come to light. Many thanks to Debbie Kocol, Dan Horn, Drew Mutch, David Parsons, Mike Ramsey, John Trainer, Dana Vihlen, Tom Crisp, Ron Ramey, Alan Fader, Marcus Lowe, and Charles Hofbauer. And a special thanks to Katy McKnight and Gary Cox, who provided not just wonderful negative feedback on certain situations, but the plot idea for the next several books. Thank you all for your insights.

Once again, I need to thank musician and songwriter, Eric Stone, for allowing me to use him as a character with his second appearance in my books. Eric used to own Dockside in Marathon, but now tours the country bringing his music to local marinas, bars, and beaches all over the country. In fact, all over the world. Just last month, he played at Bloody Mary's on the island of Bora Bora, in the South Pacific. To download his music, check his tour schedule, or book a gig, check out www.islanderic.com. In the timeline of this story, early 2009, Eric was playing in the BVI. That should give you some foresight as to where this story is heading.

Much appreciation is owed to Captain Dan Horn and all the crew at Pyrate Radio. Ever since Eric Stone first told me about this new startup broadcasting venture, I've had nothing but fun and met some really terrific people. You can listen to Pyrate Radio on my website, or head over to their website, www.pyrateradio.com, or search for it on Tune-In. But don't be surprised if you start picking it up on FM stations near the coast. You should especially mark your calendar to listen in on Saturday, November 17, 2018, from 2:00 to 4:00 PM, when Eric will be playing at my 60th birthday celebration. Portions of it may or may not be broadcast live.

I'd also like to mention Lady's Island Marina, all the folks who work in the offices above the marina and below my own, and the many sailors and cruisers who make this place their home or just a great community to spend a week or two with. Thanks for making me feel at home.

As of this writing I'm working on a new novel, Rising Charity. The title alone should tell you some things. I hope to have it published by the end of 2018 or early in January, 2019. You will find the first Chapter at the end of this story.

DEDICATION

Dedicated to the memory of Bill Stinnett, our late chow mix. Bill was abandoned in our yard when he was five-weeks old and we of course took him in. He grew to be a giant in many ways. A tall man didn't have to bend over to scratch his ears. Our other dogs could walk under him, and he weighed a hundred pounds. He also took up a lot of space in our hearts. Due to his size, we had to keep him segregated when people came over. Some were afraid of our gentle giant. Bill didn't like this but took it in stride.

When I was still an over-the-road trucker, gone for weeks at a time, it was comforting to know he was there with my wife and daughter, whom he loved dearly. In my mind, there was zero doubt about their safety when Bill was with them. He never had to prove this, but I somehow knew that he would protect them, if called upon. A more faithful and loyal, though sometimes stubborn companion, is rarely found in this life. When I came off the road, I told Bill he was retired. He didn't quite understand his new role as a retiree, though. He'd lie on the floor in front of the bathroom when Greta was showering, check the yard for intruders when we pulled into the driveway, and just watch out for us in so many ways.

He came to my wife in a dream the other night, yowling at a cat. In her dream, we all agreed that Bill still didn't like cats, even though he was dead. I feel sure we'll adopt another dog again. Who'd want a hundred-pound chow haunting them for adopting a cat?

During the writing of this book, Bill injured himself and couldn't walk. The vet made a house call and said it was doubtful that he'd survive, due to his size, and the surgery would likely kill him. He'd already far surpassed the normal life expectancy of such a large dog.

We'd known the day was coming. My wife and I, along with our seventeen-year-old daughter made the hard call. If one must die, we agreed it would be best to do so while surrounded by those you'd given all thirteen years of your life to and who loved you. The pictures below are of Bill's first and last days with us. As you can see, he was far too proud to show that he was injured. If dogs can feel emotion, I think we saw embarrassment in his eyes. Rest in peace, Boudreaux, and thanks for all the love and joy you gave us.

"Dogs die. But dogs live, too.
Right up until they die, they live.

They live brave, beautiful lives. They protect their families. And love us. And make our lives a little brighter. And they don't waste time being afraid of tomorrow."

- **Dan Gemeinhart**

If you'd like to receive my twice a month newsletter for specials, book recommendations, and updates on coming books, please sign up on my website:

WWW.WAYNESTINNETT.COM

THE CHARITY STYLES CARIBBEAN THRILLER SERIES
Merciless Charity
Ruthless Charity
Reckless Charity
Enduring Charity

THE JESSE MCDERMITT
CARIBBEAN ADVENTURE SERIES

Fallen Out
Fallen Palm
Fallen Hunter
Fallen Pride
Fallen Mangrove
Fallen King
Fallen Honor
Fallen Tide
Fallen Angel
Fallen Hero
Rising Storm
Rising Fury
Rising Force

The Gaspar's Revenge Ship's Store is now open. There you can purchase all kinds of swag related to my books.
WWW.GASPARS-REVENGE.COM

RISING
FORCE

MAPS

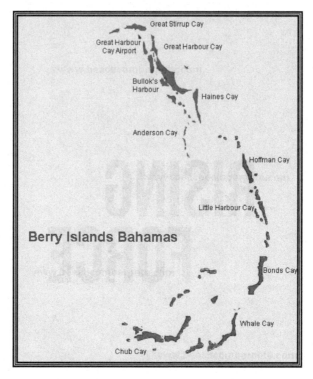

The Berry Islands of the Northern Bahamas

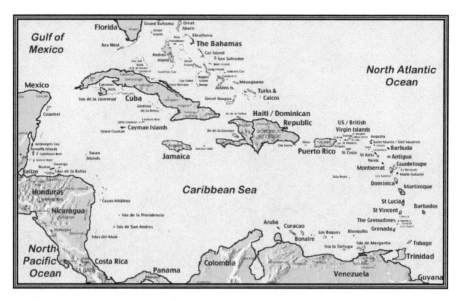

The Caribbean Sea and Bahamas

CHAPTER
ONE

I yawned; couldn't help it. The sun was well into its downward arc to meet the sea once more, the angle creating a bit of glare off the port side. The water in that direction sparkled with a million winking ripples of reflected light. There were a few scattered clouds off to the southwest and a high haze, so the odds of a beautiful sunset were dicey at best. But it was still several hours before darkness would fall. We were heading west-northwest at thirty knots, so maybe we'd pass beyond the clouds' shadow by the time it went down.

The water was calm, almost flat, with only the slightest ripples from the nearly nonexistent easterly breeze. The twin diesels droned monotonously, laying down a deep bass line to the constant swish of the bow wave. These things, combined with the calming influence of the cobalt sea all around us, were threatening to put me to sleep. My face sagged, and my entire body felt like it was wilted as well. I stared through dark sunglasses toward the oncoming horizon, my eyes half-closed and shoulders slumped forward.

The run wasn't a long one, but Tony and I were both running on just adrenaline and caffeine, neither of which were working like they had when I was a younger man. We'd made the turn at the southern tip of Eleuthera, into Exuma Sound, nearly an hour earlier. There was still a little over an hour to go to reach our next stop, the customs office at the foot of the cruise ship pier in Nassau. We'd have to slow soon, as the sound gave way to the shallower waters and coral heads south of Nassau, where this whole crazy journey had started.

"Got it," Tony said, putting his sat-phone away. "Last flight out to Miami leaves Nassau at nineteen-hundred and arrives less than an hour later."

His statement brought me out of my stupor. "Will Tasha be picking you up at the airport?"

"Yeah, I'll be home an hour after that."

"Tell her it's my fault," I said. "You weren't expecting to be gone two whole days."

Tony turned toward me in his seat. "She understands, man. I told her everything that was going on."

I pointed with my chin toward the foredeck. "Yeah, well, did you tell her about them?"

To be honest the view was spectacular. Not the clouds, sun, or sea, but the two young women lying on the foredeck. Charity had brought them out of a seriously bad situation involving murder, torture, and robbery. The girls were psychologically broken, of that I had no doubt. But outwardly, they were in the prime of life and magnificent specimens of young female adulthood.

Tony and I were taking the girls to meet up with Charity at Bond's Cay. We'd dropped her off at Arthur's Town Airport only two hours earlier, so she could retrieve her helicopter and take it back to Andros Island.

The two women on the foredeck were half my age, but far from innocent girls. Still, it had made me a bit uneasy when they'd asked if they could get some sun on the foredeck.

"Call it a lie of omission," Tony replied, yawning, "or punch-drunk from lack of sleep. Anyway, I told her everything about us helping Charity catch the people who killed Victor. She gets it."

"Probably a good idea to never bring those girls up to her."

Tony glanced at the radar, pointing out an echo several miles off to the north. Standing, I trained my binoculars in that direction.

"Think she has any chance?" Tony asked.

"Setting those two on the right course?" I scanned the horizon. "Who knows? If anyone can, it'd be Charity."

I continued to look through the binos, in the general direction of the echo on the radar screen. Finally, I spotted the boat. The large aft cabin and classic lines of an old motoryacht were unmistakable as it slowly headed north. I sat and watched the echo on the screen for a second, to make sure the echo was the boat I'd just seen. There was nothing else on the screen.

"Just a motoryacht headed north," I said, when Tony gave me a questioning glance.

"What are you gonna do after you drop them off?" he asked.

I thought about that for a moment. Whatever a person is doing on New Year's Day is supposed to be the activity

WAYNE STINNETT

they'll be most involved in for the coming year. That's why couples kiss at the stroke of midnight, though most don't even know there's a reason. If the adage was true, I was going to need to buy stock in a fuel company. I'd been crisscrossing the Bahamas for these first three days of the year, burning over a thousand gallons of diesel. Who was I kidding? It was what I'd been doing for several weeks now. Maybe that canceled out the New Year's maxim.

The current ordeal was nearly over. Having dropped Charity off at the pier on Cat Island, all that we had left to do was a leisurely cruise back toward Nassau so Tony could catch his flight home. Charity had flown her bird to Andros Island, where she had a storage lease. She'd texted Tony thirty minutes ago; Henry had been waiting for her and they were shoving off immediately to cross the TOTO to Nassau, so she could get her boat.

She was likely already under sail; she was due to meet us at Bond's Cay at sunset. After everything the two girls had been through, we'd decided early on to not put them in a situation where they might be recognized. Hence the out of the way rendezvous. Charity was good at staying off anyone's radar. At Bond's, I could finally discharge my passengers and continue my search for Savannah.

"I don't know," I finally muttered, glancing over at him.

The smirk on Tony's face told me he wasn't buying my cavalier attitude. "Yeah, right. You've been gone nearly a month, man. And you didn't tell anyone at the office where you were going. Even a blind man could see you took off looking for Savannah."

I hadn't actually made it a secret. I'd had Chyrel do some online snooping for me, which yielded nothing. I hadn't

4

told her to keep it under her hat. And, of course, Jimmy knew.

They say that in the Middle Florida Keys there are two ways of getting something known throughout the island chain in a hurry: telephone, and tell Jimmy.

I took a shot. "How's Jimmy?"

"He's taking good care of things at your place, I stopped up there last weekend. Saw Kim, too. My phone's been blowing up since you called Deuce the other day, everyone telling *me* to tell *you* to turn yours on. He might have mentioned it to someone."

"I wasn't exactly thinking when I took off," I offered.

"The heart doesn't think, man. The heart only wants. And if that desire is strong enough, it'll override the brain and make a man do things that some might find foolish. I don't think any of *us* think that. We're just worried. Had any leads?"

"Nothing," I replied resignedly.

"Only way to find someone among all these islands is from someone who's seen them recently."

"I'll keep that in mind," I said, a bit too sarcastically. "Sorry, I'm on edge. Truth is, nobody I've talked to has seen her—or none have told me anything."

Tony chuckled. "Well, you do look like some sort of wild man from Borneo, roaring in with this overpowered drug smuggler's special. I'd be surprised if anyone would even give you directions to a Tiki bar."

"What the hell's that supposed to mean?"

"*Man*, you've gotten a long way from your roots." Tony shook his head. "Before I first met you, Hinkle, Germ, and Scott had painted a picture of you that was bigger than life. Even Deuce said there wasn't anyone better at infiltrating the enemy. This boat ain't the best ghillie suit for the mission, man. Just sayin'."

Something Charity had mentioned had been eating at me. She'd said that I'd never find Savannah with the *Revenge*. I'd figured that with the advantage in speed, the search would be easier. How many places can you hide a forty-six-foot, slow-moving trawler? But, the speed advantage wasn't the benefit I thought it would be. Most of the people I'd encountered in the dozens of anchorages and ports I'd visited had been tight-lipped. Was it the *Revenge*? Cruisers were a close-knit bunch, and a high-speed sport fishing machine like my boat wasn't exactly the traditional cruising yacht.

"You should take her up on it," Tony said.

"Take who up on what?"

"Victor's boat," he replied, leaning back in the second seat. "No, it's not as fast as the *Revenge*, but you're not hunting an agile, elusive quarry. You need to infiltrate."

"She told you?"

"It'd sure blend in better." He didn't really answer the obvious question. Of course Charity had told him.

"You might have a point," I said, "but a dead man's boat?"

Tony shrugged. "He didn't die on board. And under good wind, that ketch can match just about any trawler."

He was right on that count. Having sailed Victor's Formosa, even without it being under full canvas, I could feel the speed and power in the helm. With her waterline length, nine knots wasn't out of the question. That's fast for a blowboat.

We rode in silence for several minutes. The audible and visual equivalent of the doldrums soon fell over me again. I tried to keep my mind busy, by reading the *Miles to Destination* on the GPS and calculating in my head how long it would take at our current speed. The TTD was right there on the display, too. But running the numbers in my head kept me alert.

"I think they've had enough sun," Tony said.

I looked down at the foredeck; one of the girls was turned around waving. The Revenge's handrails were low, meant for moving around at anchor, or approaching a dock; not while running at thirty knots. Considering their minimal boating experience, I'd told them to let me know when they wanted to return and I'd slow down. As I started to pull back on the throttles, the smaller woman, who called herself Moana Kapena, pointed out over the bow.

I glanced up just in time to see swirling water around something large, flat, and barely above the surface. Gulls took flight, crying and wheeling overhead, as I spun the wheel to starboard. We just barely missed the thing, and both girls slid partway to the side deck, before I straightened the wheel and brought the engines down to idle speed.

"Go down to the cockpit," I ordered Tony. "We need to turn around and see what that was."

Tony and I were both civilians now, and friends, but he understood the need for a chain of command aboard a vessel. I was the captain; everyone else followed orders quickly and without question. The *why* could be discussed later.

He climbed down the ladder, as the girls hurried along the side deck. I started a slow turn, bringing us back to a reverse heading as I stood and looked all around in front of us.

The girls came up to the bridge and, before either said anything, I pointed them forward and told them to keep an eye out. Switching on the sonar, I changed it to forward scanning, in case the thing had slipped just below the surface. I had a pretty good idea what it was going to be.

"There!" Fiona Russo shouted, pointing just off the port bow.

I saw it then; the dimensions, shape, and boxed corners sticking up and out from the sides confirmed what I thought I'd seen.

Container ships carry huge metal freight boxes to ports all over the world. The containers are then lifted from the ship by crane and placed on a truck or trailer chassis to be transported over land. I've seen them stacked six high on the decks of some ships, and probably ten deep below deck. If caught in a bad storm, many containers have been known to break loose and go overboard.

"It's a container!" I shouted down at Tony. "I'll come up on the lee side, see if you can get any numbers off it."

"What's in it?" Moana asked, just as a waft of wind carried the unmistakable, sickly odor of decomposing flesh up to us.

I held my breath, pushed the throttles forward and turned away from the container. "Maybe you girls should go down into the cabin."

"What are you going to do?" Fiona asked, covering her nose.

"Gotta report it, at the very least," I replied, watching a fin slice through the water near the giant tomb.

Moana looked as if she were about to retch. "What's that stink? A dead fish?"

"Or just take off," Fiona argued. "That's what I'd do."

"Leave it for some other sap to run into?" I asked, removing my shades. "What if it's a family with little kids?"

Tony came up the ladder. "We can't dive it. See that tiger?"

"Yeah," I replied. "We'll circle around and come up on the windward side, but I won't be able to get as close."

"Get me within reach of the boat hook," he said. "Maybe I can get an EPIRB lashed onto it."

An Emergency Position Indicating Radio Beacon broadcasts its location on the distress frequency via satellite. The ones I had on board were GPS enabled and could bring rescue services to within fifty yards. The trouble was, EPIRBs are identifiable to a specific boat, and Tony hadn't cleared through Bahamian customs.

I plucked the mic from its holder. "Let me call Royal Bahamas Defence Force first, so they don't activate a full-on rescue."

"What was that awful smell?" Moana asked again.

Tony didn't attempt to sugar-coat his response as I switched frequencies. "There's a dead person or persons inside that box."

The container had less than a foot of its top above water and could likely sink to the bottom any minute. Human traffickers sometimes used them to smuggle people—slaves really—from one place to another. The smell was unmistakably that of death. The container was probably eight feet in height and rode too low in the water for anyone inside to still be alive. There were already light threads of algae blooming on the sides. It had been in the water for at least a week.

Using the single-sideband radio, I reached the RBDF and explained what we'd found and what we believed was inside the container, making sure he understood it looked like it had been in the water for a long time and this was a recovery, not a rescue. I also asked if we should attach an EPIRB, since one of my charter clients had to meet a plane in three hours, and I couldn't really wait around.

The Bahamian officer asked all the pertinent questions; my name, boat name, home port, current GPS location, destination, and who the EPIRB was registered to. After I gave him the information, he told me to wait. I'd given him the story Tony and I had already discussed for when he got to Customs; we were transiting Bahamian waters from Miami, headed to Turks and Caicos, but one of my passengers had an emergency call and we needed to get to the airport on New Providence as quickly as possible. The radio was silent for a few minutes. I knew he was running my name and my boat through their computer to see if I was a known drug trafficker or something. After that, he'd have to get permission from higher up the food chain to allow me to activate the EPIRB in a non-emergency situation.

Finally, the officer came back on the air. "Royal Bahamas Defence to *Gaspar's Revenge*. Yuh have permission to attach di EPIRB and continue on yuh way."

I looked blankly at Tony, surprised at how easy it had been. He shrugged.

"I have two patrol boats heading toward di location," the Bahamian officer continued. "How sure are yuh of di contents?"

"It's a forty-foot container," I replied, "with sharks around it. We didn't get in the water to open it, so I'm only going on the smell. No idea what else is inside, but I know the smell of death."

"Roger dat, Cap'n McDermitt," came the reply. "Yuh clear to proceed, suh. Di patrol boats will wait on di scene for a freighter to bring di container to Nassau. If yuh like, yuh can retrieve yuh device dere."

I knew that was an invitation to sit in a *conference* room for hours on end, answering the same questions over and over. I figured it would be a better idea to kiss off the five-hundred-dollar piece of equipment; I had several on board.

Tony was in the cockpit with two boat hooks in hand, a dock line looped over the end of one of them. I stood with my back to the wheel, using the throttles for steerage. The wind, what little there was, was now over our bow. I slowly backed down on the metal container.

The slightly raised boxes on the corners of these containers have holes for securing the containers to a trailer or one to another while in transit. Tony deftly handled the boat hooks, as I tried to keep the wind from pushing the *Revenge* against the metal box. Steel and fiberglass don't mix, and I'd seen the results of a 'glass boat hitting one of those things. It took Tony a few minutes, but he finally got the loop down through the top hole and then managed to fish it out of the side with the other hook. He quickly hauled the looped end of the dock line aboard, slipped the bitter end through the eye, and pulled the slip knot tight to the container. Then he tied the EPIRB's lanyard to the end of the dock line and tossed it overboard, knowing that it would activate on contact with water.

CHAPTER TWO

"What's our time look like?" I asked Tony as he climbed up and sat beside me at the helm.

He took a moment to tap at his phone screen, then leaned over the chart plotter, shielding the sun's rays with his hand. "Still plenty of time at thirty knots. I'll be two hours early."

"Good," I said. "It'll take an hour to clear customs and get a cab to the airport."

"Was it just me?" Tony asked. "Or did that whole thing with the Defence Force go a little too easily?"

I shrugged. "Sometimes you're the bug, sometimes the windshield."

Tony shook his head. "Activating an EPIRB? Leaving the scene where someone might be dead? Sounds suspect to me, man."

The girls were sitting on the port bench seat. "Just in case the Bahamas officials stop us on the way in," I said to them, "maybe you two oughta go below and change."

"Do you think they will?" Moana asked.

I grinned at her. "It's doubtful, but sailors are sailors. If they see you two in bikinis, they just might. When we head into port, you'll want to stay inside. We're only gonna bump the dock long enough for Tony to step over, then it's about an hour to where we'll meet Charity."

"What will happen to us then?" Fiona asked.

I merely shrugged. "Just spend a little time with Charity and get to know her better. She's good people, and you three have a lot in common. Lay low with her for a while. If the Pences have the kind of reach you think they do, she can keep you hidden and safe better than anyone. Then the three of you can figure out what to do with the rest of your lives."

I waited until the girls were down the ladder before I brought the *Revenge* back up on plane. When I looked back, the gulls were landing on the container again. I doubted there were more than one or two bodies inside, not a container full of refugees or anything; the smell wasn't that strong.

Nudging the throttles back when we reached thirty knots, I again considered Charity's offer. Even if I agreed, it'd probably take months for everything to go through. By that time, I might find Savannah. Then what would I do with a sailboat? For that matter, I hadn't given a whole lot of *real* thought to what I'd do if I found her. Move her and Florence into my little stilt house? Join them on the trawler? And do what with my island, business, and boats? I had a ton of questions, but less than an ounce of answers.

An hour later, I steered *Gaspar's Revenge* around the eastern tip of New Providence Island and turned into Nassau Harbour. It was still a couple of hours before sunset, and there were boats and ships of all sizes transiting the waterway. I slowed to twenty knots, just fast enough to stay up on top of the water.

Radioing the port authority, I told them I had a client aboard who had to get home to an emergency and he hadn't cleared in with customs yet. I told him the same lie that we were transiting Bahamian waters, out of Miami. Tony couldn't show up at the airport for a flight out of the country with no entry stamp. The customs man was very helpful and said his entry would be expedited. He also said that there was a long line of cabs waiting; a cruise ship was due to arrive within the hour.

Tony climbed back up to the bridge after securing most of his gear down in the cockpit. He handed me a sheet of paper torn from a small notepad. "Here, I jotted the container number on my phone and then wrote it down for you."

I glanced at it. There were four letters and seven numbers, the last of which he'd drawn a box around.

"What's the box for?"

"Search me," he answered. "There was a box around the last number on the container, so I figured it meant something."

I folded the sheet and put it in my pocket.

Where the harbor narrowed, we passed under the high bridge carrying tourists over to Paradise Island. A few minutes later, we idled up to the customs dock. Tony had his small pack over one shoulder. He'd left his guns with me, and I'd stashed them along with my own.

Reaching out, Tony grabbed the rung of the ladder and climbed up the few steps to the pier and waved. "Hope you find her!" he shouted before turning and walking toward the customs building.

Maneuvering away from the dock, I continued west past the cruise ship terminal, toward the western harbor entrance. Twenty minutes later, we cleared the harbor mouth and I pointed the bow toward Bond's Cay.

Somewhere ahead was Charity's antique sloop, *Wind Dancer*. She'd likely be sailing a little more northerly from Nassau for greater speed, then tacking west and running before the wind for the last few miles.

"Is it okay to come out?" a voice asked over the intercom speaker.

I punched the button next to it. "Yeah, and would you bring me a thermos of coffee? Tony put it on a few minutes ago."

"Sure," came the reply, though I couldn't tell which one of the women it was.

They climbed the ladder to the bridge a moment later, both dressed in lightweight, baggy clothes designed to shield the sun and still keep them cool. Once both women were seated on the bridge and I'd refilled my mug, I pushed the throttles up just a little beyond cruising speed. The *Revenge* dropped down at the stern, the big props displacing the water under the boat. She climbed up on top of the surface in seconds, as we roared out onto the TOTO.

Call me a power or speed junky; I just like the feel of a big boat powering through the chop.

"Didn't Charity say her boat was in Nassau?" Fiona asked. "Why couldn't we have just switched here?"

"Better if nobody sees you," I replied. "She left Nassau over an hour ago and we'll be at Bond's Cay in about an hour."

"She's already there?"

I chuckled. "No, it'll take her a good three or four hours. Her top speed is about what this boat'll do at an idle."

"So we'll see her along the way?" Moana asked.

I adjusted the radar to its maximum range. "Maybe, but I doubt it. Wind's out of the east, so she'll take advantage of that and sail a more northerly course for speed."

More than a dozen echoes began to populate the screen, many moving toward the Berry Islands, as we were.

"What did Tony mean by he hoped you found her?" Moana asked. "Don't you know where we're meeting her?"

I glanced over at the diminutive Polynesian woman. "He wasn't talking about Charity."

"Who was he talking about, then?"

She held my gaze, her light brown—almost yellow—eyes seeming to convey innocence of all things. Her past told a different story. If what she'd claimed was true, she'd been kidnapped by pedophiles at the age of ten, then killed them some years later to escape. I knew she was probably the same age as my oldest daughter, Eve, who'd turned twenty-five just after I'd left the Keys; but, mentally, Moana was still little more than a ten-year-old girl.

"I've been looking for someone for a few weeks," I said. "I'll be getting back to that when we meet Charity."

"Someone who broke some law?" Fiona asked.

"No," I replied. "It's personal."

An hour and many questions later, the sun was nearing the cloud bank that still stretched across most of the horizon to the southwest. It tinged the clouds a rusty shade of red. Apparently, they were moving north also.

As we approached the southern end of Bond's Cay, I slowed and reached for the VHF mic. I hailed *Wind Dancer* three times on channel sixteen, with no reply. I didn't really expect one, though. She was likely still beyond the horizon to the east or southeast. I could probably reach her on the SSB radio—sidebands have a longer range— but opted for the satellite phone instead.

Charity answered on the third ring. "I'm under power," she said, by way of a greeting. "What happened to the wind?"

"We're just off the south end of Bond's," I said, looking at an echo on the radar screen. "How far out are you?"

"Ten miles," she replied. "I had decent wind on the first leg, but just a few minutes after tacking west, it died. It'll take me at least two hours to motor in."

"Want me to head east?"

"No need," Charity replied, her voice sounding distant somehow, though she was barely over the horizon. "You were going to anchor there anyway, right?"

"Yeah," I replied, though I had considered heading over to Chub Cay. "We'll be in the second cove on the lee side. You can't go much shallower than that, can you?"

"Roger that," Charity replied. "I grabbed some steaks at the marina store before I left."

"It's like you read my mind. We can grill on the *Revenge* before turning in."

"See you in a couple of hours, Jesse."

I ended the call and placed the phone on the dash.

An echo I'd seen on the radar had been pacing us, five miles back, for the last fifteen minutes.

I switched off the radar and turned to the girls. "Either of y'all familiar with boats?"

"I've done a little boating," Fiona replied. "Nothing as fast as this."

"Can you handle releasing the safety chain on the anchor? I can do everything else from up here."

"No problem," she said, as I brought the speed down to an idle and turned north into the natural channel on the west side of Bond's Cay.

There were two sailboats anchored in the first cove we came to. When we passed the next spit of land, I was glad to see that the second cove was empty. I turned toward an empty beach, watching the sonar. When we reached four feet of water, I reversed the engines, bringing the *Revenge* to a stop.

I toggled the windlass switch, taking a bit of slack out of the safety chain, and stood up to tell Fiona to unhook it from the anchor. But she was already bent over the rode. A second later, she turned and waved up at me. "All set!"

I released the brake on the windlass and began backing away from the beach. Once enough chain was out, I engaged the windlass brake and reversed harder, pulling the rode tight, and setting the anchor in the sandy bottom.

Satisfied, I shifted to neutral, shut down the engines, and told Fiona in a low voice to reconnect the safety chain. Sound travels well over water; normal conversation can be heard hundreds of yards away. I went down the ladder quickly and opened the salon hatch. Finn bounded out and stood on his hind legs, looking toward shore.

"How long will she be?" Moana asked, starting down the ladder.

I turned to face her just as her foot slipped. She toppled backward, and I moved quickly to break her fall. As small as she was, I was able to catch her in midair, cradling her small frame in both arms. I doubted she even weighed as much as Finn, and *he* was barely a hundred pounds. She smelled a lot better.

As I gently placed her on the deck, she smiled up at me. "Thanks."

"*De nada,*" I said, then went to the transom door and opened it. Finn came over and stepped out onto the swim platform. We were in about five or six feet of water over a sandy bottom.

"Think you can find us something to snack on?" I asked Finn, rubbing the loose fur behind his ear. He barked once.

"Then get to it, boy. These ladies are probably hungry."

Finn jumped into the water, going under for a second, before bobbing back to the surface like a cork. Labs can float effortlessly, thanks to a dense underfur that traps tiny air bubbles, making them more buoyant.

Looking around, Finn spotted the shoreline and struck out toward it at a fast swim.

Fiona joined me at the transom. "Didn't Charity say she was bringing steaks?"

"She did," I replied, "but a little snack before she arrives isn't gonna hurt."

"And your dog will find a snack?" she scoffed.

Finn reached the beach and trotted out onto the sand, his nose to the ground. "He will in a minute," I said, as Finn disappeared into the foliage. "Right now, I think he's just looking to relieve himself."

A moment later, Finn returned to the water's edge. He moved back and forth on the wet sand at the edge of the water, stopping to sniff at it here and there, before he waded back into the water. When it reached his belly, he began pawing at the bottom with his big front paws, the webbing in his toes kicking up silt. After a moment his head went under. When he came up, I could see that he had a clam in his mouth. He started swimming back toward the boat.

Moana stepped up to the transom on my other side. "What's he got in his mouth?"

"A clam."

Fiona laughed. "One clam? What do we do? Cut it up into three pieces?"

Finn reached the swim platform and deposited his find, then turned and swam in circles for a moment. Suddenly, he dove. Through the gin-clear water, we watched as he swam down to the bottom and pawed at the sand a moment. When he came back up, he had another clam in his mouth.

"Good boy," I shouted, as he dropped it on the platform with the other one.

He turned and dove again.

I looked over at Fiona. "Give him ten or fifteen minutes, and he'll bring up a good dozen. That should hold us over until Charity arrives." Glancing toward the sun, now just a few degrees above the horizon, I said, "Right now, I'm missing happy hour."

In the galley, I put four Red Stripes in a small cooler, topped it with ice, and carried it up to the bridge. The girls were already there, Fiona in the second seat, and Moana on the port bench, both facing aft.

"You like to watch the sun go down," Moana said softly. "But it makes you sad."

Taking my seat, I removed a brace of the stubby brown bottles. I opened them with a bottle opener that's always floating around on the console somewhere and passed a beer to each of the two girls, then dropped the opener in the cooler and closed it.

"Not sad," I confessed, putting my feet up on the aft rail. "Sunset is a time to reflect; to look back on your day and examine what you've accomplished. It's the best time to make plans for tomorrow, so that the mistakes you made today won't be repeated."

Fiona raised her bottle. "To better tomorrows."

We drank, and I relaxed a little. Having a pretty good idea of what was to come, I just enjoyed the daily dance of sun and sea before it did. There was a possibility that this day's events weren't quite over.

In the distance, a buzzing sound grew a little louder.

CHAPTER THREE

The sun slipped behind the clouds and was gone. I found myself hoping the clouds didn't extend far beyond the horizon, and El Sol would reappear just below them, but he didn't. It was the twentieth sunset I'd watched since leaving the Keys in search of Savannah. And it was the first I'd watched with another person during that time.

"You girls need to go below," I said, as darkness fell quickly over the water. I reached up and turned on the bright overhead lights and the anchor light. "Company's coming. Go to the forward cabin and lock the door. He won't stay long."

"Company?" Fiona's eyes showed fear. "Who is it?"

"A cop from Nassau, I think."

"A cop?" she said, as both girls moved quickly down the ladder.

I followed them down to the cockpit, carrying the nearly empty cooler and my half-empty beer in one hand.

Finn had climbed up onto the swim platform, and stood looking off to the south, ears up as high as he could raise them. For labs, that's about half-mast. At his feet, I noticed a healthy pile of top neck clams.

"Stay in the cabin until I tell you to come out," I warned the girls.

When they were halfway through the salon, I ordered Finn inside. He reluctantly obeyed. I scooped his clams into a bucket then sat down in the fighting chair to wait. The low buzzing grew louder.

After five minutes, the green sidelight and white stern light of a boat appeared out beyond the spit of land to our south. The stern light slowly disappeared as the red sidelight became visible in the gathering darkness. The boat was turning, coming straight toward the *Revenge*. I recognized the silhouette of Detective Sergeant Clarence Bingham's swift patrol boat. I wasn't completely certain in the near darkness, but I only saw one person aboard.

I swiveled the fighting chair and leaned toward the switch, mounted to the bulkhead beside the salon hatch. The bright white lights of the cockpit came on, along with the blue underwater lights around the swim platform. All lit up like this, the *Revenge* looks very inviting—and, hopefully, non-threatening.

I could hear the boat approaching, though I could no longer see it, due to the bright cockpit lights. I wasn't worried, though. I'd half-expected it after the slide the Defence Force guy had given us, though I hadn't known who would be coming.

The sound of the engine changed, as the boat's pilot shifted to neutral. "Cap'n McDermitt? Yuh look like yuh was expectin' someone."

"Come aboard, Detective Bingham," I said, raising my beer in salute. "I kind of figured you might be here to see me."

His boat entered the cone of light my boat cast around it, and Bingham quickly tied off and stepped over the gunwale. "Were yuh now?"

Reaching down, I flipped open the cooler, grabbed the last beer and tossed it to him. He caught it deftly in his left hand, and I did the same with the bottle opener in the bottom of the cooler. He caught that, too.

A slow grin came to the man's face as he leaned back on the gunwale and popped the cap, which he pocketed. "I've learned a bit more about yuh since we last met, Cap'n," he said, handing the opener back. "Did yuh know dat yuh name is a watch word to some people?"

"Watch word?" I asked, taking a long pull from my beer.

"Certain words or phrases," he began, "dey trigger some computer somewhere, for people to take a closer look. Words like *bomb*, or *hijack*—or Jesse McDermitt."

I grinned a bit. "I kinda doubt that."

"Less dan a minute after I started searching di internet about yuh, I got a phone call from di Foreign Affairs Minister himself."

"Coincidence," I said with a shrug.

Bingham took a slow pull from his bottle. "I would think di same thing. Except di minister asked specifically why I was looking for yuh."

That was mildly surprising. I knew Big Brother watched the internet, picking up on key words and phrases in all languages in the ongoing fight against terrorism. The internet is *not* private. Anything uploaded is public, whether you want it to be or not. And it's there forever.

"So, what was it the Foreign Minister wanted?"

Bingham's eyes locked on mine. "To tell me dat yuh are a hands-off ghost."

"Ghost?"

"Yuh work for di American government," he said.

I tried to keep my face neutral. While I was once loosely connected to Homeland Security, and before that an active duty Marine, these days I was nothing more than a charter boat captain, and lately not even that. But a spook? Hardly. But it would explain the events from earlier in the day, and quite well.

"Was that why I wasn't told to wait around when I found the container?"

"I wouldn't know 'bout dat, Cap'n," he replied. "I did hear dat a container was recovered south of New Providence dis afternoon with a body inside."

He studied my face as he mentioned the body.

"I called it in," I said. "I could tell by the smell that someone had died inside it. Any idea who or how?"

He continued to gaze at me, his dark eyes not giving away anything. Finally, he nodded. "One mon, tied spread-eagle on a wooden frame and propped up just inside di door. His throat was cut ear to ear, and his tongue pulled out through di slash."

"They call that a Colombian necktie," I said.

He nodded again. "Yuh are familiar with dis kind of execution?"

"Not personally. Just things I hear. The way I understand it, it's meant as a warning for other people to keep their mouths shut."

"Dat is my understanding, too," Bingham said, taking another slow drink from his beer as he continued to appraise me. "Di man has already been identified. A small-time drug distributor in America. Di coroner said dat he died at least a day before di container went overboard."

"Let me guess," I offered. "The container was bound for the States."

"To di mon's own legitimate business."

"Any drugs in the container."

"Dey are still searching," he replied. "But, from what I hear, no."

"Truth is, Bingham," I began, deciding that some transparency might get more information. "I did do a little contract work for the American government. Transportation arrangements and the like. That's all ancient history now."

"I see," he said. "I also know dat di man yuh dropped off in Nassau once worked for your government, as well. I thank you for di evidence you provided against di two men."

"I still have some contacts. Want me to see if they can find out anything about the guy in the container?"

"Your government has already been very helpful in dat regard."

He hadn't mentioned the Pences and Rayna Haywood. "That's not why you followed me all the way out here is it?"

"No," he replied, standing, and draining his bottle. "I wanted to tell yuh dat di other three weren't on dat cruise ship, like yuh said."

"Still at Half Moon Cay?" I asked, though his appearance here suggested otherwise.

"I sent a patrol boat," he said, rising and going to where he'd tied his boat. "Di three were not dere either."

"So, you came all this way to warn me?"

"I don't think yuh are a man dat need a warning," he said. "Dey stole a boat from Half Moon, a fifty-five-foot Hatteras. Di owners are still missing."

"I'll keep an eye out," I said.

Bingham untied the line and swung a leg over onto the patrol boat, letting it drift away from the *Revenge* slightly.

"Di men we arrested have begun to talk," Bingham said. "Dey both said dat besides di three dat were supposed to be on di cruise ship, dere was another woman, Fiona Russo. But I am not supposed to ask you any questions."

"Did either of those men tell you about two others in the group? A man and a woman Pence had ordered killed late last night?"

"Yes, dey did," Bingham replied, starting his outboards. "Both said dat dey saw di woman di next day, right dere on yuh boat."

"You mean they saw her on a boat that looks like this one."

He smiled broadly. "Yes, Cap'n. Dat exactly what I mean."

I moved over to the gunwale. "If I see this Russo woman, the other three, or the Hatteras, you'll be the first to know."

He merely nodded and put the engines in gear. A moment later, he throttled up and the boat was soon swallowed by the darkness. I waited until the sound was far beyond the other cove, then I went to the salon hatch and doused the bright lights. Climbing up to the fly bridge, I did the same up there, and turned on the low level red lights and radar.

Bingham's boat was two miles away and heading south at a good rate of speed. I waited until the echo was five miles away, then I went down and opened the salon hatch.

The salon was pitched in darkness, with only the red light of the coffeemaker to guide my way. Not that I needed guidance. In the galley, I turned on the red overhead lights and stepped down the companionway. Finn was sitting in front of my stateroom door, ears up, and head cocked to the side.

"Think a dozen's gonna be enough?" I asked, as I tapped on the door. Finn went past me and up into the galley. Every day, it seemed like he understood more and more.

"It's okay to come out," I said through the door.

The latch clicked, and the door swung open. Fiona was standing just inside. "You said you didn't work for the government anymore."

Turning, I made my way back toward the salon. "I don't."

"We could hear every word you and that cop were saying," she said, following me, Moana right on her heels.

Sitting at the little dinette, I opened the cabinet under the flat screen TV and took my small laptop computer out. I turned it on, and it immediately connected to the boat's wireless router, which in turn was connected to a satellite internet provider. The two women stood across from me.

"What he thinks and reality are two different things," I said. "Can one of y'all go out to the cockpit and bring that bucket of clams in?"

Fiona turned and went out through the hatch.

"What's that?" Moana asked, pointing to my laptop.

"A computer," I replied. "I have a satellite connection."

Quickly accessing the portal to Chyrel's desktop, I began to run an encrypted search. A lot of cruisers have internet forums. It didn't take long until I found one where people were talking about a boat that was stolen at Half Moon.

"What should I do with these?" Fiona asked, returning with the bucket.

"Wash 'em down in the sink," I replied, as I read the accounts from the previous day. "Know how to shuck clams?"

"I do," Moana said, taking the bucket and going to the sink.

"Leave a few for Finn," I said, looking over to where he lay on the deck at the corner of the couch. "He shucks his own." Finn's head came up, cocked sideways, as his tail beat a tattoo on the deck.

Fiona slid in next to me, looking at the screen. The blog described the same boat Bingham had reported stolen. A fifty-five-foot motoryacht had been boat-jacked while anchoring at Half Moon Cay. Several people commented on it and mentioned the boat's name: *Cruisader*, out of West Palm Beach. Of course, by the time the Bahamian authorities arrived, the boat was long gone.

Another search for the boat name and home port revealed a website, with numerous pictures of the boat and the couple who owned it, Mark and Cindy Mathis. They looked early sixties and affluent, he a retired software engineer and she a retired high school teacher. The boat looked vaguely familiar, but that style of vessel was very common.

"Think it was the Pences?" Fiona asked, reading over my shoulder.

Shrugging, I continued to scroll through the conversation. Two boats, *Saline Solution* and *Dirty Little Seacret*, had apparently witnessed the crime, and several other concerned cruisers were asking all kinds of questions. It struck me how different the conversation was compared to the stilted, one-sided interrogations I'd had with cruisers while trying to find Savannah.

"There!" Fiona said, pointing to a comment the boat called *Saline Solution* had posted an hour ago.

> *It was three people, too far away to get a description, but definitely a man and two women. They used a tender they stole from HMCR. Please pass the word on other nets, we're very worried about our friends, Cindy and Mark.*

"Time's right," I said. "This happened at Half Moon Cay an hour after the ship sailed. They could easily have hidden out on the island until *Delta Star* left, then jacked this boat as they were anchoring."

"What are we going to do?" Moana asked from the galley.

I glanced over at her and then at Fiona, sitting next to me. I couldn't quite tell if the question was what they should do to avoid the Pences, or what we should do to help bring them to justice.

"The authorities probably have it under control," Fiona said after a moment. "Not much we can do from here, anyway."

Her stock rose just a bit, in my mind. Over the next hour, we shucked and ate the clams, though Fiona struggled to get them open.

I tossed an unopened clam onto the deck in the salon. Finn clamped his favorite treat in his big paws and bit down on the opening in the shell, lining up his canines on one side with practiced ease. I explained my theory about how he was able to find them. I'd noticed several times, on different beaches, that he was able to sniff them out at the water's edge, then dig around in the nearby shallows until he found another. Little by little he'd move out into deeper water to search for more. The ones on the beach were sometimes dead and apparently didn't taste as good.

"He's a dog, sure," I explained, "but animals have instincts far beyond anything we can comprehend. I think he spots the two locations in his dog's mind and just draws a line between them, staying in the clam bed, as he moves out deeper."

It was the best theory I could come up with, having observed him hunt clams in the same way many times before.

"Charity said you were an orphan," Fiona said. "Like us."

Looking from one young woman to the other, I nodded. "Not like you, fortunately. But yeah, my parents died when I was a kid, and my grandparents took me in and raised me. They were good people. I never knew a time when I didn't know they loved me."

"How'd you lose your folks?" Fiona asked.

I can only imagine the two womens' pasts, one having been kidnapped as a small girl, the other orphaned and put into foster care, both abused and victimized most of their lives. It was a frightening thought. Among their peers, that was probably a normal, valid question. Sort of like when two military people meet, the first questions are always where you were from, and where you'd been stationed.

"My dad was a Marine, like myself," I began. "So was Pap, his father. Mam and Pap raised me after Dad was killed in action in Vietnam and my mother took her own life, shortly after she got the news."

"How old were you?" Fiona asked.

"Eight."

"Did you like living with them?" Moana asked.

Of the two, she seemed to be the most empathetic. Considering what she'd endured, it was amazing that she felt anything, let alone the feelings of another person.

"Yeah, it was good," I said. "Pap became an architect after World War Two, and they lived pretty comfortably. My dad was their only kid. Pap taught me, and my dad before me, how to build things. I remember his workshop, the smell of sawdust, and how his tools felt in my hands. Dad had dabbled in woodworking before joining the Corps. He and Pap had planned to open a boat-building shop one day. Guess I sorta filled in for my dad, but the boats were built by McDermitt and Son. Like Dad was always there with us."

That seemed to pique Moana's interest. "You built boats with your grandfather?"

I grinned. "A few, mostly sailboats."

"What's Charity's story?" Fiona asked.

I sucked down one of the clams before answering. "Maybe she ought to be the one to give you those details."

"I don't know," Fiona said. "We're about to go off with her for who knows how long. I, for one, would like to know a little more about her."

"Me, too," Moana chimed in.

"She told us the other day that she'd been raped," Fiona blurted out. "Do you know if that's true?"

I debated giving them any of the details as I knew them. In fact, I probably knew more than anyone about what had happened to Charity in Afghanistan. During the long, endless days we'd spent on the *Revenge*, hunting Jason Smith, she'd told me a lot about what had happened after she'd been shot down and captured. She cried on my shoulder quite a few times, even pounded on my chest with her fists once. Not an activity I'd want to repeat.

She'd confessed that much of what she'd told me, she'd never even told her therapists. I had never violated that trust, nor would I.

"She was an Army chopper pilot," I said. "She was shot down and captured by Taliban fighters in Afghanistan. If she wants to tell you the details of her three-day ordeal, she will. That's not for me to say."

"But you know?" Moana asked softly.

I looked at the tiny woman sitting next to Fiona. The sadness and shame, etched deeply on her soul, showed clearly in her light brown eyes. I nodded slowly.

The clams were gone, so I stood and moved around the table, gathering up the plates. I dumped the shells in the bucket and then picked it up to take outside and dump.

Moana rose and took the bucket from my hand. "Why would she tell you?"

I shrugged and looked down at her. "I listened."

She started to take the bucket aft but stopped when Finn rose from the deck.

"Don't mind him," I said. "He's never hurt anyone, except for a few wayward clams. If anything, he'll dive down and bring the shells back up to you."

Moana moved slowly past Finn. He followed her, again with his head and tail low, his way of acting nonthreatening.

"So," Fiona said, looking over at me, "you haven't tried anything with either of us. Are you gay?"

Grinning, I shook my head, as I carried the plates to the sink and washed them. "How old are you, Fiona?"

"Twenty-two."

"My oldest kid, Eve, is three years older than you. My youngest, Kim, turns twenty this summer. No offense, but you're just a kid."

"You have kids?" she asked, as Moana came back inside. "And a wife?"

Taking my seat again, I looked over as Moana sat at the far side of the dinette.

"Two daughters," I said. "No wife. Their mom and I divorced when I deployed to Panama twenty years ago."

"Twenty years?" Moana asked. "No girlfriends?"

"I remarried a few years ago," I said. "She was murdered."

"*Wind Dancer* to *Gaspar's Revenge*," came Charity's voice over the less powerful Uniden VHF radio. It was mounted in the cabinet under the TV and had only a stubby antenna mounted outside the bulkhead. It was always on channel seventy-two, which Charity knew. I only use it for ship-to-ship communication to nearby boats. She sounded very close; probably within a mile.

Rather than reach across both girls, and thankful for the interruption, I slid out and walked around the dinette, plucking the mic from its holder inside the cabinet. "*Gaspar's Revenge* to *Wind Dancer*. ETA?"

"Turning north into the channel now. Three boats at anchor here. I see your anchor light just beyond the point. Got room there?"

Three boats? I thought. There were only two earlier. How did another slip in without my noticing it?

"All alone on this side," I replied, grabbing up the small, hand-held VHF. I turned it on as I headed aft.

The girls followed me out to the cockpit. Charity's old cutter-rigged sloop could be seen in the distance, lowering her sails in the moonlight. I knew her boat was full of high-tech gadgetry, and the sails were operated by electric winches, but it was still a pretty cool sight: an antique wooden sloop sailing into a safe harbor under the moonlight.

It only took Charity a few minutes to anchor up. I heard her dinghy's engine start a few seconds after she shut down the sailboat's diesel. It idled for a moment, then Charity's voice came over the hand-held.

"Need anything besides the steaks?"

I raised the portable radio to my mouth. "All I have to drink is water, beer, and rum, and the water's running low."

"Keep your Red Stripe and Pusser's," Charity replied, sounding more cheerful than the last time I'd talked to her. "I have a pretty good red that will go well with the beef."

A few minutes later, I heard her dink's motor drop into gear and throttle up. It came around *Wind Dancer's* stern and started straight toward us, coming up on plane. She crossed the water between our two boats, then throttled down and coasted up alongside.

Tying off to the stern cleat, Charity stood, shouldered a pack, and picked up a small canvas bag. With one hand on my boat's transom, she looked up at me and smiled. "Permission to board?"

"Granted, and welcome," I said, extending my hand.

She took it and stepped over to the swim platform and through the transom door.

"Bingham was here a couple of hours ago," I said. "He arrived shortly after we got the hook down. The Pences and Haywood weren't on the cruise ship, and apparently stole a boat at Half Moon Cay and disappeared."

She paused for only a second, then grinned and handed me the canvas bag. "I don't have enough steaks for them. Besides, they're Bingham's problem now."

Charity and the girls went inside as I set up the small propane grill. I keep it stored in the engine room most of the time. It had an arm that fit snugly into a rod holder in the gunwale and held the grill out over the water. By the time I had it mounted and the burner fired up, Fiona brought the steaks out, marinating in a bowl of what smelled like teriyaki.

"She seems a whole lot happier all of a sudden," she said, as I placed the steaks on the grill.

"She's got her own way of coping," I said. "This is the real Charity. She just stows all the dirty laundry in a back part of her mind."

We dined inside, to keep the bugs at bay. The dinette only seats three, so I got out four sturdy folding tray tables, and we all sat on the couch. Finn lay on the deck in front of us, looking up expectantly whenever one of my guests speared a piece of meat.

"Give him a piece of fat and he'll be your friend forever," I told the girls.

Fiona picked a piece up from her plate and held it out to him. Finn looked over at me, as if asking permission. As a rule, I never feed him from the table, but he knew he'd always get something.

I nodded my head and Finn rose slowly, then walked toward Fiona. Stopping a good distance away, he very gently leaned forward and took the hunk of fat from her fingers. He barely tasted it before it was gone. Then he went back to where he'd been.

We talked a bit longer, enjoying the first good meal we'd had in days. The women drank Charity's wine, but I stuck with my beer.

Finn rose, and I could see Moana at the far end of the couch, reaching a tentative hand out toward him, a small piece of meat in her fingertips. He glanced at me again, and once more I nodded my consent.

Finn seemed to sense the girl's hesitation and fear. He approached very slowly, with his head and tail down. A foot away, he stopped and leaned forward, slowly raising his head and opening his mouth slightly, while stretching his neck. He looked like he'd topple forward, he was so off balance. As gently as he could, Finn took a corner of the meat with his tiny front teeth.

Moana pulled her hand back and looked over at me. "I thought you said he was an attack dog."

"No," I replied. "I said if you stayed on the couch Finn wouldn't hurt you. He wouldn't have bothered you if you'd gotten off the couch either."

"I have something for you," Charity said, pulling her backpack over to her feet.

Taking out a legal-sized envelope, she passed it to me.

"What's this?" I asked.

"The title to *Salty Dog*," she replied. "It's been signed over to you, all legal, and stamped by an ex-pat American notary in Nassau."

"I can't take this," I said, extending the envelope back toward her.

"You just did," she replied, grinning, and ignoring my outstretched hand. "Look, I can't sail two boats. Vic would haunt me if I just up and sold it to anyone, and I really don't need the money. You're getting nowhere with your mission in this stink-pot. You'll never find Savannah if you can't ask the right people. Besides, I think Vic would have wanted you to have it."

"In case you haven't noticed, I can't operate two boats at once any more than you can."

"I talked to Deuce," Charity said. "To thank him for his help. I might have mentioned that you'd need someone to run the *Revenge* back to your island. He and Julie both agreed you and *Salty Dog* are a good fit. And Andrew said he'd be on the next flight after your call."

"You should do it," Moana said. "I knew you were looking for your lover, and if something helps you find her, you should use it."

Fiona nodded her head in agreement. Charity only shrugged and said, "It's a done deal, Jesse. *Salty Dog* is your boat."

I didn't want Victor's boat, but Charity was dead set on giving it to me—and there was some truth to what they were saying. If I was aboard a cruising sailboat, other cruisers might be a bit more forthcoming and at least listen to why I wanted to find Savannah.

The rational side of my brain worried that if I needed to be somewhere fast, I'd be screwed in a slow-moving sailboat. Then again, Charity's chopper was on Andros, convenient to anywhere in the Bahamas. And the Bahamas were where Savannah liked to cruise.

CHAPTER FOUR

The first silvery light of dawn came too early. When my eyes opened, they focused on the single overhead portlight, the only light source in my cabin. Sunlight wasn't shining directly on it yet, but the lightening sky above was visible through the tinted glass. That meant the sun was at or near the horizon. The solstice had been just two weeks ago, so *early* was a relative term; the days were still quite short.

I glanced over at the clock mounted on the bulkhead. The low light made the thick hands barely visible. The local time was after seven, and the sun would be up soon.

We'd stayed up past midnight, just talking—something I rarely do these days, if I can help it. The staying up past midnight part, that is. I'm still a ways from being a total recluse. The previous three nights had me sleeping in shifts, so I'd taken advantage of the relative calm and slept quite well for a solid six hours. Another hour would have been great, but an unnecessary luxury.

Rising, I used the head, then put on clean skivvies and went up to the galley, feeling more refreshed than I had in days. My mouth was dry, the prelude to a hangover. But my mind was clear. I'd only drunk five or six beers the previous evening before the women left the *Revenge*. After the second bottle of wine was gone, Charity had taken the girls to her boat to get settled in. So I wasn't worried about walking around my own boat in just my underwear.

I went straight to the coffeemaker. I'd spared no expense on this very necessary piece of nautical equipment. It was mounted securely in the cabinet, with a latch that held the pot in place while underway, and the pot had a spill-proof top. So far, it hadn't spilt a drop, but I hadn't felt the need to test it in rough seas yet.

Pouring a mug of the Central American brew, I took a swallow, then started to go back down to my stateroom to dress—but when I looked out the side porthole in the direction of Charity's boat, it wasn't there. I looked all around. The salon has plenty of visibility to the sides and aft. The bow was still facing the beach, and I couldn't see in that direction, but she wouldn't be there, anyway.

I placed my mug on the counter and went out the hatch to the cockpit, Finn right behind me. Stepping up on the side deck, I looked forward and all around. Nothing.

Dropping down to the deck, I looked down at Finn. "You didn't hear them leave either?"

He only whined and went over to the transom door. I opened it and let him out onto the swim platform. "Don't be long," I told him. "We're leaving shortly."

Finn stepped out onto the swim platform and jumped in the water. As he started swimming toward shore, I went back inside.

My sat-phone was lying on the dinette table, the envelope under it. I picked it up to call Charity and saw that I had a text message.

Sorry for taking off. I need to move them away from civilization. All comm is off for a while. We'll meet again soon. Enjoy the Dog—C

Salty Dog, I thought. A name changing ceremony would be in order soon, whether I kept it or not. I'd agreed to accept the boat, but only if Charity would let me pay for it. She'd agreed to let me pay for it but wouldn't budge on the price of ten dollars.

She'd said that the needed parts had arrived in Nassau, and she had paid the mechanic enough to get started, but he would need a few hundred more when I got there. The boatyard had promised it would be ready by the seventh, the day after tomorrow.

Just what I needed, another hole in the water to pour money into.

Down in my cabin, I showered quickly and dressed for the day. It was forecast to be bright and sunny, so I wore loose-fitting khaki cargo pants, a baggy, long-sleeved denim work shirt that was faded nearly white, and my worn-out Topsiders. Picking up my clothes from yesterday, I transferred everything in the pockets into my clean pants, opened the port hanging locker, and tossed the dirty clothes in the basket on top of the tiny, single-unit washer and dryer combination.

When I returned to the cockpit, Finn was already on his way back. In a pinch, he can use the swim platform and

I hose it down immediately. But he prefers being on dry land when he does his business.

Once Finn boarded, I closed the transom door, then went forward and released the safety from the anchor chain. Finn found his usual spot in the corner of the cockpit, and I went up to the bridge and started the engines.

It only took a few minutes for the windlass to haul the fifty feet of chain rode aboard, and then we idled south, out of the cove. The sun was just above a clear horizon to port, and there were two boats still anchored in the first cove. I remembered both of them from the previous evening, but the one Charity had mentioned was gone.

Suddenly, in a moment of mental clarity, the image of the boat I'd seen before the container encounter filled my mind's eye. The elegant lines of a yacht built many years ago. The wide aft cabin and high stern of a classic moto-ryacht.

Could that have been the Hatteras the Pences stole? I throttled up to cruising speed as we left the channel. At the time I'd seen the boat, the time and distance from Little San Salvador were about right, if they'd headed due north.

I took my sat-phone from my pocket, knowing that I wouldn't have regular cell service here. Digging through my other pockets, I found Bingham's card and punched in the numbers.

"Detective Sergeant Bingham," he answered on the second ring.

"JM here," I said. "I may have seen that Hatteras."

There was silence on the other end for a second. Maybe he was trying to figure out who he was talking to. Finally, Bingham asked. "When and where did you see it?"

"Check the time stamp and location from when I called in the container," I said, giving him a clue, in case he hadn't figured out who I was. If he was right about my name being linked to some kind of search tag, phones might not be secure either. "The sighting was about fifteen minutes before I found the container. I'd been on a heading of three zero five degrees magnetic, doing thirty knots, for nearly an hour. The boat I saw might have been a Hatteras— definitely an older model motoryacht— about four miles to my northeast, and it looked to be about the right size. It was heading due north at trawler speed when I saw it."

There was a pause, and I heard what sounded like he was writing the information down. From what I'd given him, anyone with boating knowledge could locate the spot the container was first reported, work backward from there, use the sighting direction and distance I'd given him, and have a pretty good idea where the boat was and where it was going.

"Thanks for letting me know," he finally replied. Hesitantly, he asked, "Uh, why didn't yuh volunteer dat last night?"

"I'm not a ghost," I said. "You can ask me anything you want, and if I know, I'll tell you. I didn't mention it because, at the time I saw it, I wasn't on the lookout for it. I just remembered this morning."

"I think dey will turn up somewhere soon," he said with some finality. "Word is out all over di Caribbean. When dey do, I will see dat dey are brought to justice."

Ending the call, I punched the speed up to thirty knots, setting a course for Nassau Harbour. I couldn't shake a creepy feeling that the boat that had snuck into the anchorage last night could have been the Pences. It had been at least eight or nine hours from the time I saw the boat to when Charity told me of the fourth boat in the cove. That would have been enough time for a slow-moving Hatteras to skirt Eleuthera, then turn west to Bond's Cay.

"Nah," I said aloud. "Too much of a coincidence."

While *Gaspar's Revenge* moved out onto the ocean, I thought about Savannah. Four days ago, Charity had seen her very near here. She'd told me that another boat at their anchorage had watched Savannah leave, heading across the banks toward Chub Cay, which was only ten or so miles off my starboard bow. The desire to turn and head that way was strong; it was the closest thing I'd had to a lead so far.

But it was four days ago. Running just during daylight hours alone, Savannah's Grand Banks could have covered over two hundred miles in four days. She could be back in Florida, somewhere between West Palm Beach and the Keys, or headed down through the Bahamas chain, as far as the southern end of the TOTO. Pushing hard, she could be home in South Carolina, or halfway to the Virgin Islands.

No, I'd need to put on the proverbial ghillie suit first. Nassau was just an hour away; I could check in with the boatyard and make arrangements to splash *Salty Dog* as soon as it was ready. If that was tomorrow morning, I could make Chub by nightfall.

As I neared Nassau Harbour's western entrance, I slowed to ten knots, entering the channel. Checking that the VHF was on sixteen, I hailed the marina where I'd first run into Charity four days earlier. The dockmaster moved us down to channel twelve and said they had slips available. Fifteen minutes later, I was backed in and tied off.

I wanted to give *Salty Dog* a thorough look before I made any decision to have Andrew come out and pick up *Gaspar's Revenge*. So, after settling with the marina for one night's stay, I walked up the dock to the street. Brown's Boat Basin was directly across from the marina. There was a gate and a guard shack.

A little window slid open, as I approached. A weathered old black man sat on a stool just inside. I could feel the cold air spilling out of the window.

"Names, McDermitt," I said. "Jesse McDermitt. I'm here to take possession of *Salty Dog* and sail her back to the States." No need in anyone else knowing where I was going, and that sounded completely plausible.

"Wait dere," the man said, as he picked up an old rotary dial phone and closed the window.

A few minutes later, the gate buzzed. I pushed against the latch and it opened, so I went on through. A young black man with a bandana tied around his forehead was just coming out the main warehouse door.

"I am John Brown," he said, coming toward me with his hand out.

I shook hands with him. "Jesse McDermitt."

"Pleased to meet yuh, Cap'n," he said. "Wish dat it was under better circumstances. Miss Fleming said yuh knew di late owner and dat yuh'd be here. Di work has started; we got all di parts, but it won't be done until late today or tomorrow morning."

"Yes, she told me," I said, turning toward where the big ketch sat on the hard. "I figured I'd come early and get familiar with the vessel, if that's okay with you."

Brown fell in beside me, and together we walked to where two men were working under *Salty Dog's* stern.

"We pulled di shaft early dis morning and bench tested it," he said, as we neared the workers. "It tested true enough, but we rebalanced it to perfect, anyway. Dese mons are reinstalling it now."

He asked one of the men how things were going. The older of the two stood and wiped his brow with a handkerchief. "Very good," he replied. "Di mon dat owned dis boat took very good care of it. We'll finish before time to go home."

"Mind if I go aboard and get familiar?" I asked Brown.

"I just need ta see di paperwork," he said.

Pulling the folded envelope from my pants pocket, I opened it and took the stamped and notarized copies of Charity's power of attorney and Victor's title and registration, handing them to the man.

He glanced at them and looked up. "Yuh will need to go to dis mon's office and have yuh signature notarized. He's just two blocks down toward di bridge. Den I can let yuh aboard."

Thanking him, I left the yard and walked down Bay Street, looking for the address that was on the business card, paperclipped to the title.

The office was small, barely taking up ten feet of frontage, and right next to a bar called *Celebrity Status*. As I entered, I was assailed by a cold blast of conditioned air. There was only one desk in the front office. A middle-aged white woman occupied the chair behind it.

"You must be Mister McDermitt," she said, with a decidedly New England accent. She rose and extended a hand. "I'm Maggie Jamison. John Brown said you were on your way."

I shook her hand and said, "John Brown called you?"

"Yes, he did. My husband, Spencer, just stepped out, but should be back in— Oh, here he is now."

A man of about forty came through the door. He was dressed in island casual attire, much like his wife.

"Spence, this is Jesse McDermitt," Maggie said. "He needs his signature notarized on Captain Cook's title transfer, which you did yesterday."

"Come on back," Spencer said, his accent the same as his wife's.

Vermont or New Hampshire, I thought.

He led me down a hall to an even smaller office in back. "Have a seat," he said, stepping around his desk. "May I have the title, please?"

Handing him the envelope, I sat in a straight-backed, wooden chair, opposite his desk. He had his licenses and certifications on the wall behind him; one was a business degree from Champlain College.

"How's a New Englander wind up doing title work in Nassau?" I asked him.

"Maggie doesn't like snow," he replied. "And what Maggie wants, Maggie gets."

"I heard that!" his wife shouted from the outer office.

Grinning, he opened the envelope and pulled the contents out, shuffling through the papers until he found the one he wanted. He spun it around and placed a pen in front of me.

"If you'll sign right here," he said, pointing to a blank line, "we'll have you on your way."

I signed where he indicated, and he got a notary stamp from his desk and made his mark next to my signature, then signed below it. "If you like, I can send the proper paperwork to the Coast Guard's doc center in West Virginia to have the new title and registration done."

"That'd be fine," I said.

He got a pad from a drawer under his desk. "I'll need your tax address and the address you want them to mail the new title to."

"They're both the same," I replied, and gave him the address for the *Rusty Anchor*. For nearly ten years, it's been where I got my mail and the address I used for everything legal; I just never saw any need to change it. Besides, mail service to my island has never been established.

Spencer wrote it down and scooped up all the papers, straightening them on his desk before handing it all back to me. "You're good to go," he said, rising. "It'll probably take a couple of weeks before a new title is issued, but what you have there should be sufficient if you're stopped by Bahamian or American authorities."

I followed him back out to the front office, where I paid fifty bucks for the service and said goodbye to his wife. Leaving the office, I turned right and started back down the street toward the boatyard. Normally, *island time* moves at a much slower pace. I was surprised at how quickly things were getting done.

It wasn't yet noon, but I hadn't eaten anything but a banana all day. So when I spotted the mobile kitchen, backed up under a stand of coconut palms in an empty lot, my stomach turned my feet in that direction.

The truck looked like it had once been a delivery truck of some kind with a boxy shape and a walk-in sliding door on the passenger side. The door itself seemed to be missing, though. It was hand-painted a lime green, with bright-colored fish all down the side. There was also a large sliding window on the passenger side, which was open. The smell of blackened fish and mango filled the air. My feet moved faster.

"What's on the grill," I asked an older fellow working away inside the truck. He wore dreads, turning gray, and the beginnings of a beard, also graying.

"Mornin' Cap'n!" he said. "Blackened lionfish. But if yuh don't like dat, I and I was just puttin' togeddah some of di tastiest lobstah rolls on dis big blue rock."

"Will one lobster roll be enough for me?" I asked.

His grin told me all I needed to know. Island food trucks and stall vendors were noted for serving great local food at a fair price, and the servings were always large.

"Oh, ya, mon," he replied, handing me a fat roll, wrapped in foil. "Dat be five dollahs, 'Merican or local, all jest di same."

I pulled my clip from my pocket and peeled off a ten. "Keep the change," I said, and walked over to a small picnic table under the partial shade of a gnarled and ancient ironwood tree.

It wasn't hot, but the weather was warm and the breeze light. I was just about to get up and see if the old Rastafarian had anything to drink, when he stepped out of the van.

"Try dis, Cap'n," he said, approaching me with a large styrofoam cup, a thick straw sticking out of the lid.

"You read my mind," I said, digging into my pocket again.

He held a hand up, palm out, and waved me off. "On di house, mon. Or di truck, as it were."

"Thanks," I said, accepting the cup. "What is it?"

He shrugged. "A little ice, and some fruits all ground up in di blenduh."

I sucked on the straw. The mixture was cold, for sure, almost like a smoothie back in the States, but without artificial colors and flavors. I tasted coconut and mango and said as much.

"Aye, and a little papaya, lime, and sour orange for dat tart, tangy aftuh taste. And a banana, to make di whole thing smooth."

"Delicious," I said, unwrapping the foil from the lobster roll. "Coco bread?"

He grinned again, revealing two missing teeth. "Di wife bakes di rolls all morning. She up before di sun."

The sandwich was heavy on lobster meat, but also contained leaf lettuce, a little rice, and a few bits of vegetables I wasn't familiar with. When I bit into it there was an explosion of flavors, but the taste of the fresh lobster tail, slow roasted with butter, was the overriding sensation. It was a bit spicy, and I asked about it.

"Dat be my wife, too," he replied. "She make di sushi rice."

"Mmm," I muttered, taking another bite. After swallowing, I nodded to the old man. "Your skill on the grill is what really stands out."

He smiled and thanked me, bowing slightly before he turned and climbed nimbly back into the truck. His accent was Jamaican, but a little off. He was obviously of mixed ancestry, as his skin was the color of cinnamon and his eyes a little oval-shaped. Maybe Asian; he had mentioned sushi rice.

I finished the roll and the drink. Both were better than anything I'd had in over a month. Stuffing the foil and napkins into the cup, I deposited it in a trash can next to the truck and continued down Bay Street to the boatyard.

The man in the guard shack stepped out as I approached and pulled the gate open for me.

"Mistuh Brown had to go to di uddah side of di island," he said. "Di mons working on yuh boat will be finished soon. If yuh like, dey will pick it up with di mobile hoist and splash it dis evening."

I was beginning to get the impression that Nassau didn't want me around any longer.

"Yeah," I replied. "This evening would be great. You guys work fast here."

"Mistuh Brown say dat dere is only three ways to do a job," the guard said. "Fast, cheap, and good." Then he grinned. "But Mistuh Brown, he gwon let yuh choose only two."

I grinned at the old man. Pap used to say something very similar, and he was right. If a job is done well and in short order, it's gonna be expensive.

CHAPTER FIVE

When I got to the marina, Bingham was waiting on the dock next to my boat. In his hand was a bright yellow EPIRB.

"Thought yuh might want dis back," he said as I approached. He held the EPIRB out.

I took it from his hand. "Thanks. I'd written it off."

"Why is dat? It's an expensive piece of equipment."

I studied his face. "To avoid several hours of questions."

He grinned a bit nervously. "I was told to bring it to you."

"Foreign Affairs Minister?"

"Yes," Bingham replied.

"And you have questions you were told not to ask."

"Yuh a smart mon, Cap'n McDermitt," he said.

I considered it a moment. "Like I told you before, I used to do contract work for America's Homeland Security. But that's over and done with. I'm in the Bahamas legally, on personal business and it wasn't me who put someone in a container."

"I know dat," he said. "Our lab says dat container was in di water ten or twelve days before you found it."

"So, what is it you want to know?"

He paused a moment, then said. "I want to know where Fiona Russo and Leilani Kapena are. And I think yuh know."

Remembering what Moana had said about using her grandmother's name for years, I said, "Leilani Kapena died an old woman. More than a decade ago, on one of the islands of French Polynesia. Fiona Russo is no longer in your country."

I was only guessing at the last part, but I assumed Charity had taken the girls somewhere secure enough that they wouldn't be found.

"Di two men say dat dey saw both women on your boat."

"They saw Leilani Kapena's granddaughter on my boat."

"I see," he said. "And her real name?"

"No idea," I lied. "Just doing a favor for a friend."

"And di Russo woman?"

"Protective custody," I lied again. "Both of them."

Bingham eyed me suspiciously but didn't press the matter. I didn't like lying to the man. He was just doing his job. Leaving some doubt in his mind concerning my status with the American government might get him out of my hair faster.

"I won't keep you, den," he finally said. "It's jest dat in our questioning of di two men, we think Russo and Kapena had nothing to do with di major crimes, just petty things. With the leaders still at large, di two women might be in danger."

"I can assure you of one thing with absolute certainty, Detective." I stepped aboard and opened the hatch to the salon. "If the Pences do find them, they're the ones who will be in danger, not the two women. They are safe."

"I see," he said, waiting, as if expecting more.

Finn came out of the salon and stood looking up at the detective, his head cocked at an angle. "Be back in five minutes," I said to Finn. He bounded over the gunwale past Bingham and trotted off toward the nearest tree.

"Yuh dog can tell di time?"

"Course not," I snorted. "He lost his wristwatch last week."

I had a question of my own, and I only know one way to get the answer to a question. "Is what you believe to be my association with the American government what's fueling the haste with my departure?"

The corner of Bingham's right eye twitched just a little. "I am not sure what you mean."

I stepped over to the gunwale. "Really? I'm not ordered to wait around at the container, work on the sailboat I'm picking up is progressing far faster than it would have anywhere else in the Caribbean Basin, the paperwork is zoomed through in just one day, and a police detective is here to return my EPIRB? Island time, not."

"Did I mention dat di Foreign Affairs Minister is my cousin?" Bingham asked. It was a rhetorical question, he knew he hadn't. "We talked dis morning. He thinks dat it is wise to jest keep yuh moving. Doing whatever it is dat yuh are doing."

"I'm only looking for my girlfriend," I replied. There, I'd said it. I wanted Savannah, and not just because I might be the father of her daughter.

"Den all dat we want is for yuh to find her and leave di Bahamas."

"Are you kicking me out of the country?" I asked, incredulously.

"No, Cap'n. But if dere is anything dat we can do to facilitate yuh departure, we will be more dan glad to help."

I doubted he could help with locating Savannah. At least not until her six-month cruising permit expired and she had to renew. She might even have left the country already. But if she hadn't, he could lie and say she had, just to get me to leave.

"I'll be leaving Nassau in the morning," I said. "From here, I'm going to Chub Cay to continue my search. After that, I don't know."

He looked at me for a moment, then grinned. "I hope yuh find what it is yuh looking for, Cap'n."

Bingham left just as Finn came trotting back. I waited until the man disappeared beyond the marina office, then went down into the boat, Finn right behind me.

Getting my laptop out, I powered it up and waited for it to make all the connections. While it did, I reached into my pocket and pulled out the scrap of paper Tony had given me. I flattened it out on the dinette table and looked at the container number. I was curious and had at least a couple of hours to kill.

I quickly learned that the first three letters designated who owned the container, and the fourth letter determined what kind of container it was. The one we'd found had a U for the fourth letter, so it was a utility container, for general, unrefrigerated commodities. It was owned by one of the larger international shipping companies in the world.

After the letters were seven numbers, the last one with a box around it. That last one was a sort of mathematical check to validate the rest of the number code.

Running a search for the container number itself resulted in nothing at all. I found a website that would submit the number to the owner for tracking. Entering the number, it asked for my shipping authorization. Dead end. I put the container number in an email to Chyrel and asked if she could find any information on it. As an after-thought, I asked her if she knew of any reason an internet search of my name would set off an alarm somewhere.

Rising, I went over to the fridge for a bottle of water. The computer pinged an incoming message. It was from Chyrel.

Already ran that for T. Current shipping info for that container says it was primarily marine electronics; GPS units, radios, radar and sonar equipment, and other stuff. The ship left Taiwan on Nov 18, with stops in Cartagena and Caracas, before its final stop in Charleston. The container was lost at sea in a storm, one day after leaving Caracas, on Dec 28. The destination for that container was the Port of Charleston, then by truck to a business in North Charleston called Tropix Electronics, owned by Joel Mendoza. I checked and Bahamian authorities identified the body in the container as his. I'll let you know if I find anything on the other question. –C

So, the container had only been in the water for eight days, not the ten to twelve that Bingham's lab had reported.

Obviously, the body had been added to the shipment in Caracas, since Bingham had said the guy died only a day or so before the thing went in the drink. Caracas is one of the most violent cities in the world and a hub for shipping South American cocaine to the States and around the world.

Running a search for the dead man's business didn't throw up any definite red flags. It was a marine electronics wholesaler, selling equipment to the hundreds of boat dealers in the Southeast.

The owner was a Venezuelan-born immigrant who came to the States sixteen years ago at the age of twenty-four. He'd apparently arrived with enough money to go into business right away, or he had financial backing. Joel Mendoza did well, his business seemed to have thrived, and seven years later he'd married an American woman, giving him full citizenship.

Sidney Clark Mendoza was from a prominent family in Charleston, South Carolina and was nine years younger than her husband. The couple had two children: a boy of seven and a three-year-old girl.

I spent the next two hours packing while I considered what I'd learned. I wasn't taking everything; I'd been moving stuff aboard the *Revenge* for over two years, though not much. I'm sort of a minimalist, buying only the things I need. Going through my meager dresser, I put all my clothes in the bottom of the same seabag I'd been issued in boot camp, nearly thirty years earlier. They didn't even fill half of it. The smell of the canvas seabag brought back old memories—days of camaraderie and adventure, challenges, and victories.

He was a smuggler, I thought, while going through the drawers. I didn't know a whole lot about the marine electronics business, except that everything I'd bought for my boats had always been expensive. The photos I'd seen of Mendoza and his wife seemed to have them living an opulent lifestyle, at the very least. *Did he earn that from his business?*

And just why in the hell was I so interested? True, I'm a naturally curious person; as a kid, I loved puzzles and riddles. Pap had a million riddles and never gave me the answers. I could ask questions, and sometimes did so for weeks, until I'd solved his riddle. But there was something about the way Bingham had described where the body was located that bothered me. He'd been tied to a frame just inside the container, so that his body would be displayed when someone opened the doors. The Colombian necktie was a clear message to whomever that was. Mendoza, or maybe the person who found his body, had said something that he shouldn't have.

On top of my clothes, I placed a few mementos that hung on the bulkhead in my cabin; a couple of framed pictures of me with my folks from when I was a kid, a slightly older me with my grandparents on the day I graduated high school, and me with the president, when he came down to the Keys for a little fishing.

Kneeling at the foot of my bed, I punched in the code on the electronic lock's touchpad and raised the bunk. I then added three Penn fishing reel boxes to the half-full seabag. Opening a fourth one, I took out four thousand dollars in American currency, shoving the bundles into both cargo pockets of my pants. Then I closed the box and put it in the bag as well. Reaching under the bunk, I removed a flyrod case, placing it beside the seabag. Then I closed the bunk storage compartment and carried the seabag and case up to the salon.

Taking a break, I went to the marina office to pay for a second slip for tonight, right next to the *Revenge*, explaining that a friend would be coming to pick up my Rampage, as I was moving aboard a ketch.

"Di boat dat belonged to di young Cap'n dat was killed last week?" the dockmaster asked.

"Yeah," I replied, unsurprised that he knew why I was here. "I'm taking it back to the States," I lied.

"Dat was a shame. I met di mon only once, but I could tell by di way he kept his boat dat he was a good mon."

When I got back to the *Revenge*, I called Deuce's office. Julie picked up on the first ring. "Are you *ever* planning to come home?" she asked, instead of the typical *hello*.

"One of these days," I said. "Why? Can't your husband get anything done without me?"

"Funny, Uncle Jesse," she said. "Actually, everything here's going very smoothly in your absence. But we all miss you. Any leads?"

I assumed everyone now knew that I was traipsing around the Bahamas like a love-sick puppy.

"Charity was with her New Year's Day," I said.

"Sorry to hear about Victor. How's Charity handling it?"

I thought about that a moment. "Better than you'd think. She has a mission."

"Oh, God."

"Nothing like that," I said. "I guess you could call it a humanitarian mission. Anyway, Savannah was reported to be leaving High Cay early the following morning, four days ago, heading across the banks toward Chub Cay."

"So, what can Livingston and McDermitt Security do for you?"

"Is Andrew free for a day?"

"You bought it?" Julie asked, hardly concealing her excitement.

She and Deuce had moved aboard a forty-two-foot Whitby ketch when they got married. They both loved the boat, and even with a son on the way, they had no plans of moving ashore. Unlike a lot of *dock queens*, the *James Caird* had put a lot of water under her keel since Deuce and Julie got married about two years ago.

"She wouldn't let me say no," I replied. "Besides, it'll blend in with the rich, old yachties a lot better than the *Revenge*."

"Ha!" she exclaimed. "A lot more twenty-something, blue-collar types live on boats than you'd think."

"That's what I'm finding out."

"Andrew just left, but I can have him on the first flight out in the morning. It'll be noon or later before he can get there. He'll have to spend the night and leave on Wednesday."

"Thanks, Jules. Tell him the key will be with the dockmaster."

"Good luck, Jesse," she said. "I hope you find them."

Saying goodbye, I ended the call, then finished packing some things from the galley. About an hour before sunset, I went back up to the marina office to pay for another night for the *Revenge*, so Andrew wouldn't have to pay it.

Just as I was about to enter the office, I heard a big diesel from across the street. If you've hung around some of the larger marinas, the sound of a Travelift is pretty familiar. They're giant machines, with four wheels at the ends of long struts, enabling it to straddle a large boat.

Turning around, I went out to the street. The big mobile boat hoist was moving into position across the street, towering over all but the tallest masts. Several workers threw large cradle straps under *Salty Dog's* keel, then went around to the other side to connect the ends to the massive block pulleys.

Slowly, the cables on both sides raised the blocks, which then lifted the big ketch like it was just a toy, hanging free on the straps. I watched as the larger main gate retracted and the Travelift moved toward it at a very slow crawl. The workers went out into the street to stop traffic, but there weren't any cars, so they just stood in the street and waited for the crawler to get across.

A few minutes later, the boat hoist moved out onto two narrow concrete docks, spaced as far apart as the gantry's wheels. Once in position at the ends of the piers, it slowly lowered *Salty Dog* into deep water next to the marina.

I went back inside the office and paid for another night, leaving the spare keys with the man, and telling him that a friend by the name of Andrew Bourke would arrive in the morning to take my boat back home for me.

Then I went out to where the Travelift was just driving off the dock. John Brown was there, helping two of his workers tie *Salty Dog* off to the work dock.

"How much do I owe you?" I asked, as he finished tying off a line to a rusty bollard.

"Miss Fleming already paid for most of di work, Cap'n. Di total only came to five hundred more dan we figured, by adding di extra workers."

"Maybe Detective Bingham should pay for the extra labor," I said. The surprise in his face was evident. "Don't worry about it," I said. "Not your fault." I counted off twenty-five twenty-dollar-bills and handed them to the man.

Brown took the money and shoved the bills into his pocket. "I am sorry, Cap'n. I just do what dey say." He handed me an unsealed envelope. "Here is di receipt and itemized list of parts and services."

I peeled off five more bills and extended my hand to him. "I run a twin-engine powerboat and it's been years since I maneuvered a sailboat. Can a couple of your guys meet me over on the other side of the marina to help me get her into a slip?"

He took the offered tip, called to one of his workers, and told him what to do. Then he turned back to me and handed me a float with a key attached to it.

"Will ya need help moving it over dere?"

The *Salty Dog's* bow was pointing out into the harbor. "No," I replied. "Just when I get over to the slip. It's the one next to my Rampage."

Looking past me, Brown let out a low whistle. "Dat is a fine machine, Cap'n."

He shook my hand, and I stepped aboard the big ketch. Starting the engine, I looked at the simple analog gauges on the pedestal. Oil pressure was good, and the ammeter showed that it was charging the batteries. I let it warm up for a minute while I untied the lines.

When I pulled the ketch away from the work dock, I idled straight out into the harbor about a hundred yards. Not knowing how the boat would turn under power, I wanted plenty of room.

Salty Dog turned easily as I spun the big wooden wheel. A conch shell lying on the deck rolled slightly against the bulkhead. Visibility over the bow was a lot less than

I was used to on the *Revenge*, but better than a lot of sail-boats I'd been on. Forward of the cockpit, the cabin roof of the pilothouse extended only two feet above the wide side decks and ended just before the mainmast. Forward of the mast, there were a pair of doghouse hatches, side-by-side and low to the deck. Other than that, there were the typical air intakes, white and standing a foot high, but mostly there was just a lot of open deck area. A wooden storage box was on either side, just forward of the main, both built to resemble the doghouses. A very clean and uncluttered deck.

With help from Brown's two workers, I managed to get the big ketch into the slip without incident. Once they left, I stepped across the short finger pier between *Salty Dog* and *Gaspar's Revenge*, and opened the salon hatch.

Finn came out into the cockpit and stood with his paws on the gunwale looking over at the sailboat. He was also curious by nature, and I had no doubt he saw me bringing the ketch in.

"That's our new home for a while," I told him, as I ducked inside to grab my seabag and case. I placed them on the deck in the cockpit, then went back inside to get the boxes from the galley.

When I came out, I locked the salon hatch and lifted my belongings up onto the dock. Finn was at *Salty Dog's* bow, looking at the older boat. He turned toward me and cocked his head.

"I agree, Bubba, it's gonna take some getting used to."

I stepped up to the side deck and went aft to the cockpit. Finn jumped over onto the ketch and started sniffing around. Suddenly, I realized we were going to have a problem.

If we were on the water for a long time on the *Revenge* and Finn needed to go, he could use the swim platform, though he was very uncomfortable doing it. *Salty Dog* had no swim platform. In fact, away from the dock, the boat had at least three feet of freeboard at the lowest point along the side deck.

While Finn snooped around on the foredeck, I scratched my head, trying to come up with a solution.

"Yuh didn't say yuh had a dog, Cap'n."

I turned and saw John Brown approaching. "Yeah, we've been together almost a year," I said. "But I just realized a dog on a sailboat presents a few challenges."

"I might have di fix for one," he said. "But how dat big, yella dog gwon get up and down di companionway, I don't know."

"A fix for what problem?" I asked.

"To where di dog gwon do his business. We make something yuh might be interested in. Sort of a cat box for dogs dat fits into one of di showers."

"A litter box?"

"It has a fine mesh with fake grass dat look and feel very real."

"Grass?" I asked.

"Di pee go right through," he said. "Just wash it down good. His poop yuh can just shovel into di commode or just spray it down till it breaks into pieces dat will go through di mesh. We redo di drain so it go into di black water tank."

"Does it work?"

Brown chuckled. "Ya, mon. I live on a boat with two dogs. Dat's how I got di idea. Come over to di shop, I show you."

Inviting him aboard, I went below, and Brown handed my gear down to me. Then we went to the forward head and he measured the shower.

"Dat a big one," Brown said, as we went back up to the cockpit. "I got just what yuh need, Cap'n."

I locked up, and Finn and I followed him across the street. He guided us around behind the big warehouse repair shop, to a spot where dozens of various sized boxes were stacked.

Finn sniffed around the plants growing there. "No," I told him, pointing to an overgrown area in the back of the yard. "Go on over there in the weeds."

Brown watched Finn trot away. "He a good dog, Cap'n. I guarantee dat he will like dis."

He went to the end of the row and measured the last two boxes. "Dis one," he said, taking the one next to the end and handing it to me.

It was hard, but lightweight. "Fiberglass?"

"Yes, suh," Brown said. "Di legs on di corners let it sit up above di shower floor, so a flex pipe can connect to di drain in di floor. Den we just go into di bilge and attach di shower drain to di black water pipe from di commode."

"How much?" I asked. "Installed. Tonight."

Brown smiled. "I can have two men carry one over right now. Dey will put it in and do di plumbing in less dan an hour, for five hundred."

CHAPTER  SIX

As the sun slipped toward the horizon, I started exploring the boat. Starting on the foredeck, I opened the storage boxes. The port box held four fenders and a single folding deck chair. The one on the starboard side held the same, minus two fenders that were hanging over the side of the boat. I glanced toward the sun. It was only ten minutes or so from setting, so I pulled out a deck chair and unfolded it on the foredeck.

After going down to the galley, I sat down in the folding chair with a beer for what had become my and Finn's daily ritual. He seemed a bit confused and kept looking over at the *Revenge*. Finally, he lay down beside me on the deck, forelegs crossed, head up, and looking around.

The sun was a few degrees above the hilltops, between a derelict schooner with used tires hanging off the side for fenders, and a newer sport fisherman, the tuna tower nearly as tall as the schooner's foremast. Beyond them, downtown Nassau was silhouetted against a rose-colored sky with the hills rising up behind it. The view was like something you'd see on a tourist postcard as the dark red sun slid down between the two boats, setting behind the hills of Nassau.

"Pretty anti-climactic for the buildup," I said, scratching Finn's neck as the sky quickly grew darker.

Finishing my beer, I put the chair back in the storage box. Finn bounded over to the side deck and down to the dock, jumping toward the *Revenge* in a halting gait.

"No, buddy," I said. "We need to go below and unpack some stuff."

The hatch to the pilothouse was forward of the helm and to starboard. I waited there until Finn reboarded, then I went below. The steps were steep, but not straight down like a lot of other boats. The companionway was more like the stairway in a two-story house, and the seven steps to the bridge deck got wider as you went down.

I figured that I could live out of my seabag and boxes until I got familiar with the boat's layout. But there were a few places I needed to locate: places to hide my valuables. Charity probably knew all of them and had certainly taken all of Victor's personal stuff off the boat.

All boats have hiding places. She'd told me of one, under the main engine. Knowing where it was and how to open it made it a simple matter. I was impressed at the simple ingenuity of it. The panel simply snapped into place with a spring-loaded stainless-steel ball, which was fitted into a brass sleeve and machined into the wood panel. Once it was in place, you could barely see it with a flashlight, and it looked and felt just like a part of the cross-bracing under the engine.

Remembering a pair of Pelican boxes I'd seen on the workbench, aft the cramped engine room, I carried one of them up to the pilothouse and unpacked a few things. One of the Pelican boxes was large enough for the four Penn reel boxes, but I only put three in it. Then I took the watertight box down and stashed it in the starboard hiding spot, below the engine.

I also remembered something else. Something that had seemed odd when I'd been aboard before. Opening the fourth box, I took the Sig Sauer out and checked the chamber, though I knew it was empty. Taking one of the magazines from the box, I slid it in and put the gun and the second mag in my cargo pocket, before going up on deck.

I knew that the top of the helm raised up, and beneath it was a suite of high-tech navigation instruments. But on the starboard side, I remembered there being too much of a gap below the tilt-up lid and the cabinet door below it.

Kneeling beside the wooden pedestal, I opened the cabinet. Inside were an assortment of cleaning and polishing items, lubricants, and neatly folded rags. I reached my hand inside, palm up. There was a panel above the drawer, about four inches below the countertop. I couldn't feel any release or anything, but when I pushed against it, there was a click and the panel gave slightly. When I lowered my hand, the panel dropped down with it, hinged on the inboard side. It was a perfect hiding spot for my Sig.

I looked through the contents of the drawer again and found a bottle of mineral oil. I opened it and sniffed, just in case. Satisfied, I took one of the rags, unfolded it, and poured a few drops of the oil onto it. Then I refolded the rag and rubbed it together to distribute the oil better.

Looking around to make sure nobody was watching, I pulled the Sig and spare mag from my pocket and wrapped them together in the rag. Placing it inside, I raised the false panel and it clicked into place. Then I closed the drawer and went around to the helm seat.

The cockpit wasn't completely recessed into the deck like some sailboats; there was a low fiberglass rail around it and the benches were nearly flush with the deck. Only the footwell was recessed. In my mind, I traced the below-deck area and guessed that the footwell was over the engine room and the helm seat was above the workshop, allowing a bit more head room down below. The helm seat was high enough to allow the captain to see over the heads of his passengers, even while seated.

The seating in the cockpit wasn't cushioned, and both the port and starboard benches were hinged with recessed stainless-steel latches. Lifting both sides, I located the cushions, along with extra dock lines and what looked like several neatly folded tarps, undoubtedly to keep the sun off the cabin roof in the summer. Rummaging under the tarps, I found a long, heavy-duty electrical cord.

There was an electric pedestal on the dock, so I dragged the shore power cord out and looked around the cockpit. The plug was on the port side of the helm. Going below, I checked that the main breaker was off, then returned to the cockpit and connected the shore power and water line, turning both on.

Back in the pilothouse, I turned off all the breakers, then turned on the main. Satisfied, I switched on the breakers I'd need for the night and heard a low hum behind the panel. When I opened it, I found an inverter with the red light on showing that the batteries were being charged.

Going forward, I switched on lights in the lower salon. Ahead were two hatches, each with nautical scenes carved into the wood. Opening the one on the port side, I looked through the cabinets in the head and found nothing. A hatch on the far side led to the forward stateroom. The starboard hatch opened into a short gangway with a closet to starboard and another hatch beyond. Opening the closet door, I found a hanging locker large enough for an extensive wardrobe.

I continued forward, opening the hatch at the end of the gangway and switching on the light. There had probably been a guest stateroom there, but now instead of a bunk it had a desk built against the starboard hull with a large storage area in the bow, aft the chain locker. An old guitar case lay on a wide shelf against the port side, with a tool box and bench under it. In the forepeak, several sails lay neatly folded and stacked on the deck. I assumed they were spares, since all the sails on the masts were on rolling furlers.

Leaning over the sails, I opened the small hatch to the anchor locker, the foremost part of the interior of the boat. Though it was dimly lit from the single overhead light in the cabin, I saw nothing but two chain rodes, each piled up in separate compartments with a divider between them.

I turned my attention to the tool chest and the drawers beneath the workbench; it struck me as odd to have a separate work area in the bow. The one aft the engine room seemed more than adequate.

Opening the drawers of the toolbox, instead of the usual assortment of wrenches, sockets, and screwdrivers, I found large sewing needles, spools of lightweight braided line, pieces of leather, grommets of assorted sizes, and other sail repair items. Checking the drawers below the work-bench, I found more of the same, along with several rolls of sail fabric.

"I didn't know I'd have to learn to sew," I said aloud.

Turning, I opened the guitar case, only to find an old acoustic guitar. As I lifted it out, the strings vibrated, making a deep, resonant tone. There wasn't anything hidden below the guitar, except some sheets of paper and a battery-powered tuner.

Mom had played guitar when I was a kid. I'd tried to teach myself by watching her, and she'd taught me a few simple chords, but I didn't get very far with it before she died. Then I'd just given it up.

I strummed the guitar's strings. It sounded good, with a mellow resonance that reminded me of long ago times. Finding the right finger positions on the frets, I strummed one of the two chords I remembered. It sounded like it had been recently tuned. But, then again, I was hardly the guy to make that call.

I put the guitar back in its case and turned toward the little office. As an afterthought, I picked up the case and moved it through the narrow gangway and leaned it against the bulkhead by the lower salon hatch.

The little office space was just what it appeared to be. There was a laptop computer on the desk and a small printer next to it. Opening the big bottom drawer on the left, I found neatly labeled hanging files. I thumbed through them. They seemed to be bios on people.

Victor Pitt had once been a covert CIA operative, so it didn't strike me as unusual that he kept reports on people. I pulled one out at random and looked it over. Oddly, it didn't contain much more than a physical description.

Looking through several more, I saw they were the same, with an occasional one having more detailed information about where the person was from and what they did for a living.

Closing the file drawer, I opened the drawer above it. It held nothing more than blank printer paper. The one above that had typical office stuff: a stapler, a box of paper-clips, two boxes of pencils, and a couple of pens. The top two drawers on the right were practically a mirror image of the left, except that instead of blank printer paper, there were hundreds of printed pages. I took out the top twenty or so sheets and thumbed through them. It looked like a book, minus the binding and cover.

Was Victor a writer? I wondered.

I opened the laptop and turned it on. It took a moment to boot up and when it did there were only three icons on the desktop. I double clicked on the first one and a document opened. It too appeared to be a book. I looked down at the page count and it was just over a hundred pages long.

Too short for a novel, I guessed. I scrolled to the bottom and the end of the lengthy document was hung in mid-sentence, as if he'd been called away from his desk while writing.

Carrying the guitar case aft, I laid it on the large sofa in the lower salon. Across from the comfortable-looking seating area was a large-screen television with speakers mounted in custom carpentry below it. The TV was flanked by two cabinets. I opened the one on the left and found four racks of CDs. The two racks on the left held music CDs, and quite a few of them were Jimmy Buffett. The other two racks seemed to be filled with movies. I looked back and scanned through the music collection, not rec-ognizing many names. Then I saw two CDs by Eric Stone.

That kind of surprised me. He was a bar singer in Mar-athon, or so I thought. I'd met him a couple of times when he'd been working at the *Rusty Anchor*, just before I left. I took one out and looked at the cover. It was the same CD that Kim had bought just a month ago.

I opened the cabinet on the right, found a stereo system, and turned it on. Pushing the eject button on the CD player, I put the Eric Stone CD in and hit play.

Eric began singing about a magnetic compass, a north-ern girl who escaped from the snow, and the sailing life. It sounded pretty good, so I let it continue as I looked through the other cabinets.

There were no hiding places in the cabinets that I could find, but I didn't expect there to be; a little too obvious. I hide stuff in plain sight on the *Revenge*. Rod and reel boxes are common on a fishing boat, and most of the ones under my bunk are just what they appear to be. Others, not so much.

In the deck were two large hatches. I opened the first and found it to be nearly full of canned food. The second one was less than half full of boxes of dry foods. No hidden latches or false bottoms. I was reminded that I'd need to pick up a few things before departing, but there seemed to be enough food for at least a week.

Turning, I looked at the guitar case on the couch. The couch itself looked like a regular living room sofa, but it had been carefully trimmed and redesigned to fit the contour of the starboard hull. I removed the cushions, saw that it was a sofa bed, and pulled it open. The foot of the bed almost reached the custom cabinetry of the entertainment center on the port side. The thin mattress didn't look all that inviting, but if someone needed a place to crash, it would work in a pinch. I'd slept on worse many times. Raising a corner of the mattress at the head, I saw that there was space below it. I peeled back the mattress and removed two slats that snapped in place.

The false bottom below the mattress didn't look obvious and had I not been searching for hiding places, I might have overlooked it. I felt around inside but couldn't find a latch of any kind. Remembering the three spots I'd already found and how they were simple snap-type panels, I pushed against it. The panel clicked and rose up a fraction of an inch, just enough to get a fingertip under the edge.

I lifted the panel out and found a black towel wrapped around something. The familiar scent of gun oil reached my nostrils. I pulled it out and unwrapped the towel, revealing a Mossburg Mariner shotgun. The stock was glossy and all the metal parts were finished with a marine grade coating that shined like chrome. The short barrel extended no farther than the tubular magazine. I pumped the forestock slightly and saw that the chamber was empty but the magazine was loaded. Turning the extraction port toward the mattress, I racked out eight shells. They were alternating slugs and double-aught buckshot. The ultimate deck sweeper.

The shotgun had been cleaned and oiled recently. It's a chore, but living in a salt air environment, I clean all of my weapons every week, and keep them stored in ziplock bags when I can.

There appeared to be enough room below the false panel for my fly rod case also.

The second song on the CD began, with accompanying gulls calling during the intro. Eric sang about a cold day in Nashville and playing in a lounge, before heading south because ballads, beaches, bars, and boats are what he's all about. It was a sailing song, and I found myself enjoying his laid-back style.

Going up to the pilothouse, I retrieved my rod case and put it under the sofa bed along with my new chrome-plated Mariner. After closing it up, I went back up to the bridge deck and brought two boxes of dry goods down and refilled the deck storage areas.

Stepping back up to the upper salon and galley—or bridge deck, or pilothouse, depending on whether you were anchored or underway—I went straight to the lower helm on the starboard side. The woodwork was beautiful and well maintained. The throttle controls were simple, and the wheel much smaller than the one in the cockpit. Sitting at the raised helm seat, I could easily see through the low windshield, but the view over the bow left a lot to be desired. In fact, the horizon would be obscured by the hull for a good fifteen degrees to either side of the bowsprit. I didn't expect to be piloting from here much, though it was good to have in the event of a sudden storm.

Above the helm was a slim cabinet with VHF and single-sideband radios. VHF radios have a limited, line-of-sight range, but with the antenna mounted on the masthead, it would have a range of nine or ten miles. Twice that to another boat with its antenna at the same height. The SSB radio was different. It bounced a high-frequency radio wave off the ionosphere and, depending on the power and frequency used, its range could be thousands of miles.

On the dash in front of me, clustered in a diamond pattern in the middle, were the usual engine gauges for temperature, oil pressure, and voltage output, with the tachometer at the top. On either side of the gauges were a combination radar and depth finder on the left and GPS chart plotter on the right.

I searched the upper salon carefully and found another hiding place built into the bulkhead on the port side, just above the navigation station. It was only a few inches deep and opened with the same spring-loaded ball bearing that the others had. Closed, it wasn't noticeable in the least. Inside were shelves spaced six inches apart from the top of the desk to the trim around the cabin top. The shelves were empty. A good place to stash money or more guns, but little else, due to its shallow depth.

Aft the nav station was a small dinette for four. Aft that was the galley, which extended beyond the companionway, ending in a large pantry. That took a while to search. My earlier estimation of being off the grid for a week was off by at least a month.

Continuing aft from the bridge deck on the starboard side, I went through all the drawers above the combination workbench and laundry table and found nothing. Next to it was a stacked washer and dryer, like you'd find in an apartment. Small, but still a lot bigger than what I had on the *Revenge*. I'd already searched the engine room and attached tool and parts storage area, so I continued aft.

Opening the hatch at the end of the gangway, I was amazed. The master stateroom was nearly as big as the salon on the *Revenge*. And the bed was practically double the size. At six-three, bunking on a boat has always been a problem for me, but here I'd be able to stretch my arms and legs out fully and not reach the sides of the hull. The bunk was full-beam width, narrowing at the stern, where the three large, rectangular portholes allowed a lot of natural light in. I guessed the bunk to be nine feet at the forward edge, and at least as wide as a king-sized bed. Over the bunk was a large portlight hatch, tinted to keep the sun out.

Outside, I heard a commotion: voices raised in anger. My hand went to my cargo pocket, but I'd stashed the Sig at the helm. I'd brought over two other handguns, but they were in the Pelican box under the engine, and the Mossberg was forward, under the sofa bed.

When I stepped up to the bridge deck, I could hear the voices a lot more clearly through the open companionway hatch. Finn stood in the middle of the pilothouse, ears up and the hair all down his neck and back standing on end.

I was tied off on the port side of a finger dock, bow to the pier, putting the hiding spot and my Sig on the other side of the boat, away from the dock and the direction of the commotion.

I held my hand up, palm toward Finn. "Stay here."

Halfway up the companionway, I stuck my head out into the night air. The voices were coming from the other side of the *Revenge*. I moved quickly to the helm and opened the cabinet, cursing myself for not stashing another gun down below where it could be quickly accessed.

Retrieving the Sig, I inserted the mag. As quietly as possible, I racked a round into the chamber and decocked the gun, before putting it in my right cargo pocket.

I looked back down into the cabin; Finn sat at the bottom of the steps, looking up. I quietly closed and latched the bat-wing doors to make sure he stayed down there.

The arguing had stopped, but there was still a lot of noise coming from inside the boat docked on the other side of the *Revenge*. I couldn't see it, but it sounded like things were being tossed around inside. I stepped over onto the dock, then dropped down into the cockpit of the *Revenge*, going straight for the engine room hatch with my keys in hand. I keep a powerful hand-held spotlight mounted just inside the engine room. Unlocking the hatch, I opened it and grabbed the light.

Stepping over to the gunwale, I looked forward. The boat next to me was a small sloop, no more than thirty feet. The *Revenge* was backed in, and the sailboat was pulled in forward, so her cockpit was up near the fore-deck of the *Revenge*.

Aiming the spotlight at the sailboat's cabin, I flicked it on. The light pierced the darkness, turning night to day on the small sloop. "What's going on over there?" I shouted.

There was silence for a moment. Then a suitcase popped up from below, clattering to the cockpit deck, as a man's head came up out of the cabin.

"Kill the light, asshole," the man said without turning around.

I didn't blame him. The spotlight in my hand was two-hundred thousand candle-power and looking directly into it would ruin your vision for a few minutes.

"How about you move out to where I can see you first," I replied, my right hand on the butt of the Sig in my pocket.

Instead, the man disappeared below. A moment later, another suitcase was toppled onto the deck with the first. The man slowly rose up from the cockpit but didn't turn to face me. He was smallish in both height and build.

"I ain't gonna let you blind me," he said, his voice raspy like a three-pack-a-day smoker. He was American, but I couldn't tell for sure where he was from. Somewhere in the mid-Atlantic states, maybe.

"What's with all the noise?" I asked.

"What's it to ya?"

"I don't like noise when I'm resting," I growled back.

"It's over," the man said, lifting one of the suitcases and dropping it onto the dock. "She's gone, and I hope the bitch never comes back."

I kept the light on the man, as he tossed the second bag onto the dock, then went to the helm and started the engine.

"You wanna kill that light, so I can cast off?"

I reached over to the salon hatch and flicked the bridge lights on above me, then switched off the spot, but I didn't put it away.

The man turned and looked up at the bridge, then moved toward me to untie the bow line. "This ain't none of your business anyway," he called up to the fly bridge.

I didn't say anything, just watched him from the shadows below the fly bridge overhang. The man was young, maybe twenty-five or thirty. He had long, light-colored hair, which he wore in dreads. He didn't have quite enough fuzz on his face to call it a beard. His clothes were worn, and he just had a semi-permanent disheveled look about him. In the subdued light, I couldn't make out any facial features. He kept his head down, as if hiding his face for some reason.

Without another word, he untied the lines and backed the sloop out. Within minutes, he was leaving the marina and turning east, away from the bridge.

Once he was a good distance away, I stepped up to the dock and went to where he'd tossed the luggage. The suitcases showed a little use, but they were both high-end matched pieces. Apparently, they belonged to the woman he'd just abandoned, though I hadn't seen anyone leave. I moved them to the center of the dock, then returned to the *Revenge*.

Not my circus, not my monkeys.

CHAPTER SEVEN

After putting away the spotlight, I'd gone back over to the *Salty Dog*. I wasn't going to be caught unprepared again. I'd finished unpacking a few things, then stashed another Sig in the aft stateroom and a Glock in the hiding spot in the pilothouse.

Around twenty-hundred, curiosity had gotten the best of me and I went back over to the *Revenge*. The suitcases were right where I'd moved them to on the dock. I don't know why, but I fetched a small cooler with a six-pack of Kaliks and took it up to the fly bridge. Kalik is a decent lager brewed in the Bahamas, and here it's cheaper than any other brand.

Just before midnight, I was on my third beer, and yawning. It had been a long day, and I wanted to get an early start. Sitting in the darkness, debating going to bed or drinking one more beer, I heard footsteps on the dock. I could just make out a figure moving along the main pier.

It stopped at the finger dock for a moment, then ran out to where the suitcases were sitting.

"Dammit, Benny!" The voice was obviously female.

The woman sat on the larger suitcase, mumbling something. After a moment, I heard the unmistakable sound of her sobbing.

I switched on the red overhead lights, so as not to diminish my night vision. The woman on the dock noticed the faint glow on the dock and looked up.

"Is someone there?" a frail-sounding voice asked.

"He left a couple of hours after sunset."

The woman stood and looked up. "Did he say where he was going?"

Rising from the helm seat, I moved to the ladder and climbed down, switching on the red lights in the cockpit, mounted under the overhang.

"No," I said. "He didn't say much of anything at all. But he headed east out of the harbor."

She took a hesitant step toward me. "Do you have a phone?"

"You have friends in Nassau you can call?"

"No, not here." She was close enough that I could see the tears in her eyes. "But I have a friend up on Chub Cay who I can call."

Fishing my cellphone from my pocket, I leaned across the gunwale and extended it to her.

"Thanks, mister." She turned and walked toward the end of the dock, past her luggage.

After a moment, I could hear her talking in a low voice. Though I couldn't tell what was being said, I recognized the pleading in her voice. She started back toward me, and I heard her say, "I'll find a way," before ending the call.

She was young, probably younger than the guy that dumped her. In the dim light of the bridge, I could tell she had a pretty face, with light-colored hair pulled back in a ponytail. Maybe five-six or so, with a slim build. She was wearing faded jeans and a white pullover with exposed shoulders and sleeves that tied just above her elbows.

"I'm Kat," she said, handing the phone back. "That's with a K."

"Short for Katherine or Katrina?" I asked.

"Kathleen."

"I'm Jesse," I said, taking the phone with my left hand, and extending my right. She shook hands quickly, then snatched it back as if realizing that I could easily pull her off the dock. "Someone coming for you?"

"I have a friend on Chub Cay," she repeated. "But her boat's not running, and she can't come for me for two days."

I paused for a moment, looking into the girl's eyes. What I needed to do was get to sleep and set sail early in the morning. Instead, I was debating if the girl was going to be okay, or if she was some sort of looney.

"This is my boat," I said. "And I own the ketch on the other side of it. I can let you sleep here, if you want. But I'm leaving at first light."

"How do I know you're not some kind of sicko?"

"I could ask the same of you," I replied. "But I'm not the one standing at an empty dock with nowhere to go."

She stood there a moment, then looked up toward the bow of the *Revenge*, some forty feet ahead of us. "I don't guess sickos go around in fancy boats like this."

"I can put on some coffee," I offered. She considered it another moment, then took a tentative step forward. "Probably oughta bring your luggage aboard," I said, stepping out into the light in the middle of the cockpit.

She turned and went to her bags. As she carried them toward me, she said, "You're sure I'm not putting you out?"

"You are," I replied. "But I have two girls about your age and I just don't see how I can leave you stranded on the dock and be able to sleep."

She handed me the luggage, then stepped down to the cockpit and looked up at me. "Wow, you're really big."

Turning, I unlocked the hatch and put her bags inside, switching on the interior lights. "I've moved most of my stuff over to my ketch," I said. "That's where I'll be sleeping. If you're hungry I can whip up something to eat."

"I'm not real hungry," she said, following me into the salon and looking around. "This is really nice."

"Thanks," I said. Under the inside lights, she looked malnourished, her eyes slightly sunken, but still pretty in a familiar sort of way. Like a woman you'd known since childhood might be. "Make yourself at home. The staterooms are forward, take your pick. Head and shower are to starboard. I'll go over to *Salty Dog* and rustle up something to eat. You afraid of dogs?"

"I love dogs," she said. "And the truth is, I haven't eaten since yesterday."

"Then go get cleaned up," I said. "Come over to the ketch next to this boat when you're ready. I promise I'm not a sicko."

I remembered seeing that *Salty Dog* had been connected to shore power at Brown's and I'd already found a box of frozen hamburger patties in the freezer. Hopefully, the patties were still good. I pan seared three of them, though I wasn't terribly hungry. While they cooked, I opened the hatch in the galley to let the smoke and heat out. There were chips in the pantry. Normally, I'd opt for fresh vegetables, or at least fried potatoes. But that would take too long.

As I moved the patties onto a rack to drain off some of the grease, the girl called out from the dock, "Hello?"

"Come, Finn," I said, as I started up the companionway. "You might as well meet our guest now."

She was standing on the dock, wearing shorts and a tee-shirt. Both were worn, but looked clean.

"Come aboard," I said, as Finn joined me in the cockpit. "This is Finn."

She stepped aboard cautiously. I noticed the handle of one of my galley knives sticking out of her pocket. I felt pretty certain she stole it for defense reasons, but just in case, I stepped back to arm's length. My arm, not hers.

"You're in no danger," I said. "I know all bad guys will say that, too. But I really do have two daughters your age and it'd bother me if I didn't at least offer you the necessities."

"Is he friendly?" Kat asked, looking at Finn.

"He is, but he's a little confused right now." I nodded toward the *Revenge*. "We've been living on that boat for a while, and it's our first night on the ketch."

Kat extended the back of her hand to Finn, as someone familiar with dogs would do. He sniffed it, wagging his tail, then took a step forward to allow her to scratch his neck.

"Well," I said, "that confirms *my* impression that you're not a dangerous psycho. Dogs have good instincts about people."

She squatted and scratched both sides of Finn's neck, which was just pure nirvana to him. As she did so, the carving knife fell out of her pocket, clattering on the deck. She looked up, horrified.

"You can hang onto that, if it makes you feel more secure. But I would like it returned before I leave tomorrow."

"I'm sorry. I just—"

"Don't worry about it. I've been in strange places with strange people, where I couldn't tell the good ones from the bad. Come on down, I made a few burgers."

Around bites of the rather large hamburgers, Kat told me about her relationship with the man who abandoned her, telling me his name was Benny, but she didn't think it was his real name. He'd struck me as an unsavory character, at best, and her description of him removed any doubt. He was a simple thief and con-man. A boat bum who lived fully over the line and off the grid.

"What about you?" she asked. "What's your story? You own two high end yachts here in the Bahamas, but you're from the States?"

"I have a few other boats back home in the Keys." I nodded toward where the *Revenge* was tied up next to us. "Mostly work boats like *Gaspar's Revenge* over there. I do charters, fishing and diving mostly. A friend is arriving tomorrow to take the *Revenge* back home for me."

"You're a charter captain?"

"Sometimes," I replied, recalling a waitress asking me the same thing ten years ago in Key Largo. "I don't have to charter a whole lot to get by."

"You said you were leaving tomorrow? Taking this boat back to Florida, too?"

I knew what was coming. She was American, but had no discernible accent, which I pegged for Floridian. She wanted to go back home and needed a ride.

"No," I said. "I'm cruising the Bahamas, looking for someone. I could arrange for my friend to give you a ride to Florida. But he won't be leaving until day after tomorrow."

She chewed a handful of potato chips, but I could see something in her eyes: fear or dread. "No, I don't want to go to Florida. Where are you going tomorrow?"

I didn't want a passenger and I didn't need company. I wasn't the greatest sailor in the world; I'd only sailed a few times since I was a kid. Back then, I'd sailed a lot with my parents, and later with Mam and Pap, even helping Pap build a few boats. But single-handing a sixty-one-foot ketch would be a bit of a learning curve. If I was going to screw something up, I wanted to do it alone.

"Your friend in Chub Cay? Will you be safe with him?"

"Her," Kat corrected me. "She works at a marina there and has a tiny room available, over the store. She said I could stay as long as I wanted, and she'd even get me some work."

"The person I'm looking for," I began. "She was last seen headed toward Chub Cay. That's where I'm going in the morning."

"I know how to sail," Kat offered, hesitantly. "I can help crew in exchange for a ride. I don't take up very much space and can stay out of the way. It's only a day's sail."

"You've made your mind up that I'm not a dangerous fugitive?"

"Bad people raise bad dogs," she said, extending the last bite of her burger to Finn.

He looked at me, licking his chops, and I nodded. He inched closer and delicately took the morsel from the girl's hand.

She smiled. "Dogs have good instincts about their owners, too."

I smiled back, and even though I didn't want the company, I knew I couldn't leave her stranded if she had a safe place to stay on Chub.

"I accept your offer to crew, then. But this boat only has one stateroom. There's a sofa bed in the lower salon and this dinette converts to a bunk. Or you can spend the night on my other boat. Just don't steal any more knives, okay?"

She looked down the forward companionway. "The couch looks plenty big enough. I'd rather not be alone."

"You sure?" I asked. "The *Revenge* has a state-of-the-art security system. You'd be perfectly safe there."

Kat removed the carving knife from her pocket and slid it across the table. "What's your last name, Jesse?"

"McDermitt," I replied, leaving the knife where it was.

She finished her second hamburger, and I ate about half of mine, giving the rest to Finn. He was like a bottomless pit when it came to burgers.

Kat rose from the table, picking up both plates. "I'll clean up, Captain McDermitt. But I need to get my bags from your other boat."

Grinning, I said, "I'll get your bags. I want to sail early, so we need to get some shut-eye."

Leaving the *Salty Dog*, I crossed over to the *Revenge*. The salon hatch was locked. She'd apparently locked it from the inside, when she left. I opened it and went forward to my stateroom, checking everything along the way. She seemed like a nice enough kid, but you just can't tell. Finding nothing amiss, I turned off the main breaker, picked up her luggage, and returned to the *Dog*.

When I stepped down into the pilothouse, Kat was opening the cabinets in the galley, holding two plates in her other hand.

"One more to the left," I said, carrying her bags on down to the lower salon.

She put the dishes away, then followed me down, going over to the couch and opening the guitar case. "You play?"

"Not really," I replied. "It came with the boat."

"Hey, this is a Silvertone," she said, taking the guitar out and lightly strumming a few chords.

The CD player was still playing, apparently having started over at the end. Eric was singing a tune about being a reggae guy. It was fading to a close, and he was narrating about smoking a spliff.

"You like Eric Stone?" she asked, easily playing along with the music for a moment. "I've seen him play a few times."

"He was playing at a friend's bar when I left Marathon last month."

She put the guitar back in the case and lifted the smaller suitcase, putting it on the couch. Opening it she dug through the contents and produced a small wooden box.

"Thank God he didn't find it," Kat mumbled, sliding a side of the box open and pulling a small metal tube from the box. "Do you party?"

I could smell the pungent contents of the box and recognized it as marijuana.

"Tried it once," I said. "Wasn't real crazy about the way it made me feel. Kinda nervous and awkward."

"Mind if I take a lift?"

I did. But a lot less so than in the past. Jimmy smoked pot all the time, as did a lot of other people I knew. It seemed like it had gone from an underworld drug to common usage in my lifetime. Or maybe I saw it that way because it just wasn't very prevalent in the Corps.

Kat seemed to sense my negativity. "I don't have to. But, it wouldn't stink up your boat. This is good weed, and it doesn't take much."

I remembered the time I'd smoked it. A tiny fleck of the stuff in a pipe had me seeing stars.

"It's okay," I said. "As long as it doesn't smell up the place. But, do me a favor, keep it in your pocket at all times. If any cops come near, throw it overboard."

"There are a lot of different strains of weed," she said. "Not all of them make you feel paranoid. Some are good for creativity. Others for just chillaxin'. It's even used in pain management."

Paranoia was exactly what I'd felt. I don't like not being in control and tried not to drink enough to feel that way.

"Another time, maybe," I said, turning to go up to the pilothouse. "If you need anything, I'm in the aft cabin, okay? The head's right through that hatch on the port side."

She nodded as she pushed the metal tube down into the larger side of the little wooden box.

"I'll be up at first light," I added.

I left her in the lower salon, and Finn followed behind me. He started up the companionway to the cockpit, but I stopped him. "We're sleeping down there," I told him, pointing toward the gangway that led to the aft stateroom. I knew he wanted to go back to the *Revenge*; Finn doesn't like change.

Stepping up on the first step, I pulled the batwing doors closed, and slid the overhead hatch into place, latching them both. Then I went aft, toward my new bunk.

As I got ready for bed, I heard the music stop and a moment later, I heard a guitar playing a soft melody. I listened for a few minutes, remembering how I used to fall asleep to Mom playing. Kat was good. She played and sang softly. I couldn't make out the words to the song, but I could tell it was a love song. She stopped for a moment and I heard the flick of a lighter. Sniffing, I couldn't detect the smell.

What the hell have I gotten myself into? I wondered. Jimmy could function normally when he smoked pot. But I'd seen enough people turn into lazy couch potatoes to know that it affected some folks differently.

Or maybe it was like Kat said, different kinds did different things to people's minds. At any rate, I'd given her the okay. What I should have done was toss the pot overboard, like I had with Jimmy that first time. I guess I'm getting more tolerant of petty crimes in my old age. At any rate, the smell of pot drifting through an island marina was hardly out of the ordinary

I stretched out on the bunk and put my hands behind my head. For a few minutes, the sound of tiny waves lapping at the hull was all I could hear. Then, almost as a backdrop to the gentle swish of the waves, Kat's soft voice and music filtered into the cabin, barely audible.

I looked around in the near darkness. This had been Victor Pitt's boat and his bunk. No doubt he and Charity had made love in this very spot. I'm not a materialistic guy. A boat's a thing, same as a house or a car. The sheets were new; still had the straight-line wrinkles from being folded up. I closed my eyes and silently thanked Charity for that.

CHAPTER EIGHT

Waking, I could see light through the three aft portholes, the gray light of predawn. I wasn't disoriented, I knew exactly where I was and how the boat was situated. In a few minutes, the sun would rise over the mouth of Nassau Harbour and stream directly into those portholes.

Stretching, I thought about the trip that lay ahead. It was about forty miles to Chub Cay. Calculating the boat's hull speed by estimating the waterline length, I guessed that I could make forty miles in less than six hours if the wind was favorable. This time of year, it would be out of the east and I'd be sailing northwest on a beam reach. So, maybe six to eight hours to reach Chub. I'd have ten hours of sunlight; more than enough time, even if I had to motor the whole way at four knots. Still, I wanted to depart as soon as it was light enough.

Time in the islands is measured by sunrise, sunset, and the daily influx of tide. Sure, you could sail on a low tide at zero-dark-thirty, with a light wind, but your odds of a smooth passage go up substantially if you work with the elements that our forefathers harnessed before us. I'd already checked; high tide was an hour after sunrise. I'd have a following current through Nassau Harbour.

Rising from the bunk, I went to the in-suite head, then dressed for the day. The cockpit was covered with a large Bimini, so I opted for cargo shorts and a tee-shirt. Basically, the same thing I always wore. Opening the stateroom hatch, I let Finn trot ahead of me up to the pilothouse where I opened the companionway hatch to let him out.

"Use the bathroom and get back here," I whispered to him. "I don't want you wandering around in the dark."

I'm not sure how dogs interpret human speech, but some seem to understand more than others. I preferred to think that Finn knew what I was saying much of the time.

Leaving the hatch open, I went to the forward companionway to check on my guest. I could see her feet and calves, a sheet twisted around them, as she lay sleeping on the sofa. Another step forward and I froze. Apparently, Kat slept in the nude. The sheet was pulled down across her flat belly, exposing her breasts. She had no tan line that I could see.

Turning on my heel, I made my way to the galley to set up the coffeemaker. My face was flushed; I could feel it. True, she was a grown woman, of that there wasn't any doubt. But, she couldn't be much more than half my age. Both my daughters were grown women, a thought that I constantly had to push out of my mind.

Rattling some pots and pans, I tried to make enough noise to wake her, without it seeming obvious I was doing so.

"Timezit?" I heard Kat mumble from the lower salon.

I leaned with both hands on the counter, staring hard at the coffeemaker, trying to will it to brew faster. "Sorry if I woke you," I said over my shoulder. "It's about half an hour before sunrise."

Please don't come up here naked, I thought. I really didn't need any drama, especially with a young girl.

There were rustling sounds from below and a moment later, Kat emerged, wearing a white bikini top and white shorts. The sallowness of her eyes was still there, but her face seemed to have more color.

"Sorry I overslept. I had a lot of thinking to do and playing lets my mind wander. Your Silvertone sounds cool."

"Just waiting on the coffee," I grumbled. "I'm really not at my best until I have my first cup."

"My dad's the same way," she said, which for some reason made me feel immensely old. "I can cook, too," she offered. "If you have things to do to get ready, I can bring coffee and breakfast up to you."

When I glanced over at her, she seemed fresher. The gaunt look that had been in her eyes last night was diminished slightly. But she could still have stood to put on a good ten pounds or so. Her ribs were showing below her bikini top.

"You haven't eaten much lately, have you?"

"Benny wasn't exactly the best provider," she said, leaning a hip on the counter and crossing her arms. "I've decided I'm better off with him out of my life."

"Had you been together long?" I asked, pushing away from the counter. "I'm sorry, that's none of my business."

"It's okay. I hooked up with him down on Crooked Island a few weeks ago. A friend of a friend. He was meandering toward the Berry Islands, so I hitched a ride."

"There's eggs in the basket," I said, pointing them out. "And sausage in the icebox."

"Aye, aye, Captain," she said, attempting a salute.

I started up the companionway. "Coffee first, though."

Finn greeted me, then sat down and looked over at the *Revenge*. It was like he was wondering when we were going to go home or something.

"This is home now," I told him, as I went to the helm, fished the key from my pocket and started the engine. It was an old Ford Lehman and the tach showed it had just over three thousand hours. About a fourth of its life expectancy. Probably not even that, if Victor was as fastidious about engine maintenance as he seemed to be about the boat as a whole.

Kat came up with a large mug and a thermos. "I don't like coffee very much."

"Lucky for me," I said, with a wink.

"Food'll be ready in a few minutes."

I could tell she wanted to say something. I just sipped at the coffee and waited for her thoughts to quit spinning around in her head and exit her mouth.

"Do you plan to hurt this person you're looking for?" she finally asked. "'Cause you look a little scary."

I almost choked on the coffee. "No," I said. "I'm not planning to hurt anyone."

"So it's someone you like? A girlfriend?"

I gave that some thought. My affair with Savannah, which might or might not have resulted in a child, had been years ago.

"Something like that," I said. "Maybe—I don't know. It was a long time ago."

"You're not married, then?"

"No," I replied.

"Well, you're not gay; I'd have picked up on that."

Lifting an eyebrow, I looked over at her, "You're the second person to ask me that this week. No, I'm not gay."

"So, why didn't you come to my bed?"

If she'd struck me with a feather, she'd have knocked me right off the boat.

"Kat, how old are you?"

"Twenty-five," she replied.

"I'm forty-seven."

"We're talking about sex here, right? Not a relationship. You're not currently attached, not gay, not dead, and probably still too young to need help from Pfizer."

I really didn't know how to take that. Sitting in the helm seat, I looked up at her, somewhat embarrassed even to be discussing it. I said the only thing I could come up with. "Some things just aren't done."

"That's kind of old-fashioned," she said, turning toward the hatch. She stopped before going down and looked back at me. "I bet without that beard, you're pretty cute."

She turned and went back down to the galley, leaving me speechless. I glanced over at Finn, and he was looking at me quizzically, his head cocked slightly to the side.

"Yeah," I whispered, scratching his neck. "We live in strange times."

I'm never sure around women. Or at least I'm always sure I'm wrong, if that makes any sense. A woman Kat's age wouldn't be remotely interested in a man twice her age. It was just weird. Most of the people I knew were older. Had society become more liberal about age and relationships?

The truth was, having been raised by my grandparents, I probably did have some old-fashioned notions. It was Pap who told me about girls and sex. I was thirteen, and it was the Seventies. He had been thirteen during the Depression years. So the morals and values I learned as a kid, and carried into adulthood, were those from a time long past.

Going to the open hatch, I called down to her. "Can you locate the electrical panel and switch off the non-essential breakers?"

A moment later, she yelled up that the AC and water heater were off, and I stepped over to the dock. Going to the pedestal, I turned off and disconnected the shore power and water, then stepped back aboard and stored the gear under the bench.

"We're on battery power now," I called down as I went forward to untie the lines.

Returning, I glanced down the companionway. Kat was standing in front of the stove, swaying to the beat of the music coming from the lower salon. For just a moment I felt a stirring, then pushed the thought aside, and got to work.

When she came up to the cockpit again, we were idling away from the dock. "I already ate," she said, placing a plate piled with scrambled eggs and sausage on the port bench. "You didn't say how much you wanted, so I just guessed. Want me to take the wheel so you can eat?"

Shifting over, I picked up the plate and dug in. I hadn't realized how famished I was. Kat took the helm and started a wide turn into the channel toward the high bridge. The early morning sun revealed a dark tan, which the white bikini and shorts accentuated. She stood at the wheel, instead of sitting, and she looked quite comfortable. I could tell she was no stranger to a boat.

I ate quickly, washing it down with copious amounts of Hacienda la Minita coffee. I let Kat continue to steer as we passed under the high bridge to Paradise Island. She slowed as a cruise ship began to maneuver alongside the outer dock, half a mile ahead of us. I watched the activity on the ship closely and judged that it would bump the dock about the time we passed alongside. Kat had a sharp eye.

"Tell me about her," she said, turning toward the north side of the channel, just to give the cruise ship some added room.

"Who?"

Kat took a pair of white-framed sunglasses from her pocket and slipped them on. "The woman you're looking for."

"We met nine years ago," I said, wondering why I was talking about Savannah to a stranger. "She moved on a few weeks later."

"Nine years ago? You don't take a hint very well."

"She has an eight-year-old daughter now."

"Oops," Kat said.

"Yeah, oops. I guess I just want to know if she's mine."

Kat's face was expressionless behind her shades. "Nah," she said at last. "That's not the vibe I'm getting."

I tried not to roll my eyes. "Vibe?"

"You're still in love with this woman, carrying a torch for almost a decade."

Sliding the last bite of food into my mouth, I chewed and swallowed it. "How could you know that, if I don't even know it?"

"It's a gift," she said. "Had it all my life. My dad said I was an old soul. I don't exactly know, I just feel things that others don't seem to."

As we motored sedately past the cruise ship, I retook the helm, and throttled up slightly, pointing the bow toward the western mouth of the harbor. Kat went below to clean up the galley.

Raising the top of the cabinet, I switched on the GPS chart plotter, and laid in a course for Chub Cay. Kat returned to the cockpit, just as we were turning into the open ocean.

"Galley's all set," she said. "I checked the rest of the boat to make sure everything was secure. I put your laptop in the desk drawer. Are you a writer?"

"Me? No," I replied. "The laptop came with the boat, too."

"It looks like everything else is secure down there," she said, looking around the cockpit at the sheets and halyards. "And it looks like your boat is all rigged for single handing. What do you want me to do?"

"To be honest," I said, "I've never sailed this boat before."

"A boat like this is a breeze," Kat said, cocking her head, and smiling at me. "More sails, yeah. But they're smaller and easier to handle. I'll take the winch drum and haul in the slack in the halyard, while you hoist the main."

Once clear of the shallows near the harbor entrance, I turned into the wind, dropped to idle speed, and loosened up the main and mizzen sheets. I went to the mainmast and, while I did the grunt work on the main halyard, Kat quickly took up the slack, matching my rhythm easily. We then did the same on the mizzen sail. The windspeed indicator said we had twelve knots of fresh morning wind, so I decided on just the fore staysail. In a lighter wind, we could unfurl the genoa, but I thought that might overpower my ability under these circumstances. Slow is smooth, and smooth is fast.

With the sails set and luffing in the wind, I spun the wheel to port. *Salty Dog* fell off the wind and the sails snapped, filling with air. Kat manned the sheets, quickly adjusting the sails for a broad reach, and the *Dog* heeled over slightly. I reached down and shut off the chugging Lehman.

The near silence was exhilarating. The big ketch heeled like a plow horse leaning into the harness. The feeling in the wheel was one of strength and solid mass. While the Formosa ketch was fiberglass, it was built solidly, and had considerable weight in the full keel.

Kat sat on the windward bench seat next to me and looked at the navigation equipment. "Cool, all high-tech but keeping with the rustic lines of an old sailing ship."

I couldn't help but laugh. "I think your dad was right about you being an old soul, Kat."

"At this speed, we'll make Chub by mid-afternoon."

A quick glance at the chart plotter confirmed our arrival time. "So long as the wind holds," I replied. "Nothing to do now but relax and enjoy the ride."

Standing, Kat scanned the horizon in all directions. We were more than a mile off the western tip of Paradise Island and moving away. "I'm glad you mentioned that," she said, sitting back down, and pulling her wooden box from her pocket. "I want you to take a lift with me."

"Get high? In the morning? Naw, but thanks."

"This strain is different than any you might have tried," she said. "It was developed for a slight euphoric affect. Perfect for chillaxin'. And like you said, there's nothing to do for a few hours."

"Developed?" I asked. "I thought it was just pot."

"It is. But growing it has evolved a whole lot."

Reaching past me, she took the cover off what appeared to be a remote stereo controller, which I hadn't even paid any attention to. She pushed a few buttons and soon, a steady island beat began to reverberate through the speakers in the cockpit.

"I loaded four CDs in the changer," she said, twisting the little tube into the box. "This is Bob Marley's *Legend* album."

The song was familiar. I'd heard it in bars and on boats all around the Keys. He sang of loving and treating his woman right. The beat was a little faster than the rhythm of the bow cutting through the waves.

Putting the little tube to her lips, Kat lit it and drew deeply. The tube was shaped sort of like a baseball bat, but just three inches long. Like a bat, it tapered; getting smaller at the mouthpiece. The tip glowed for just a second and she exhaled a small cloud of blue-gray smoke, which disappeared in the wind. Then she leaned over the side deck to blow the ashes out of the tube.

Stretching her legs out on the bench, she dug the tube in the box again. After a moment, she offered it to me.

"I don't know, Kat. I don't think it's safe."

"We're on the ocean, old man," she said, raising her white sunglasses and winking. "What are you gonna run into?"

Before I could respond, she put the tube in my hand. "I promise, this won't be like what you smoked before."

I looked in the end of the little tube. The shredded gray-green pot didn't even fill the tip. It looked like about the same amount that Wilson Carmichael had me smoke that one time. I'd been trying to infiltrate his group and had to do it to fit in. This was different. I wasn't being forced.

"I don't think so," I said, pushing the tube back toward her.

"Jesse, there's not enough in there to do much of anything. It's just a taste. This weed is very mellow and will put you in touch with this boat like you've never been before. I promise you won't get hooked or anything like that."

Looking at the tube again, I reached over and took her lighter. I lit it just as she had and with the first small puff, I felt a hot ash hit my tongue. I spat the ash out and inhaled deeply, trying to make sure I got a lot of clean, salty air in my lungs at the same time. The only other time I'd done this, it was extremely harsh, and I'd felt like I was going to cough up a lung.

Exhaling, I felt like a wave of cool water washed over my face and head. I couldn't help it; I smiled.

"See," Kat said, putting the little tube away. "Half a bat is all it ever takes a newbie."

The feeling was both intense and relaxing at the same time. Kind of like a shot of really good eighteen-year-old rum. I looked over at Kat, relaxing in a supine position with her arm draped across the cockpit combing. I remembered the first time I'd taken the helm of this boat. Charity had been relaxing in the exact same position.

"How long does it last?" I asked.

"Not long," she said, not looking toward me. "Look out there over the bow. Let your eyes and mind drift toward the horizon. Feel the ride."

Looking out over the foredeck, which was canted a few degrees off horizontal, I watched the horizon rise and fall, as *Salty Dog* rode up the shoulder of one glassy wave after another. Occasionally, the cleaving of a wave caused a mist of sparkling water to cascade out over the glassy water. The scene was hypnotic. It would be, even without the pot, I knew. But somehow, my mood was elevated, and the scenery of the deep, blue sea all around us, with puffy white clouds stark against the clear azure sky, seemed to take on a different character.

I began to feel the tiny pull and give of the wheel as we crested each wave and accelerated ever so slightly down from the crest. I felt like I was an integral part of the boat.

I smiled again, feeling the rising sun on the side of face and the taste of seawater on my lips. A broad reach and a following sea. A fine vessel beneath my feet and a pretty girl for company.

"I listened to you playing last night," I said, my own voice sounding like someone else speaking. "You're really good."

Kat smiled, but kept her eyes on the far horizon. "I picked it up when I was little," she said. "Dad played in a band."

I noticed that she'd mentioned her father several times, but never her mother. I asked about her.

"She's a stay-at-home mom; blond and very pretty. Dad's seven years older than she is and calls her his trophy wife. I have a little brother, still at home. I left as soon as I turned eighteen."

Marley began singing a song about skanking, another tune I was familiar with. When he sang about taking a lift, I nearly laughed. I knew that he'd died nearly twenty years ago. Kat probably hadn't even started school then, and I'd been on my first tour in the Marine Corps. I guessed it was still island slang for getting high.

The math was suddenly hard. The view of the horizon over the bow, the neat clean lines of my new vessel, and the wind in my face were a distraction. She'd been on her own for six years, I guessed.

"Mind if I get some sun?" she asked.

I lost track of how long I'd been calculating her years alone, and how much money it would take to live without a job. "Sure," I replied.

Kat rose from the bench and moved forward along the starboard side deck, one hand on the cable rail. I worried for a minute. We should both be wearing flotation and using safety harnesses attached to the jack line that encircled the cabin. My worry quickly dissolved as Kat reached the foremast and wiggled out of her shorts. She wore a bikini bottom under her shorts. Then she reached behind her back, tugged the strings of her top, and pulled it off over her head, dropping it and her shorts into the starboard storage box. Stepping quickly up onto the boom, Kat leaned back against the mainsail, facing the sun, now a good fifteen degrees above the horizon. It wasn't hard to see why she had no tan lines.

At first, I was aghast. I couldn't figure out her intention. My heart quickly slowed, my mind accepting her for what she seemed right at that moment. A young woman, enjoying life on her own terms.

I grinned as Marley began singing a pleading song that I'd also heard many times, asking someone to please not rock his boat.

And you should know, you should know by now, dat I like it like dis.

Improvise, adapt, and overcome. The mantra of the Corps. How does a middle-aged man adapt to a young, half-naked woman lying on his mainsail?

But really, what was there to adapt to? I looked beyond Kat at the horizon, felt the surge in the wheel when riding the face of a low roller, and could smell and taste the sea.

It all came together in a hypnotic display to all five senses. Six, if you counted the spirit. I could sense how those first mariners might have felt when leaving the safety of a harbor. The doubt and anxiety of venturing into the unknown. But the only half-naked women they took to sea were the figureheads on their bowsprits.

"That comfortable?" I shouted forward.

"Set the autopilot and come see for yourself!"

So, I did. Within a minute, I'd stripped off my shirt and joined her. I was never one for sunbathing. I get enough sun just being out in it most of the time, without seeking to intentionally deepen my tan.

Kat moved out on the boom a little farther, allowing me room nearer the mast. Once I was standing beside her, I relaxed, putting most of my weight on the sail. It felt kind of like laying in a hammock.

The wind passed over both of us, tugging at our hair and my shorts. We couldn't see where the boat was going, but like she said, it was the ocean and nothing was around for miles.

"Chillaxed?" she asked, touching my forearm.

Somehow, the touch didn't feel sexual at all, even with her half-naked, lounging on the sailcloth just inches to my right. I could feel the movement of the boat through my feet and all down my back and legs, resting against the mainsail. The constant movement of the sail felt like an all-over massage, lulling my mind away from any dread or apprehension.

"Perfectly appropriate word choice," I replied, watching the horizon rise and fall with each roller we crossed.

My breathing had long since synched with *Salty Dog's* motion. Occasionally, a wave would catch the bow as it was going downward and send a fine mist into the air, sweeping back and cooling my face and skin with its touch.

"I told you, old man."

I didn't take the comment as a dig or insult. I am old. And suddenly I realized that maybe it didn't matter. Though I'd only met this young woman, I was thinking of her as nothing but a fellow traveler who just happened to be female and very liberated about herself.

That familiar feeling I'd had when I first looked at her in the light returned. I recalled running into a woman several years ago, someone I'd known all through my school years. As a kid, she'd been sort of gangly, all knees and elbows. She wore braces all through the fourth grade. She was a friendly girl—not ugly, but not pretty. She liked fishing, boating, and hanging out with the other kids in our neighborhood, mostly boys.

I'd been on emergency leave, home for Pap's funeral. She came, as did most of the folks in our neighborhood, young and old. My eyes told me she'd been a late bloomer; she was drop-dead gorgeous. But, my mind still saw the gangly adolescent girl who liked to tell fart jokes and could out-fish most of the boys.

I looked over at Kat, with neither desire or embarrassment. She just seemed familiar somehow.

After about twenty minutes, I felt like it was time to get out of the sun and turn to the serious matter of sailing.

My back was sweating, and the mellow feeling the pot had given me was beginning to wear off. I didn't feel the need to repeat it. Nor did I discount the possibility.

"It's herb," Kat said, reading my thoughts, but not moving her head. "God put it on the Earth; it's a part of the Earth and grows inside her. It draws all it needs from the Earth. How we use the things God gives is up to each of us, Jesse. If eyeglasses enhance failing vision, is using them wrong? The herb enhances your inner vision. So how could it possibly be a bad thing?"

"In moderation," I said.

"Of course. Drunkards and gluttons become poor, and drowsiness clothes them in rags. That's from the Bible, you know."

As I stepped down off the boom, my body suddenly felt leaden and heavy, as if I'd awakened from a long nap. I went back to the helm as Kat put her clothes back on.

Dropping down onto the bench beside me, she looked at the instrument panel. "Wow, almost two hours in the sun? That might have been a bit much. But it felt good, and morning light isn't as strong as midday."

"Two hours?" I said, startled. I looked down at the clock and GPS. We were twenty miles out of Nassau, nearly halfway to Chub Cay. I knew I hadn't fallen asleep. I remembered the whole experience with perfect clarity. Yet, I'd lost over an hour of time. Or had it lost me?

In the cupholder, my sat-phone blinked that I had an incoming message. I picked it up.

Arrived. Leaving at first light. Hope you find what you're searching for

- Andrew

CHAPTER NINE

A rain squall arrived while we were still five miles out, moving in the same general direction. Not a howling storm, just the typical downpour associated with tropical and sub-tropical waters. As the sun heats a land mass, be it a continent or an island, it creates an updraft. The updraft pulls in cooler air from the sea, air heavily laden with moisture from evaporation. As the humid air rises into the atmosphere, pressure and temperature decrease, causing the vapor to condense into raindrops, which fall back to the ground, flow down a river, and back into the sea, to do it all over again. Wash, rinse, repeat.

The wind died to almost nothing, as fat raindrops pelted the deck and beat out a rhythm on the Bimini top. Kat and I were soaked to the skin by the time we got the sails down and the engine running. But it was a warm day, so I didn't care. I'd been wet before, and so far I hadn't drowned.

In Okinawa, I had a platoon sergeant who always said, "If it ain't rainin', we ain't trainin'." Sergeant Russ Livingston loved to play in the rain. So I just took it in stride, knowing that a fresh towel was right inside the cabin.

Surprisingly, Kat seemed to revel in the sudden downpour, leaving the relatively dry cockpit and dancing on the foredeck in the rain. She raised her face to the sky, like a kid trying to catch raindrops. I was beginning to think she was a bit nuts. But she was fun to be around, and an excellent sailor.

The crossing had been uneventful up to then, except for the pot and half-nude sunbathing. We'd eaten lunch under sail and talked about the pot experience and a variety of other things. Kat struck me as a very intelligent, though quirky, young lady. We'd listened to music from Victor's CD collection, which contained quite a few artists Kat said were some of her trop-rock favorites. She'd even brought the old guitar up on deck to play along with the songs she knew. I found myself enjoying the stories the musicians sang about, stories of sailing, beaches, bars, and women. And I found I still loved sailing.

We finally idled into the anchorage with the rain still falling. Kat directed me past a few boats lying at anchor, toward a small building on stilts. It looked like there were slips for maybe twenty boats, and only a handful of those were occupied.

A man and woman walked out onto the pier, waving and directing us to a slip away from the other boats. Neither was wearing rain gear.

The man's hair and beard were neatly trimmed. He was dressed only in red and black baggies hanging low on his hips. The woman wore shorts and a tank top, which was plastered to her skin by the rain. Her hair was dark blond and soaked, hanging loose around her face. Water dripped from the ends whenever she moved her head. Both were slim to the point of malnourishment, much like Kat. But the sinewy lines in the man's abdomen and arms told me these were people who lived primarily from the sea. A very low-fat diet.

With the bow line in her hand, Kat stepped off the boat and into an embrace with her two friends. They quickly broke apart and helped get *Salty Dog* into the slip with practiced ease.

After shutting off the engine, I stepped down to the dock, Finn at my side. Finn's mostly yellow lab, so the rain meant nothing to him at all.

The man came forward and offered his hand. When I took it, he pulled me in for a man-hug and a quick pat on the back. "Name's Brayden, mate. Welcome to Chub."

He was an Aussie, or Kiwi maybe. His attitude was one of genuine warmth and openness.

"Jesse," I replied, as the woman stepped up and hugged me tightly.

"Thanks for bringing Kat out of the clutches of that den of vipers they call Nassau," she said stepping back. "*And* the douche bag she's been hanging with. I'm Macie; short for Mackenzie. Will you be staying over for a while?"

She was a friendly woman, probably in her early thirties. I detected a touch of a New England accent in her voice

"Not sure," I replied. "At least for the night. Maybe two."

"You can pay as you go here," she said. "But don't be surprised if a night or two doesn't turn into a month. When I first came here, it was just to lay over for two days. That was two years ago. Is your dog good with other dogs?"

"He's sometimes a little goofy," I replied. "But he's never hurt anything other than clams."

"My dog's running around here somewhere," Macie said, reaching down to give Finn a scratch. "He's a little old but loves to run and play."

The rain abruptly stopped, the same way it had started. After a short moment, the sun came out, and steam immediately began to rise from the dock planks.

"Don't like the weather on Chub?" Brayden said, raising his arms wide, palms up. "Just wait a few minutes."

Finn whined and looked up at me.

"Go ahead," I told him. "But stay close."

He trotted toward shore ahead of us. Then, with his nose to the ground, he tore off toward a stand of trees behind the building, following a zigzag course.

I followed Kat and her friends as we walked toward the office. Kat was the younger of the three, but only by a handful of years. All three were within an inch in height, about five-seven. And all were probably within thirty pounds in weight, none over one-fifty.

The marina office was small, just a corner of a building that was also small. The rest of the building had shelves of stuff boaters needed, as well as a few canned and boxed foods. It was the only building for several hundred yards. Some scattered homes, raised high on stilted legs, were beyond the stand of trees Finn had run toward.

A chalkboard beside the counter showed the tides, predicted wind speed, and temperature for the day—but it was a day in June, more than half a year ago.

"The slip's fifty dollars," Macie said, drying her hands and face on a towel. She passed out more from beneath the counter. "Extra days are thirty a day for as long as you want, or one-fifty a week in advance, or if the bug sinks his teeth deep into you, four hundred a month. Mooring balls are fifty a month, and anchoring's free. We don't have any amenities, but that's not why people come here."

"Sounds reasonable," I said, taking a small roll of bills from my pocket, and counting out four twenties. "What's the main attraction?"

"Care for a beer, mate?" Brayden asked. "It's close enough to five. We're right on the north end of the TOTO. Big game fishing's the name of the game."

I noticed right away that I was already being accepted differently than I had been in other marinas and anchorages aboard the *Revenge*. Or maybe these folks were just friendlier. I knew billfish were the big trophy catch in the Tongue of the Ocean, but not until early summer. So, a bona-fide marlin fishing machine like *Gaspar's Revenge* just wouldn't be running around out here this time of year. Indeed, every boat I'd encountered was a sailboat or slow-moving trawler.

When summer arrived, this little marina would probably be full of boats just like the *Revenge*. Even then, I didn't think the locals would be as open and hospitable to tourists and charter crews. This time of year, the only people around would be like Savannah: cruisers.

"Sure," I replied, accepting the dripping Kalik that he pulled from a cooler. He passed out two more, before getting his own.

"Lessee, it's Thursday, right?" Brayden asked Macie.

"Wednesday," Kat corrected him.

"Better still! It's lobster night." He turned toward me. "A bunch of us will be getting together around a fire on the sand when the sun gets low. Cruisers and boat bums, mostly. Care to join us?"

"Don't mind if I do," I replied. "Who's supplying the lobster?"

"Me and you, if you're game, mate. Pick you up at your boat in twenty minutes, eh?"

"Sounds great," I said, then turned toward Kat. "Want me to bring your bags up?"

"Uh, yeah," Macie said. "About that. Your loft isn't ready yet. But with you here to help, we can get it livable tomorrow, easy. There's a bunch of boxes and stuff up there right now."

"No worries," Kat said. "You have room in the boat, right?"

"Well, not exactly. The vee-berth's been converted to storage."

Kat and Macie both turned toward me. "The couch is all yours," I offered.

"That big ketch doesn't have two cabins?" Brayden asked.

"It did," I replied. "But the forward stateroom was converted to an office and the bunk removed. The sofa pulls out into a queen-sized bed, but the mattress doesn't look very comfortable."

Kat smiled at my discomfort. "The couch is fine, Jesse. It's really very comfortable."

"Go make your vessel secure, then," Brayden said to me. "Where we'll be diving to get the little buggers is only about fifteen feet, so just bring a mask and fins, eh?"

I thanked them for the beer and headed back down the dock toward my boat. The remnants of the clouds, which had poured down on us for an hour, were moving off to the west, dissipating quickly. The area around the small marina was mostly tall sea grass, scattered cocoplum bushes, and a few coconut trees, all bent slightly to the west by years of wind and rain. The sand at the water's edge was glaringly white, and the water just off the beach was gold, giving to light turquoise, then cobalt blue where it got deeper. I knew that, just a mile or so to the south, the bottom disappeared to more than half a mile deep.

Looking beyond the marina, I saw no movement around the small dwellings to the northeast. There were only a handful of full-time residents on the island, but I'd heard that like many of the Berry Islands, it was for sale, and there was talk of some rich Texas developer planning to build a resort here.

Standing at the foot of the pier, I looked around. The wind had come back up, tickling the sea grass into a dance. It felt invigorating against my skin. The air was fresh and clean, with a salty tang. The little stilt houses and marina blended well with the natural surroundings; it was an idyllic little island, painted in neutral pastel colors of yellow, tan, green, and white. It would be a damned shame when they brought bulldozers and cranes in here.

Just as I reached my boat, Finn came trotting out onto the pier and barked. He was in the company of a shaggier version of himself. Both dogs were panting, and I noticed the other one had a black tongue. Probably a chow mix.

"Found a playmate?" I called back to Finn as I stepped aboard.

Finn barked again, he and the other dog waiting patiently at the foot of the pier.

"Don't go far," I said. "We'll be here until tomorrow."

As if they both understood, the two dogs went bounding off toward the beach and, no doubt, a dinner of clams. I often wondered if they communicated in any other way besides sniffing each other's butts.

Hey, Finn, let's go play.

Okay, but we gotta stop and ask my dad first.

I checked the lines, adding two spring lines just in case of a blow. Tides here only changed about eighteen inches from the highest high to the lowest low, and it was low now. So I left enough slack in the lines, knowing they'd tighten as the tide and boat rose. Then I unlocked the cabin hatch and went below.

Kat's bags were on the couch in the lower cabin. I went forward, opening all the hatches. The slip was oriented perpendicular to the prevailing wind, and soon there was a little air movement through the boat. I wasn't worried about the lack of electricity. Though it felt like it was in the eighties before the rain came, the temperature at night in these islands was usually in the low sixties in January. I anticipated a comfortable night.

Grabbing my snorkeling gear from under the bench seat at the dinette, I started up the companionway. Macie was standing on the pier.

"Thanks again for bringing Kat," she said.

Closing the hatch, I locked it and turned to face her. "It was no trouble at all. She more than pulled her weight."

A small outboard started on the other side of the marina and Macie looked that way. She had something on her mind, so I waited.

"She's kinda gullible, you know."

"No, I don't," I replied, wondering what she was getting at. "But I only met her last night. She struck me as sort of a free-spirited girl."

"Yeah," she said, and paused for a moment. "Free spirits can get walked on by certain guys."

"The guy she was with didn't strike me as anyone to write home about."

"I wasn't talking about Benny. But yeah, he hurt her. I can tell."

I looked down at Macie. "I see. You're wondering about my intentions toward your friend?"

Laughing, Macie cupped a hand over her eyes against the sun and looked up at me. "Kind of a weird way of putting it, but yeah."

I stepped down to the dock next to her and grinned. "I'm much too old for games, Macie."

"Age is nothing but a number, Jesse. Kat was just dumped and she's very vulnerable. She's the type who wears her heart on her sleeve." She paused and looked me up and down. "And you are a hot guy, regardless of your age."

I couldn't help but laugh, though her gaze and comment made me uncomfortable. "There was a time, in a faraway place, I'd have taken her hand. But my own daughters are her age, and I don't see women of a certain age the way I once did."

Macie grinned up at me as the outboard approached. "I'll take you at your word, then. I think you'll like most of the people coming tonight."

Turning, we both walked toward the end of the pier as Brayden approached. "Is tonight a special occasion or something?" I asked her.

"Yeah," she replied, as the little boat turned and lightly bumped the dock. "It's Wednesday."

"All set, mate?" Brayden asked, holding a dock cleat in his hand.

"Yeah," I replied. "I believe so."

Stepping down into the small, wooden boat, I dropped my gear at my feet and sat on the middle bench.

"Be back in a coupla hours, love," Brayden said, pushing away from the dock and reversing the engine.

Macie waved as Brayden turned and pointed the little boat toward the marina entrance. His skiff was a hand-made wooden boat, with a high bow and wide beam. It looked and felt sturdy as we motored out toward the ocean.

Once away from the marina, Brayden asked, "She have a talk with you about Kat?"

"Yeah," I replied. "Nothing to worry about from me. I'm searching for *my* lady. Or I hope to think she'll one day *want* to be my lady."

"Ahh, I get it, mate. Hard to love a lady who loves the sea."

The little boat rounded the point and Brayden turned west. The sturdy wooden skiff bounced on the small rollers, but not so hard as to cause pain or anything.

"This lady you're looking for," Brayden shouted over the outboard. "I take it she's been in this area?"

Turning around, I faced aft. This was the way in I'd been looking for. A local waterman. Someone who knew the daily comings and goings of anyone who came near Chub Cay. Maybe Savannah had stopped here, maybe she hadn't. The only way to find out was to ask.

"A friend met her up on Hoffman's Cay about a week ago, and she was headed in this direction in her Grand Banks trawler. Her and her eight-year-old daughter. Savannah and Florence Richmond."

Brayden studied my face a moment and seemed to come to a decision. "Tall, blond lady? A bit younger than yourself?"

"Yeah," I replied, unable to hide the anxiety in my voice. This was the first lead I'd had. "You saw her?"

"She was here a coupla days, mate. Anchored off on the lee side. Left last Sunday."

"Any idea where she was headed?"

He studied my face again. People have said I shouldn't play poker, as I'm not good at hiding my feelings.

"They were waiting on weather," Brayden said, as he slowed the boat. "You wanna grab that anchor? We're coming up on a sandy patch."

When he brought the little boat down off plane, I turned and went to the bow, watching the water. I saw a patch of light yellow sand just ahead and off to port and pointed at it. "There?"

"That's it," Brayden replied and turned the boat. "I think I remember her telling Macie that they were headed for the BVI."

When we were over the sand, I lowered the anchor quickly, and Brayden backed away until fifty feet of line was out. "Tie her off, mate."

Once anchored, I turned around and faced him again. "The BVI, huh?"

"Boat like that," he said. "It'd take at least three weeks, unless she moved night and day."

"No," I replied, looking off toward the island while studying the map in my head. "She runs only about eight hours a day, never in a hurry. Probably closer to a month with stops along the way."

"Need gloves?" Brayden asked, slipping his fins on and extending a pair of mismatched gloves toward me. "I have extras. Sorry they don't look the same."

"Form follows function," I said, taking the gloves. "Thanks."

"You've caught lobster before?"

I grinned. "Yeah, a time or two."

Once we both had our fins and masks on, we rolled off either side at the same time, then reached up into the boat and grabbed the two bright orange goodie bags.

"All 'round that sand patch where you dropped the anchor," Brayden said, rolling onto his back and beginning to kick his fins. "It's gonna be loaded with bugs."

I rolled over and followed. "I knew Savannah a long time ago."

"About nine years ago, I'd wager," he said. "Judging by the girl's age. She yours?"

"I don't know," I replied, "but I'd like to."

"They stayed pretty much to themselves, but I got the impression she was a smart girl. Her mum, too." Brayden rolled over and looked down, then lifted his head out of the water. "Here we are, mate. We only need nine, eh?"

I put my face down and looked at the bottom. The anchor lay almost centered in the patch of sand. All around the ledges of coral and rock were dozens of lobster antennas.

When I looked up at Brayden, he was grinning. "Let's make it an even dozen, eh? I don't know about you, but I'm famished on Wednesdays."

With that, he doubled over and started to the bottom. I followed right behind him. Free diving for lobster in just fifteen feet wasn't difficult. When I reached the bottom, I immediately saw that the biggest obstacle would be in choosing which ones to catch, while not scattering the others. The shallow ledge was teeming with lobsters. Instinctively, I headed away from Brayden, kicking slowly so as not to burn up the air in my lungs or scare the lobsters.

I caught two in just a few seconds, then a third eluded my grasp. I kicked slowly toward the surface and paused for only a second, inhaling and exhaling quickly. Brayden was coming up as I went back down.

Moving slowly along the edge of this lobster honey hole, I was amazed at the size of some of them. It was like shopping; I was able to pass over the ones I knew were undersized and avoid the monsters that could break a man's wrist. The nice, fat four- and five-pounders didn't need to be measured.

Brayden and I both surfaced together after three dives. "How many ya got?" he asked.

"Four. You?"

"The same. Two more each should do it."

I gave him a thumbs-up sign, and we descended together. On the bottom, I bagged another lobster quickly, then a second one kicked so hard he almost twisted my wrist before getting loose. Grabbing another one from under the ledge, I put it into my bag.

As I turned, something caught my eye about fifty feet away. Brayden was heading to the surface. Rising, I looked over again. There were several large objects resting on the bottom, gently swaying in the easy surge. They seemed out of place, but too far away to see exactly what they were.

"I think we're good," Brayden said, his head bobbing on the surface.

"I saw something down there," I said. "Something out of place about fifty feet off to the south."

"Let's get these bugs on the boat," he said. "Then we'll go have a look-see."

Within minutes, we'd dropped our heavily laden bags into the boat and were returning to the anchor site.

"What was it you saw?" Brayden asked.

"Not sure," I replied. "Two or three large objects, all drifting in the current near the bottom."

When we reached the sand patch, we turned south and snorkeled away, looking down at the bottom. I saw it again and pointed. Brayden and I dove, kicking slowly toward whatever it was.

Still twenty feet away, I realized what I was looking at. The backs of three sea turtles, with their shells removed, and the raw meat of their bodies exposed. Brayden kicked closer, moving toward the first carcass. I settled in beside him.

It appeared that sharks had been feeding on the carcasses, taking small bites out of the exposed muscle and a rear flipper. I looked all around but saw no movement in the water. There didn't seem to be any other injuries, so I couldn't tell how the animals had died.

Brayden straightened the flipper of one of them and pointed out a metal tag in the fleshy part of the skin. Quickly drawing a knife from a sheath on his ankle, he cut the flesh away from the tag and removed it, stuffing it into the pocket of his baggies.

Just as we turned to swim up and back to the boat, I almost collided with a black tip shark. Black tips aren't usually aggressive and, as sharks go, they're considered rather small and harmless. Fortunately, he dodged me more than I dodged him. He was bent on getting to what was left of the turtles.

Harmless or not, I knew there was blood in the water and that might attract other sharks. Bulls, hammerheads, and tigers are found throughout the Bahamas. And they're neither small nor docile.

We both stayed near the bottom as we finned toward where we knew the boat was. More sharks appeared, circling the three carcasses and darting in and out for a bite. I looked toward Brayden, my lungs burning for air, and we both jerked a thumb toward the surface and rose quickly.

Levering ourselves aboard from opposite sides, we fell into the boat, breathing hard.

I pulled my mask off. "I counted at least five black tips and a bull."

Brayden nodded. "We probably spooked them when we arrived."

"Any idea what happened to those turtles?" I asked.

"Bloody poachers!" Brayden said, yanking on the pull cord. "And recent, mate."

CHAPTER TEN

S itting in the forward cabin aboard *Salty Dog*, I connected my sat-phone to my own laptop, leaving Victor's in the desk drawer. Though I wasn't crazy about the
electronic devices, I had grown to see the convenience of
them. As a kid, I'd spent hours, sometimes days, looking
up stuff at the library. Today, it takes only an internet connection and a few minutes. The sat-phone could be used to
connect to the internet, but I found the small screen difficult to type anything on. Chyrel had shown me how to
use a phone as a modem. The satellite data rates weren't
much more than making a voice call.

On the short ride back to the marina, Brayden had
told me of quite a few dead turtles that had turned up in
the area. They were all hawksbill turtles, one of the most
endangered sea turtles on the planet due to their beautiful shells, which are used to make jewelry and eyeglass
frames. That had been all the poachers had taken in each
case. I saw it the same way I viewed killing an elephant or

rhino just for the tusks and horns: a deplorable lust for money. People mistakenly quote the Bible, saying that money is the root of all evil. But money can be used to do good just as well as evil. It's the *love* of money—greed— that is the root of evil.

According to what I found using the computer, there were fewer than fifteen thousand nesting-aged female hawksbills left in the whole world. On a global scale, since these turtles are found in all tropical oceans, that's teetering on the edge of extinction. Imagine a body of water that's fifteen thousand miles long and three thousand miles wide, with that few individuals able to propagate a species. That's one turtle in three thousand square miles of ocean. It'd be like being the only person in the whole state of New Hampshire, trying to find the only person in the state of Vermont.

The shell of an adult hawksbill could weigh twenty to twenty-five pounds and was worth a hundred dollars a pound. Not a lot of money back in the States, especially with them being so difficult to locate. But those three dead turtles had made someone a helluva profit for just a few minutes work.

The boat moved slightly, and I heard the unmistakable sound of Finn's claws on the deck above. A moment later, he came into the gangway and sat on the deck just outside the little office.

"Where'd your buddy go?" I asked him.

Turning his head aft, he looked toward the main companionway, his tail swishing on the deck.

"We're going to stay the night here and it looks like we're going to a beach party. Think you can supply some clams?"

Finn cocked his head at the mention of his favorite snack, his eyes bright and mischievous. "Just a few," I said, closing the laptop, "so you and your friend don't mooch all the lobster."

I followed Finn aft and up on deck. The sun was low on the horizon, bathing everything around me in a light golden hue. The wind was back up to its usual ten knots, tugging at my hair and beard. There wasn't a cloud to be seen anywhere. There's something very seductive about watching the sun set over water, especially if you're on an island.

Chub Key is much larger than my island. It's shaped like a dog's leg, with the longer, southern part of the island being about four miles long and a mile wide in places. The northeast dogleg is only a couple miles in length, and a good outfielder could throw a baseball across some of it. The marina is located at the western end of the island, along with most of the homes, where the twenty or thirty permanent residents lived.

I'd showered and changed into comfortable Dockers and a white long-sleeved button down with the *Gaspar's Revenge Charter Service* logo on the left breast pocket. Like most of my clothes, the shirt had seen better days. Since shoes and sand don't mix, I opted for bare feet. I'm not what you'd call a fashionable guy.

Down on the beach, a few hundred yards from the marina, I could see people standing around something large and black. I couldn't make out who any of them were, but two were women in bright-colored sundresses, which were snapping in the brisk breeze.

With Finn walking beside me, I made my way to the foot of the pier, where we turned and followed the shoreline around the point. Crossing the dune there, we reached the gathering place.

"You must be Jesse," a man in a guayabera shirt said. He was next to what I now saw was a beat-up charcoal grill. He stepped toward me, extending a hand.

"Guilty as charged."

He was about my age, with graying hair, and a slight build. Like me, he was also dressed for the cooler weather nightfall would bring. I noticed the women had blankets and sweaters stacked on a nearby log.

"Name's McKay. Cory McKay."

"Irish or Scott?"

"Irish, lad," he replied, his blue eyes twinkling.

"What's the craic?" I asked in my best Irish brogue. "Name's McDermitt, of Clann Dalaigh."

McKay's grin broadened, his cheeks reddening. "Aye, the craic's ninety, it is."

He turned to the two women who were talking on the other side of the rusted-out grill. "Lea, come meet one of my kinsman."

The two women were both younger than McKay; that was obvious. The light breeze pressed their flowered dresses to their bodies in all the right places. One was a blonde and the other had dark hair and even darker eyes.

McKay slipped an arm around the dark-haired woman's waist. "Lea, meet Jesse McDermitt. His ancestors come from the same seaside town in Northern Ireland where mine are from. Jesse, this is my bride, Lea."

Lea smiled and extended her hand. "Very nice to meet you, Jesse." She turned to the other woman and introduced her as Carol Jessup.

I guessed Lea to be maybe a decade older than Carol. I shook hands with both women, then McKay put a beer in my fist.

"Y'all are recently married?" I asked him, taking the first pull.

"Depends on how you look at time," McKay replied. "We tied the knot more than a year ago and have been honeymooning ever since."

Another man approached, carrying a large bag of charcoal for the grill. Carol introduced him as her husband, Tommy.

"You staying long on Chub?" Tommy asked, tearing the bag open and pouring the briquettes into the grill. I was worried that the weight might collapse it, but it held together.

"A day or two," I replied. "I'm on my way to the BVI."

"That's your ketch that came in during the downpour?"

"Yeah," I replied without elaborating.

"Nice vessel," Tommy said. "We're in the cat, out in the anchorage. Cory and Lea are aboard the trawler, *Eastwind*."

Two men approached the group, both in their early thirties, with long, dark blond hair. Between them, they carried a large cooler. Behind the two men came Kat, Macie, Brayden, and another young couple, who were holding hands.

I was introduced to Mayhew and Gaston Bourgeau, brothers from France, sailing together. The other couple was David Young and Carmen Novac. The couple looked to be the same age as Kat and obviously in love. Aside from McKay, I was older than the group by nearly two decades.

The grill was lit, and everyone moved away from it. "Just in case it falls apart," McKay said.

"You should have brought your guitar, Jesse," Kat said, moving over next to me and taking my arm in both hands.

It seemed an obvious ploy to distance herself from the French brothers. Three couples, three single men, and one single woman. I could see the dynamics easily enough. Kat was on the rebound and didn't want anything to do with the younger Frenchmen, both shining physical examples of young male adulthood. Land sharks.

"I can barely play three chords," I said, grinning. "But if you'd like to play, I'll gladly fetch it for you."

"I'll go with you," Kat said, turning me by my arm.

As we walked away from the group, I glanced down at her. Her hair was damp, and she smelled fresh from the shower. As we walked back up the beach toward the docks, she continued to hold my arm, bumping close with every step.

"The French guys seem to think they're God's gift to womankind."

I patted her hand on my arm. "I kinda got that impression."

She looked up and smiled. "I'm just going to use you to keep them away from me. Hope you don't mind." She wasn't asking.

I'd only known the girl a day but felt close to her, nonetheless. Not in a romantic or sexual way, just sort of like travelers on the same ride. Which, in a way, was what we were.

"I remember that age," I said. "I thought at the time that I was ten feet tall and bulletproof, and that the whole world existed for my own personal amusement."

"What happened to that guy?"

I smiled down at her. "He got married, had kids, went to war, and survived. A lot of the world's not a pretty place, and people aren't always what they seem."

Kat glanced down at my forearm. I'd rolled my sleeves slightly, and the lower half of my Force Recon tattoo was visible. "You were in a war? Vietnam?"

Laughing, I put an arm around her shoulder and pulled her into a fatherly kind of hug, "I'm not *that* old."

When we reached the boat, I unlocked the hatch and we went below. "Think this crowd likes rum?" I asked, as she disappeared down into the lower salon.

"We're all pirates," she replied, coming back up with the guitar case. "In one way or another."

Slipping down to my cabin, I opened the bottom drawer of the little dresser, and took out an unopened bottle of fifteen-year-old Pusser's Royal Navy Rum. Though I'd only met these people, I felt that they, and certainly the setting, deserved the best.

Turning around, I almost collided with Kat at the hatch. "Oh my God," she exclaimed. "This cabin is huge."

I stepped back to allow her in. She went to the edge of the bunk, looking from one end to the other, before turning toward me. "This thing's decadent, Jesse."

I felt my face flush. "Well, yeah, it's big, I guess."

She shoved both my shoulders with her hands. "Big? A basketball team could fit up there."

Then she looked down at the bottle. "Whatcha got there?"

"Pusser's rum," I replied. "The official rum of the Royal Navy."

"Is that what you did in the war?"

"The Royal Navy?" I asked, chuckling, and herding her toward the hatch. "No, I'm not British. It's just good rum."

"So, what did you do?" she asked, once we got back up to the dock.

"When?"

"You said you went to war."

"I retired from the Marines, almost ten years ago," I replied. "The US Marines."

"The Marines? Whoa..."

"Lots of guys do," I said. "No big deal."

"But retired? You're not old enough to retire."

"Thanks, but it's only twenty years of service. And the pension isn't enough to be completely retired. I own a charter service back home."

As we walked back up the dock, Kat asked about the turtles that Brayden and I found. "He showed me the tag," she added.

"I looked on the internet," I said. "Those three shells probably netted the poacher six or seven thousand dollars on the black market. Other than that, Brayden probably knows more about the poaching."

Kat shuddered. "It's awful that someone would do that to some defenseless animal just for the shell."

"You get no argument from me on that," I said, as we started along the shoreline.

Finn and the dog he'd been playing with came trotting toward us. Both dogs jumped and started around us, as if conveying the unabridged all-important news of the day in body language.

Kneeling, Kat took the other dog under the chin and lightly wrestled him to the ground for a belly rub.

"How's my Bill?" she asked in baby-talk.

Finn barked, and the other dog wiggled and sprung to his feet. Then the two took off racing down the beach at a dead run.

"That's Macie's dog," Kat said.

"Bill?"

"Yeah," she said. "Just Bill. Simple name for a simple dog."

She handed me the guitar case and trotted ahead, toward the cooler. I picked up my pace and when I reached her, Kat handed me an icy Heineken. "I'll trade you."

"Deal," I said, opening the case and handing her the old Silvertone.

The group had moved away from the grill while waiting for the charcoal to get ready. A pile of driftwood stood at the ready inside a ring of rocks. The wood was dry, but the charred edges of the rocks and ashes below the wood told me this wasn't the first beach fire here.

"Play that song you're writing," Macie said, moving over, and patting the log she was sitting on.

The others were sitting on similar logs, or in the case of the Bourgeau brothers, right on the sand. Cory and Lea McKay had brought their own, low-slung beach chairs. I took a knee next to Kat, then lowered myself into a semi-seated position, my right knee up and left leg curled under me. It's the seated position for rifle target practice. Easy to get into and quick to get up from.

Kat spent a moment tuning the guitar, then began to play a few chords. The old guitar sounded like it had found itself a home here on the beach. The tone carried fluidly around the gathering, before being lifted and carried away on the breeze. She played effortlessly, as my mom had. But where mom's singing voice was deeper and sort of sultry, Kat's was bright, like a silver bell, as she began to sing about islands in the sea and a beach far away.

The chords she played were simple, but clever, as she strummed the guitar. I looked around, and the others seemed to have similar expressions, the sort I like to think Armstrong had after he stepped on the moon and looked around. Occasionally we all experience something for the first time, something bigger than life, that we're certain nobody else has ever experienced. The brothers were speaking low to one another, and one of them, the younger one, glanced over at me for a moment.

To say that Kat was *good* would be putting all good singers on a pedestal they just didn't rate. Her voice was clear, and each note she sang rang perfect to my ear. I'm not a musician or anything, I just know what sounds good to me.

Everyone clapped their hands as the song ended abruptly. Kat turned to me. "It's not finished yet."

"But, you've added more to it since last time," Macie said, smiling brightly, and placing a hand on Kat's bare knee. "I really like the new second verse."

"I wrote it last night," Kat said.

I remembered her playing the previous night and how I'd fallen asleep listening. At the time, I thought she was just learning, as she stopped and started over. She'd been writing her song.

Finn approached, Bill close on his heels. He dropped a clam at my feet, then the duo trotted back to the water's edge.

The young girl, Carmen, leaned forward on her log, looking down at my feet. "What'd he bring you?"

"A clam," I replied. "They're probably not hungry anymore."

"I love clams," she said, elbowing her boyfriend.

"He'll likely bring more," I said. "It's a game with him."

While Kat played a couple more songs, Finn returned repeatedly, dropping little top neck clams at my feet. Soon, Bill began to bring some to me, as well. As the sun neared the horizon, there were nearly three dozen in a pile at my feet.

Kat stopped playing, as one by one, we all turned our eyes toward the setting sun. There was nothing between us and the horizon except a few gulls wheeling across the reddening sky above the dogs. The air was cool and clear, and even though it had rained buckets earlier in the day, the humidity was low.

Though I'm sure everyone there had seen it many times before, there was a collective gasp as the refracted light gave the impression of the water reaching up and grabbing the dark orange orb as it reached the horizon. The lower half of the sun began to flatten out in the ocean's grasp, as if it were struggling to stay aloft.

Closing my eyes, just before the last instant, I wished for the same thing I always do. A long life and happiness for my kids.

Opening my eyes, I saw the last of the sun disappear in a pale green flash, and I smiled. It was the sixth time I'd seen this odd display of light, moisture, and air.

Brayden raised a chipped and faded conch shell to his lips and blew out a long, low note. Other horns, both natural and mechanical, joined in from the anchorage, each person celebrating the magnificent sunset in their own way.

"I think the grill's ready," Lea said to her husband.

Cory McKay rose from his chair, and Gaston Bourgeau joined him. The two walked toward the grill with the cooler of lobster tails.

"How long has everyone been here?" I asked, looking around the group.

"Macie and I for two years, like I said earlier," Brayden began. "Lea and Cory got here about a year ago, with plans to sail the northern Bahamas right after their marriage."

"Cory was a doctor," Lea said. "When we dropped anchor here, it was only to stay a few days. After two weeks, he told me he was going to give up his practice. That was last summer. We cruise to other islands now and then, but always return here."

"We sailed into Chub four months ago," Carmen said.

David took her hand. "Probably the most memorable four months of my life."

"We arrived two weeks ago," Mayhew Bourgeau said, his accent heavy and speech uncertain. "We are sailing around the world."

"Off and on since I crewed with Macie and Brayden," Kat said. "I think I'll stay a while now."

"Carol and I have been here for three months this time." Tommy said. "Last year we spent all winter here. Sure beats Buffalo. But we're heading out in the morning to visit friends on Hoffman's Cay."

"This *is* an exceptionally beautiful island," I said, uncorking the rum. I held it aloft. "To islands in the sea."

Taking a swig, I passed the bottle to Kat. She did the same, and it went around the circle, as the night quickly grew darker. It wasn't yet eighteen hundred, but it *was* the dead of winter.

"Give them about ten minutes," Cory said, returning from the grill. Taking the bottle from Lea, he looked at it. "Fifteen-year-old rum? You do know how to win friends, McDermitt." He took a sip and passed it to Gaston, who handed it to me without drinking.

Cory doused the bottom of the driftwood with a heavy dose of charcoal lighter and tossed a match in. Within seconds, the beach fire blazed forth, the pungent smell of the accelerant hanging in the air until the wind carried it off. The fuel burned off quickly, and the flames began to crackle and change color. Some driftwood pieces burned red and others blue or green. Different woods absorb salt and other trace elements in the water at different speeds, and it's these things that create the vivid colors of a beach fire.

Excusing myself for a moment, I went over the dune to where a small palm tree stood. Two of the lower fronds were dying and looked to be perfect for my needs. Using a folding knife, I cut them away from the tree and cut the fronds from the petiole.

Returning to the fire, I put the flattened sides of the petiole sticks together, and used them as makeshift tongs, putting a clam between the ends and placing it on a long piece of wood near the flames. As I was moving the last of the clams into place, the first ones were beginning to open, steam coming from the shells.

"You're a handy pair to have around," Carmen said, as Finn plopped down in the sand beside me.

He appeared to be more exhausted than hungry. He hadn't had anyone to play with like this in a long time. Bill lay down behind Macie and looked to be equally worn out.

"Sometimes you have to improvise," I replied, lifting the open clams away from the flames, one at a time, and placing them on a flat rock beside the fire. "Let these cool for a minute."

The clams made for a good appetizer and disappeared quickly. Kat played another couple of songs before dinner was ready. The place settings were rustic: pieces of flat wood siding, with banana leaves covering them. The meal was a single lobster tail, served over a bed of rice Lea had cooked earlier and carried over in a heavy steel pot. The whole thing was garnished with several slices of fresh pineapple. Back in the States, people would pay fifty dollars a meal for the experience. We ate with our fingers.

Macie leaned across Kat conspiratorially. "Brayden said you're looking for a woman who came through here last week."

"A woman I used to know," I replied earnestly. "It was many years ago. I let her go and often wish I hadn't."

"Was the boat called *Sea Biscuit*?"

"You remember her?"

"She only stayed a couple of days," Macie said. "Waiting on weather. She shared a bottle of wine with me one night when I was waiting up for Brayden. He'd gone out fishing. Nice lady."

"Yeah," I replied, wistfully. "We got along well. I'd like to think we can again."

"She's on her way to Tortola," Macie offered. "She said she wanted to be in Cane Garden Bay by the first of February, if I remember right."

"That's what? About a thousand miles from here?" Kat asked.

"Seven days," Brayden said. "Cruising non-stop, day and night."

"But I don't think she was in a hurry," Lea said, "and her daughter was so bright and fun."

Three weeks to cover what could be an easy ten-day run at six knots, I thought. Sounds just like her. She'd probably have to stop for fuel at least once, I doubted her boat had a thousand-mile range.

After dinner, banana leaves and remnants of food were brushed into the fire and the boards tossed shoreward for the next time. Brayden produced a joint and lit it, passing it to Macie.

I leaned toward Kat. "Is his the same as yours?"

"No," she whispered back. "It's better and will make you feel all happy inside."

Kat accepted the joint from Macie and took a small puff, inhaling deeply. Then she passed it to me. Knowing that it would have a whole hell of a lot more pot in it than the little tube Kat had given me, I took a very small puff and then sucked in as much air as I could. I nearly coughed, as my chest began to expand, but following Kat's example, I let the smoke out quickly.

The initial feeling was the same as earlier in the day. Like a rush of warm water, it radiated across my face, then up and over my head. I passed the joint to Gaston. As he'd done with the rum, he handed it to Cory. I was surprised that Cory and Lea both smoked it, him being a doctor. So I asked him about it.

"There are far more benefits to marijuana than there are detriments, Jesse," he said. "Well, aside from the delivery method, that is. Smoke damages the lungs, no doubt, but one or two inhalations a day does a lot less damage than sitting next to this fire for an hour. Besides, it's fun, and aside from the smoke, it doesn't hurt anyone. In my learned opinion, as a practitioner of the ancient art of healing, it's more harmless than rum."

When the joint got back to Brayden, it was half gone. He pinched the end quickly with his fingers, crushing out the ember. I understood why. The effect was immediate and deeply satisfying, like a double shot of smooth, over-proof rum. Just without the burn. I felt pleased about everything: my full belly, the company I was in, the feeling of the damp sand under my leg. Even the stars in the sky seemed to be dancing merrily.

Topics of conversation came and went, like the waves on the beach. We laughed and told stories about ocean crossings and islands visited. I mostly just listened. Now and then, someone would request a song and Kat would pick up the guitar and sing. The songs were a mix of reggae, folk, and what she called trop-rock. Most were tunes I'd never heard before, but I recognized a couple of them. The others seemed to know them all and some sang along. Kat explained where and how she picked up some of the songs. A few she'd learned from cruising musicians in tiny, out-of-the-way bars on some faraway islands.

This whole community seemed to be highly mobile, yet traveled at a snail's pace, stopping for days, weeks, or months, whenever the situation warranted it. They talked of other cruisers they knew, where they were, and the last time they'd been heard from. Many of the same names kept popping up. Indeed, they were a tight-knit community, talking regularly with others over SSB radios. I somehow felt relaxed and happy to be in their midst.

The Pusser's bottle went around again, and more beers were plucked from the icy depths of the cooler. At some point, Brayden relit the joint, and it went around again. In the back of my mind, I knew that it was illegal. But, I'd done a few things in the past that stretched the bounds of the law, things that I'm far less proud of but would do again given the same circumstances. We weren't hurting anyone.

Somewhere around midnight, with the moon halfway down the western sky, the Bourgeau brothers excused themselves, saying they had work to do tomorrow. I considered that a moment. I had something to do, as well. I had a good idea where Savannah was going to be, and when she'd be there. It was a big ocean to search, and Tortola was a very small island. Part of me was wishing I still had the *Revenge* nearby. But another part was looking forward to the challenge: ten days at sea, sailing solo. I could easily be in Tortola ahead of her.

"Did you call that in?" Cory asked Brayden. "That turtle thing?"

"I did, mate," Brayden said, sitting forward. Discussion of the poaching brought my mind back to the present. The pot was starting to wear off, but the haze of the rum was still there. "After a bit of ducks and drakes, being shuffled from one department to another, I reached the Bahamian Interior. They're sending someone out in the morning to take statements." Brayden looked across the fire at me. "Will you still be here, Jesse?"

"Yeah," I said, reaching a decision. "I think I'm gonna stay a few more days."

Kat smiled and put the guitar in its case. "I'm tired," she said. "It's been a long day."

CHAPTER ELEVEN

I t was late when I woke. Bright sunlight streamed through the overhead porthole. By the angle, I could tell the morning was nearly half over. The previous night's events were hazy after midnight. I don't drink to excess very often, but I'd felt at ease last night and probably overindulged. Add to that the fact that yesterday was the first time I'd ever gotten high on pot. At least, the first time I'd willingly done so.

My mouth was dry, so I put on a pair of shorts and a faded yellow *Rusty Anchor* tee-shirt, then stepped up to the pilothouse to get a bottle of water from the fridge.

Kat was just turning on the stove. She was wearing my shirt from last night. It looked huge on her little frame, and I couldn't tell if she had anything at all on beneath it.

"Sleep okay?" she asked, handing me an empty mug, then filling it with coffee.

I took a tentative sip. It was strong, the way I like it. "I don't think I moved an inch after laying down."

"Thanks for letting me borrow your shirt," she said, as she placed six strips of bacon in a pan. "I usually sleep nude and don't have anything clean."

"Don't mention it," I said, looking around. "Where's Finn?"

"Bill came to get him an hour ago. They're around somewhere."

"You didn't have to make breakfast."

"It's the least I could do," she said. "If you hadn't been there the other night, I'd still be in Nassau. God, I hate that place."

I took another sip of coffee. "Is this the place you and Benny were headed to?"

After several minutes, Kat placed the bacon on a straining rack and poured the grease from the pan into a glass.

"Yeah, sort of," she replied, adding what looked like half a dozen whisked eggs to the skillet. "Benny was coming from Puerto Rico. He bought a bunch of scrips and was taking them to Miami to sell to a guy he knows there. Truth is, he never planned to come here. He just said that to get me to go with him."

"Scrips?"

"Prescription drugs," she offered. "Vicodin... Darvon... Demerol. I don't really know what kind, and he didn't tell me any of that until we were underway."

"And he was taking them to sell in Miami?" I asked. "Why?"

Kat shrugged, as she moved the eggs around the skillet. "Higher price, I guess. Or just for the thrill of being a smuggler, maybe. Benny was like that."

There was obviously more she wasn't saying, due to the incident on the dock in Nassau. I knew there was a huge epidemic of prescription drug abuse in the States, and assumed it was probably the same all over the world. The pharmaceutical companies made far more than could possibly be prescribed, and out-of-date meds were often sold on the black market.

As she scooped the eggs onto two plates, I sat down at the dinette with my coffee. Kat slid the plate with the larger mound of eggs in front of me then sat down across the small table.

"Anyway," she said, shaking a little salt onto her eggs, "when I found out, I told him I didn't want any part of it, or him. I convinced him to sail straight through. His boat doesn't have autopilot, so one of us had to be at the helm. I didn't even want him touching me anymore."

"So you jumped ship in Nassau?"

Kat placed her fork on her plate and looked at me. "It worked great for two days. Near Nassau, he suggested we do it at the helm. That's when I told him I didn't want anything to do with him."

"You don't have to tell me what happened," I said.

"I kicked his ass," she said, conviction in her eyes. "Bloodied his nose and blacked his left eye. Then I sailed into Nassau."

I nearly choked on a mouthful of bacon. Perhaps there had been more to the reason Benny didn't let me see his face than what he let on.

"You beat him up?" I finally got out.

"I'm no easy target, Jesse."

Hearing a chirping noise, I rose and went aft to my cabin, with a newfound respect for the girl. The idea of her whipping Benny, as small as he was, then commandeering his vessel was sort of swashbuckling.

My sat-phone was on the charger. I had a text message from Andrew telling me that he was under way and would arrive at the *Rusty Anchor* before sunset to meet up with Jimmy. My first mate's knowledge of the local waters surpassed even my own. Jimmy would take the *Revenge* the last thirty miles to my island. The message was time stamped nearly three hours ago. I'd slept through the alert tone and several reminders. I sent a quick reply, thanking him again, though I knew he wouldn't get it for another hour, when he got within cell range of the Florida coast.

"Anything important?" Kat asked, when I returned to the pilothouse.

"Just my friend telling me he was leaving Nassau on my other boat."

We ate in silence. I could tell Kat had something on her mind, so I ate unhurriedly to give her time to collect her thoughts.

"What do you really do?" she finally asked.

I glanced up, arching an eyebrow. "What do you mean?"

"This boat's one thing," she said. "It's beautiful, but it's older. So probably didn't cost more than a house back home. But that other boat is big money. I've met a few charter guys; most couldn't rub two pennies together after making the payment."

"I work because I like to, not because I have to; I owe nobody. And because I don't have to work, I often don't. I live frugally, living mostly off of my retirement and investments."

"Yeah, I asked Cory about that. He's smart. He said your retirement couldn't be enough to live on and I should watch out."

Taking a deep breath, I placed my fork on the table, and looked deep into Kat's eyes. I was unaccustomed to discussing how much money I had, or where it came from, with someone I didn't know very well. Or, for that matter, even trusted friends.

Opening my phone, I pulled up the internet and did a search for a news story in the *Abaconian*, the local paper of the Abaco islands. When I found it, I opened the story to the group photo that was taken at the stern of the *Revenge*, with chests of emeralds and gold coins, all propped up in front of my friends. I was on the bridge, just visible behind them.

"A few years ago, me and some friends found something that'd been lost for over four hundred years."

Kat picked up the phone and looked at the picture, zooming it in. Then she scrolled the screen, stopping to read here and there.

"You found a treasure ship?" she asked.

"Yeah. So, like I said, I work because I enjoy working."

Picking up her mug, Kat swallowed the last of her coffee. I could tell by the look in her eyes that there were more questions.

"When you were in the military?" she said. "What was your job?"

Drinking down the last of my own coffee, I looked at her over the rim. The difference between us was vast, I could see. There were career military people, like myself, then there were those who served one or two tours. Others might have had a sibling, parent, or child in the military. Others still might have had a sibling or parent who served, or known a veteran or two, or remembered Billy from high school who left for the Navy and never came back. Then there were the sheltered few.

I kind of figured that Kat, and maybe some of her friends were in the last group. Those who have never had contact with someone in the military, or a veteran. And that's okay. Less than half of one percent of the population serve. The other ninety-nine-and-a-half percent are protected by those serving, and many don't even know to what degree that protection extends, or at what cost to that half percent. Those who serve do so for that reason: so people like Kat would never experience a night without peace.

"I was an infantryman, Kat. Just before I retired, I taught promising young Marines how to shoot straight."

"Brayden said you were a sniper. Said he could tell by the way you sat down at the fire."

Having worked with Deuce and his team, and now owning part of a security company, I felt a bit ashamed that I had let something like that give me away.

"How would Brayden know?"

"I'm not sure," she replied. "I think he was in the New Zealand army or something."

"I was a Marine, Kat. The Marines have a motto: Every Marine a rifleman. Even the cooks and clerks had to know how to shoot. Now I'm just a former treasure finder who likes boats—a boat bum with a little coin saved up."

Picking up my fork, I continued eating nonchalantly, hoping that would be the end of it.

"Are you really gonna do what you said last night?" she finally asked.

Swallowing a bite of eggs, I thought back on last night's impromptu gathering on the beach while I chewed. I couldn't remember saying anything about anything I had planned that would concern Kat.

"I'm not sure I know what you mean."

"You got pretty wasted," she said, pushing the eggs around her plate some more. "Do you remember coming back to the boat?"

I didn't. I remembered some of the conversation after the French brothers left, and remembered Kat saying she was ready to turn in. But, I got the feeling that we didn't leave right away, and I definitely couldn't remember walking back to the boat, or anything after that, until I awoke. Had anything happened once we got back? After all, she *was* wearing my shirt.

I took a swallow of my coffee before answering. "Yeah, I guess I did have a bit too much. I don't usually get that bad off, especially around people I barely know. I'm sorry if I said or did anything out of line."

Her face took on a mischievous expression. "What if I told you we did it in that big bed of yours?"

I felt my face redden, and she laughed.

"Don't worry," she said. "Nothing happened between us; but I did nearly carry you back here."

I took a sip of coffee and raised it to her. "Thanks. So, what kind of alcohol enlightened pearl of wisdom did I drop last night?"

"You said you were going to find the people who were killing the turtles and reefs and make them pay."

"Reefs?" I asked.

She laughed again. "You really were bombed, huh? Brayden told us about reporting the turtles and then David brought up an ongoing problem they've had around here. Someone's been breaking off huge portions of reef and live rock. Brayden thinks they've hauled away tons of live rock in just a couple of weeks. You seemed very interested."

That's a lot of material to haul off, I thought. Coral reefs are slow growing communities of tiny animals. They can't move about, and the calcium skeleton of hundreds of years of growth is as hard as rock and doubly treacherous to boaters. The collection and sale of limestone rocks with attached corals, tube worms, and other organisms is strictly regulated, and most of it is grown in artificial farming tanks.

"That was just the Pusser's talking," I said. "I'm just one harmless old guy."

But, she'd piqued my curiosity. A couple of years ago, someone had intentionally destroyed many patch reefs in the backcountry of the Keys, near my home. They'd done it intentionally, to flush me out.

"Yeah," she said, drawing the word out. "Older, maybe. But, I get the sense that you could be miles away from a harmless guy, if you set your mind to it."

"So, what are your plans for today?" I asked, changing the subject.

"Cleaning out my loft. In fact, I told Macie I'd be there at nine and it's nearly half past that now."

"Need some help?" I asked, then quickly shoveled down the last of the eggs.

We cleaned up the breakfast dishes, then Kat went below to change clothes. When she returned, she was wearing a tight-fitting workout top that ended before her ribcage, and a pair of cutoff jeans.

"If you need to wash some clothes," I offered. "There's a machine in the aft passageway."

"Thanks," she said, smiling. "This is the last of my clean clothes, so I'll take you up on that when we get finished."

We walked up the dock to the marina office and went inside. There wasn't anyone around. Kat went to the drink cooler and took two bottles of water, tossing me one before making a note on a pad sitting on the countertop.

"That's about all I can offer for pay," she said. "Macie must be out back."

"Payment accepted," I said, following Kat out the back door.

I glanced down at the pad. Names were scribbled, along with items like water and canned corn. The honor system.

Behind the building, under the shade of what was left of someone's mainsail, Macie, Brayden, and Cory McKay were sitting around a small table, with a portable single-sideband radio in the middle of it. Two cords extended from the radio; one was connected to a heavy extension cord that went through the door we'd just come out of. The other cord, an antenna coax, snaked around a mast attached to the side of the building, and soared at least fifty feet above the ground.

A woman's voice was coming over the radio, and Macie put a finger to her lips and motioned us to sit. I held a chair for Kat and then dragged a bucket over, flipping it to sit on.

The woman on the radio was giving the sea conditions off the lee side of Cat Island. I'd listened in on SSB nets on occasion. They had a set time and frequency to broadcast the news of the day from wherever the net was located. People who were planning to visit the area, had friends there, or, like me, were just bored for something to do, could listen in.

Cory reached over and switched the radio off. "That's it for now, I guess. No news is good news, right?"

"What's going on?" I asked.

"That was the morning net from Cat Island," Brayden said. "Some mates have disappeared over there. Someone bloody boat-jacked them last weekend."

The couple that the Pences and Haywood stole the boat from, I thought, while trying not to let on that I knew something. I didn't know why I wanted to keep that information to myself, but I did.

"Still no word?" Kat asked, concern evident in her voice.

Cory shook his head. "Mark and Cindy, nor their boat, have turned up anywhere. Jenny said there was an unconfirmed report to the Defence Force that a boat matching their description was spotted the day after the abduction, heading north toward Spanish Wells."

"These people are friends?" I asked.

"Mark and Cindy Mathis," Macie replied. "He was a software developer and she, a teacher. They took early retirement three years ago and bought a Hatteras, up in Galveston. It was an old yacht but had been completely refitted and modernized. I doubt they've spent more than a month ashore since then. They were here for six weeks last fall and decided to visit the BVI. Sweet people."

"I'll catch up with all of you later," Cory said, standing. "Today's what? Hogfish day?"

Brayden nodded toward me. "You up for some spearfishing, mate?"

"Sure," I replied. "But I don't have a sling."

"Gotcha covered," Brayden said.

Cory started off and called over his shoulder as he wound through the small palms and buttonwood bordering the back of the marina. "Lea caught several conchs and is going to bring fritters."

"I gotta jet, too," Brayden said, following Cory. "David and I are cleaning his bottom."

"Jesse said he'd help with the loft," Kat offered, as she rose and started for the back entrance.

I jumped up from my bucket and grabbed the door.

"Good," Macie said, following Kat. "There's some heavy boxes up there."

Once inside, the two women turned down a narrow hallway behind the marina office. There were two doors on the left, marked for men and women. At the end of the hall, stairs turned back the opposite way, above a closet marked with a sign saying *Parts*.

Macie flicked on a switch at the bottom of the stairs. Up above, a flickering light came on in a loft area above the little office. The stairs themselves were shadowed and quite steep.

"If you have some receptacles, wire, and switches," I said, "I might be able to rig up lighting in the stairwell and a separate switch up there for the loft."

"There's lots of scrap wire and electrical parts in a parts bin downstairs," Macie said. "Not house wiring, just individual strands for boats. People leave what they don't need and take what they can find. Everything's solar and batteries here."

"That'd work," I said. "If the wires are long enough."

The loft was a mess. It looked like it had been used for a catch-all since the arrival of the Spanish armada. There were boxes of all sizes, most of them stacked along two walls. Several were open, out in the middle of the small space, revealing nothing but junk and papers. As if someone pulled a box from the stack to find something and never put it back. Even the open boxes were dust-covered. The labels on some of the boxes dated back to the seventies. Boat parts, ripped fenders, tangled dock lines, and torn sails were strewn everywhere like flotsam after a sinking. I stripped off my shirt, and we got to work.

Macie went over to the boxes. "Anything marked two-thousand-three and older, we can toss."

"You sort, and I'll carry," I said. "Where do you want them?"

"Just downstairs for now," Macie replied. "We can carry them out to the fire pit later."

The loft was hot, with bare walls and rafters, but it would be cool at night. The boxes weighed thirty pounds or so, and after the fourth trip downstairs, I'd built up a sweat and could feel the burn in my calves.

I found the parts bins, and each time I went down, I came back up with anything I could find to hodge-podge together another light.

When the boxes were either gone or stashed in the corner, the women turned to cleaning, and I started in on the lights. I mounted a boat's live-well switch to the bare planked wall. It's a three-way switch where the middle position is off and the other two either fill or drain the tank. In this case, one would turn on the stairwell light, the other would turn on the overhead light in the loft, and the off position turned everything off.

The light receptacle was the challenge. There were a few to choose from, but no matching bulbs. I looked all through the shelves downstairs in the store and then went out to *Salty Dog* and started rummaging through the work area aft the engine room. I found exactly what I was looking for: a pair of LED lights, complete with bulbs. The fluorescent light in the loft would have to go. One of the tubes was burned out anyway.

"Take a break, big guy," Kat said when I returned. She patted the floor beside where she and Macie were sitting, their backs against the bare wall.

Moving the bucket that I'd planned to use as a step-stool closer, I accepted a bottle of water from Macie and sat down across from them—not in a shooting stance this time.

I drained half the bottle and held it against the back of my neck. "I found a couple lights just sitting around on the boat, collecting dust. They use a lot less electricity, but the bulbs are more expensive to replace."

"LEDs?" Macie asked.

I nodded. "They last a helluva lot longer than regular bulbs or fluorescents and use a lot less energy."

Kat pulled her dugout from her pocket and twisted the little bat into the main part of the wooden box. She passed the tube to Macie, who lit it, inhaling deeply. When she loaded it again and offered it to me, I held my hand up, palm out.

"Not if I'm gonna be working with electricity."

Kat shrugged and lit the little tube, exhaling a small blue-gray cloud of smoke that hung in the air with Macie's.

"So, you're going after her?" Macie asked me.

"Who?"

"The lady who came through here last week with her daughter."

"Well, thanks to you, I know where she's going and when she'll get there. I thought I might hang around here another day or so."

"The poachers?"

I raised an eyebrow in surprise. "That's part of it. But, to be honest, I haven't sailed in decades. Crossing from Nassau was the first time in a long time."

"Really?" Kat asked. "I wouldn't have guessed that. And if I'd known, I probably woulda *second*-guessed my decision to accept the ride."

"What can you do about the poachers?" Macie asked.

I glanced at Kat, then back to Macie. "Probably nothing," I said honestly. "Those turtles are so rare, the people who killed them have likely moved on."

"Brayden thinks it's the same people tearing up the reefs."

I took another swallow from the water bottle. "There aren't a lot of anchorages around here that could hide a boat big enough to remove tons of reef material. They'd be hiding in plain sight."

"Plenty of coves all through the Berries," Macie said.

True, I thought, thinking how close Andros Island was. "Anyone around here have a fast boat that can make Andros?"

"Not really," she replied. "Sometimes Brayden and I will take the mailboat to Nassau. It stops in Fresh Creek on the way."

"When does it arrive here?"

"Fridays, about nine," Macie said. "It does a hundred-mile loop out of Nassau, getting to Fresh Creek a couple of hours after leaving here. From there, it returns to Nassau. Why do you want to go there?"

"Just an idea," I replied.

Getting back to work, I soon had the lights installed and the switches working. The tiny LED bulb in the loft didn't provide as much light as the old fluorescent tube, but for a living space it was more than adequate. The added light in the stairwell made visiting the restroom at night a lot safer.

By early in the afternoon, we'd moved a vinyl-covered bench seat from someone's boat into the loft. It was in good shape, clean, and would double as a sort of foot locker. For a bed, Kat planned to use just a simple hammock someone had made from a jib. But then Lea McKay called out from downstairs and brought up a brand new, queen-sized inflatable mattress, still in the box.

"We've had this laying around forever," she said. "I thought it'd make a nice sun pad for the boat, but we just never used it."

Kat was pleased and very appreciative. It suddenly dawned on me that she and several of the others probably couldn't rub a pair of quarters together. Yet, others in the community, like the McKays, were obviously of greater means, and everyone lived together in harmony. The world, as a whole, could benefit from the example.

After Lea left, I went back to work, securing the wires to the exposed timbers using bent nails. It would never pass a fire-marshal's inspection, but unless someone yanked on the wires, there was no danger.

When we finally finished, the tiny loft looked livable. Kat hung the jib by three corners to create a hanging chair and we unstacked the boxes in the corner and arranged them on the floor, so the air mattress could sit on top of them. With a cotton sheet over it, it looked like a regular bed.

There was a vent up high at the gable end, and I pointed to it. "If you can scrounge up a fan and mount it to blow the air out, it'd be cooler during the day."

"It's a bedroom," Kat said, then grinned wickedly. "Mostly for sleeping. I doubt I'll be up here during the day at all."

"Hey, Jesse!" Brayden called out from below. "Time to go catch dinner, mate."

Saying goodbye to the women, I started down the stairs. "Where are we going?" I asked Brayden.

"A great little reef I know, not far from here. I've always been able to spear a few hogfish there. You know hogfish?"

"Best tasting fish in the sea," I replied.

CHAPTER  TWELVE

Brayden had his boat tied up at the end of *Salty Dog's* dock. As we approached, another boat came through the cut into the little marina. I recognized Detective Bingham's patrol boat instantly. It turned and came straight towards the *Salty Dog*.

"Bloody wallopers are never around when needed, and always late for appointments."

I'd heard the derisive Kiwi term for a police officer before. New Zealand cops don't carry guns, but they do carry a truncheon, or baton, which were sometimes wielded excessively.

We walked to the end of the pier, where the uniformed officer at the helm expertly brought the stern of the boat sideways to the pier.

"Why is it dat I am not surprised to see yuh still here, Cap'n?" Bingham said as he stepped off the boat, leaving the lines to his subordinate.

I didn't fail to notice that he hadn't used my name. It was obvious he still thought I was something I wasn't, and maybe didn't want to blow my cover if I was, and working at whatever he thought I did.

"You two know each other, Jesse?" Brayden asked.

"We've met," I replied. "Detective Bingham, this is Brayden, the guy who called in the report on the dead hawksbills."

Stepping forward, Brayden extended his hand. "Brayden Walker, mate."

"Australian?" Bingham asked.

"Don't be ridiculous," Brayden said with a half-grin. "An Aussie couldn't sail this far from home in two boats. I'm Kiwi."

"Who was with you when you found the dead turtles?"

"Captain McDermitt here," Brayden said, jerking a thumb toward me. "We were diving for prawns about this time yesterday."

Wiping at his brow, Bingham looked toward the marina building. The hottest part of the day had passed, but it was still in the eighties. And he'd probably been on the boat most of the day.

"We can go inside my boat to get out of the sun," I offered.

Inside, I waved a hand at the dinette. "Have a seat, Detective. Want something to drink?"

"Watuh, if it's not too much trouble."

"Beer for me," Brayden said.

I took two cold Kaliks and a bottle of water from the fridge, and placed them on the table. Sliding a chair over, I joined Brayden and Bingham.

Bingham produced his notepad and dug into his pockets until he found a pencil. "Yuh are certain dese dead turtles were hawksbills?"

"They didn't have a top shell anymore," Brayden said. "I was pretty certain of what they were at the time I reported it. One was tagged, and I called a mate in Florida who works with turtles and he ran the number and confirmed it. Definitely hawksbills. I found three more last week. Same thing."

"Could it have been a boat accident?" Bingham asked. "A big ship maybe?"

"Not a chance," I said. "Their entire shells had been removed, and there didn't seem to be any other injuries."

"I see," the detective said, looking at me. "Is dis why yuh are here?"

I was beginning to get a little irritated. I had no idea who he, or his cousin, the Foreign Affairs Minister, had talked to, but somebody had stepped off the pier and no boat was there.

"Like I told you before, Detective. I'm here on personal business and have no ties to any agency other than my own private business."

Bingham nodded. "Livingston and McDermitt Security. I know."

"So, you blokes know each other pretty well then?"

I turned to Brayden. "This guy's got it in his head that I'm some kind of secret agent or something." Then I turned back and glared at Bingham. "If I was, would I be telling that to a civilian?"

Bingham asked a few more questions. It was obvious he was only here because nobody else was available. But

I guess to a cop who has gangs running wild in his own town, a few dead turtles would seem like a waste of time. Fortunately, there were people in the world who saw value in all life. I felt that those here on Chub Cay were among them.

Once he'd finished asking his questions, Bingham rose and went to the companionway, stopping to face me. "How much longer are yuh planning to stay here, Cap'n?"

"I'll be in the Virgin Islands before this month ends, Detective. Other than that, I go where the wind blows and lay where the sand's warm. Why do you want me out of here so bad?"

The detective looked me straight in the eye. "Every time I see you, dere is a dead body involved."

Tromping up the steps, Bingham exited the boat. Brayden and I went up after him and stood on the pier. He signaled the uniformed officer on the patrol boat, who immediately started the engines.

"I'm beginning to think there's a little truth in what you said last night, mate."

"I was drunk," I said.

"You were more than that. My crop frees the mind. Kat said that was only your second time?"

The patrol boat roared off, and the two of us walked toward Brayden's skiff. I untied the lines, while he pumped the ball on the fuel line to start the outboard.

"Third, actually. But the first time wasn't of my own accord."

"Some of what I grow isn't really for first timers, mate."

Tossing the bow line into the front of the boat, I stepped down, and took the middle seat facing Brayden. "What exactly did I say, anyway?"

Idling away from the dock, Brayden pointed the little boat toward the open sea. "After the Frenchmen left, and it was just the eight of us, I brought out my good stuff and you passed that fifteen-year-old rum around several more times. Since there was an empty chair, you sort of staggered over to it, and then Kat joined you."

"Huh?"

He grinned at my discomfort. "I think she's hot for you, cobber."

I was completely bewildered. Kat hadn't mentioned any of that. And what did that have to do with something I might have said?

"Whoa, back it up," I said. "Kat's younger than one of my kids. No way I'd do anything like that."

Brayden laughed heartily. "Oh, you were the perfect gentleman, mate. You fell asleep."

"Wait—what? Back up and tell me everything that happened after the brothers left."

"You talk in your sleep, Jesse," he said, leaning forward for emphasis. "The combination of rum and weed opened your mind up and what was in there just spilled out of your mouth."

That was very troublesome. There are things I know that nobody else in the world knows. Places where bodies could be found, and the names of those who put them there. Several weren't very far from here, at the bottom of a blue hole.

"What exactly did I say in my sleep, Brayden?"

"It was hard to make out," he replied. "Kat was on your lap and repeated what she could make out. You mumbled on and on about how you and some others worked for the government. Someone named Deuce and Charity. We just sort of figured those were code names or the like."

"Code names?" I had to think fast. Adding mostly truth to a lie is the best way to diffuse a situation. "I was a marksmanship instructor in the Marine Corps, but retired almost ten years ago. Deuce is the son of my old platoon sergeant of the same name, Russell Livingston, Junior, or Deuce. I helped finance his security business. You know, installing alarms and escorting celebrities in Miami."

He met my gaze evenly. "And taking down drug lords and terrorists in Cuba on your days off?"

I could actually feel the blood drain from my face.

"That struck a chord," Brayden said with a smile. He brought the little boat up on plane, put his feet up on the gunwale, and shouted over the engine. "Relax, mate. Your secret's safe here on Chub."

Instead of going west, as we had the day before, Brayden turned the little boat east, following the shoreline. The marina and houses quickly dropped out of sight behind us, and the idyllic, natural shoreline was all there was to see.

I said something about going into Cuba with Deuce? That could be a real problem. It had been nearly three years ago, but I was sure the Cuban authorities would love to know who botched their gun-running operation.

After ten minutes, we reached the promontory at the east end of the island. There, the long, narrow island turns to the north, like an inverted number seven.

"It's gonna be a bit rough for the next couple kilometers," Brayden said, as he continued almost due east into open water.

Open water and I were no strangers, and I trusted the man's ability. But the boat we were in was no more than fifteen feet and nearly flat-bottomed. To say it was a bit rough was an understatement. We both held on as Brayden leaped the boat from one wave top to the next.

Another island lay ahead; the sparsely inhabited Bird Cay. As we neared the lee shore, the waves diminished; Brayden slowed the boat, looking back toward Chub. He turned north, always watching the point a mile away. I knew what he was doing. He was using the east and west points of Chub Cay's southern dogleg to line up his course to wherever it was we were going. Finally, he turned due east again and dropped to an idle.

"Take the bow," he said. "There's a wreck up ahead. We're gonna anchor about fifty meters past it."

Kneeling on the forward deck, I looked down into the gin-clear water. The bottom looked to be about thirty or forty feet. I scanned left and right, looking for anything out of the ordinary. Finally, I spotted a dark shape off to starboard and pointed toward it.

"Good eye, mate," Brayden said.

As we passed over the hulk, I recognized it. Lying on the bottom was a huge crane; its boom, twisted and broken, lay off to the left.

"The victim of an overzealous developer back in the seventies," Brayden explained. "Or at least that's what I'm told."

We continued another fifty yards into the wind. The boat was so small, the light breeze coming over the island would push it more than the current. When he nodded, I dropped the anchor in about twenty feet of water. Stretching my arms to measure the length of anchor line as the wind pushed us back toward the crane, I measured out an estimated scope.

"Some developer wanted to dredge this little cove, so he could bring his big yacht in. The Bahamas are carbonate islands, formed when sea levels rise and fall. They're brittle in some places and pretty damned hard in others. The crane operator on the barge had been drinking and underestimated the load he put on the crane."

Brayden held his arm out, elbow crooked so his hand pointed straight up, and let it slowly fall, punctuating the end. "Kersplash!"

"What happened to the barge?"

"Who knows?" Brayden said, looking over the side to see the crane just below us. "That's enough rode."

I tied off the anchor line and looked down. The massive body of the crane was directly under the boat. We were within a mile of the shore.

"People still live on Bird Cay, right?"

"So how come there aren't a bunch of other boats here?" he asked rhetorically. "It's a long swim. Bird Cay folks use nets and lines from shore for the most part."

I considered that a moment, in respect to trying to locate the poachers' big boat. This crane was huge, and easily seen if you came near it. A lot of people don't realize just how immense the ocean is.

"So not a lot of people know this thing's here?" I asked.

Brayden shrugged. "I guess not very many. You've spear-fished before, yeah?"

"I prefer a pole spear," I replied. "But I have a few spearguns."

"Only Hawaiian slings in the Bahamas, mate." He handed me a hand-carved piece of dense hardwood, about six inches long and half as thick. It was round and had a hole drilled through its length, just big enough for a spear shaft.

The wood was old, scratched and dinged, but it was clean. The spear and the surgical tubing that propelled the shaft both looked fairly new. The rubber tubing was attached to both sides of the wood with hundreds of turns of light braided twine. The tube's loop had a leather pocket to hold the butt of the six-foot spear. He'd probably lost the original steel boot. You shoot it much the same way as you would a bow and arrow.

"Same as yesterday," he said. "Enough to feed ten people and maybe one or two more."

"You believe me, don't you?" I asked, slipping on my fins. "About Kat I mean."

Brayden eyed me warily. "She's a good friend, Jesse. If someone hurts her, I'll hurt them. I'm no pacifist." Then his demeanor softened. "But she's an adult and can make her own decisions. Yeah, I believe you're uncomfortable with the situation. Your problem is, is she?"

"Well, I'm definitely not gonna smoke any more of your pot."

He laughed, perching his mask on his forehead. "Do or don't, mate. Nobody judges here. And if you blow up the poachers' boat, nobody here will say a thing about it."

Before I could reply, he gave me a thumbs-up, pulled his mask over his face and grabbed his sling and spear. Then he rolled backwards off the boat, causing it to rock. I did the same on the other side. On the surface, I threaded my spear through the hole, holding the shaft and the wooden block loosely in my left hand as I followed Brayden.

Diving, we finned slowly toward the crane directly below the boat. I kicked slow, clearing my ears with every third stroke. The body of the crane was resting on its tracks, the roof only ten feet below the surface. But that wasn't what drew my attention.

The massive boom was a spearfisherman's dream. It extended away from the mammoth tracked body, broken from its mount, and stretching out more than a hundred feet. It was a honeycomb of twisted and broken metal, with at least a couple decades of soft and hard coral growth along the entire length. Whether the metal frame had broken apart when it fell, or by the constant push and pull of the water, I couldn't tell.

All around the boom, a massive school of yellowtail snappers moved in and out of the thousands of openings in the coral growth that was slowly encapsulating the intricate steel structure. Moving around the base of the artificial reef formation, dozens of hogfish cruised the bottom, rooting through the sand for small shrimp, crabs, and worms, the same way their namesake does on land.

Brayden was finning slowly toward the right side of the boom, his left hand extended and his spear notched and pulled back. I moved diagonally across the boom, heading toward the other side, while bringing my own spear up and notching it in the leather pouch.

I heard the soft thwap of his sling but was already closing in on a platter-sized hog and kept my attention focused on the fish. My legs moved slowly, allowing the fins to do the work, so I could conserve oxygen. I closed on the big hogfish, my spear out in front of me, pointing at the lighter brown patch just behind his eye. Five feet away, I slowly drew the thick surgical tubing taut, taking careful aim, before releasing the shaft. It hit the fish right where I'd intended. He twitched only once, dead before he felt a thing.

Retrieving the spear, I headed to the surface, pulling the fish up with me. I took a quick breath, then swam with my face down, back toward the boat. There, I slid the hogfish off the pole and into the bow of the boat.

Pulling my mask down under my chin, I looked around. Brayden was on the surface, twenty feet away, with his face down. He arched his body and submerged.

I put the spear back through the wooden tube and swam to where he'd disappeared. Taking a deep breath, I dove down after him. Apparently, he'd missed on his first dive and was near the bottom, stalking another fish. I again moved to the other side of the boom, and soon found another hogfish that was too busy rooting in the sand to notice the danger he was in.

In the Keys, getting a couple of hogfish with a speargun in a few hours of diving was fortunate. They're usually solitary fish. Though I've seen them in loose groups, I'd never seen this many in one area.

We worked quickly and efficiently. Neither of us scored with every dive, but it soon became obvious to me that Brayden was an exceptional free diver. The two of us moved up and down effortlessly, spending more time on the bottom than on the surface. We soon had a dozen fresh hogfish in the boat.

Levering ourselves into the boat at the same time, we prepared to leave. "Take only what you can eat?" I asked, knowing that the boat limit in the Bahamas was sixty pounds or twenty fish. We weren't close to either limit.

"Yeah," Brayden replied. "That, and most everybody's freezers are full."

"And tonight's celebration?"

"Thursday," he replied with a smile. "How many Thursday's d'you suppose a man has, mate? It's a *seventh* of your whole life. If you live to be seventy, ten years of that life was on a Thursday." He winked. "That's a good enough bloody reason to celebrate it in my book."

As we started back, I moved the fish into a cooler and centered it in the boat. I didn't want Thursday's celebration dinner going overboard on the rough ride back.

Again, I bent and held onto both gunwales, as the boat bounced over the waves, headed back to Chub Cay. Halfway across, just as we crested a wave, I caught something out of the corner of my eye to the north.

Turning my head, I watched for it again. It made the ride rougher, not being able to anticipate the waves, and I nearly lost my grip. I saw it again, two miles away. It looked like a barge and small tug.

"What is it?" Brayden shouted.

"A barge," I called back to him. "Off the north end of Bird."

Soon, we neared the point on the southeast tip of Chub and the wave action subsided. I took the bow line in my hand and, with my legs spread wide, I stood and looked back over the starboard side.

"There," I said, pointing. The tug had her stern toward us, threading the passage between Cockroach Cay and Whale Cay.

Brayden stood, levering the tiller up and extending the handle.

"Right on the horizon at five-o'clock. What's beyond there?"

"Bond's Cay," Brayden replied. "I've a friend anchored over there with his family. Let's get back and I'll get *Cattitude* on the radio."

Brayden brought the boat up on plane and we zipped along the shoreline in just three or four feet of water. When we arrived back at the marina, there were only a couple of hours of daylight left.

"Go contact your friend," I told Brayden. "I'll take care of cleaning the fish."

He took off toward the marina building and I lifted the cooler out. Finn and Bill passed Brayden on the dock, on their way out to greet me. The two dogs met me at *Salty Dog's* rail.

Placing the cooler on the dock, I looked down at them. "So, what are y'all's plans for this evening?"

Finn barked, and Bill looked over at him, then he too looked at me and barked, as if to say, *What he said.*

I looked back at Brayden's boat, thinking I might as well leave my flippers and mask on board, as it seemed that Brayden was the hunter for the group. And I'd likely be helping him tomorrow.

Am I staying another day? I asked myself. Somewhere south and east of here, Savannah was making her way toward the Virgin Islands. There wasn't anything keeping me. It felt as if the two days here had melded together. I could see how the transients here ended up staying.

"Yeah," I told Finn. "We're staying another day. Go have fun with your new friend."

He barked again, then turned and bounded toward the foot of the pier, Bill running right alongside.

Stepping aboard *Salty Dog*, I went below and retrieved a long, thin filet knife, then carried the cooler downwind to another dock where no boats were tied up. I placed the cooler on the deck at the end and got to work. Hogfish filet nicely, and then each filet can be skinned with a long slow movement of the blade with the skin side down.

Hearing footsteps, I turned and saw Kat approaching. "That our dinner for tonight?"

"And then some," I replied. "Twenty-four good-sized filets for ten people."

"We'll wrap half a dozen and give them to David and Carmen. They're leaving in two days."

"They're on that little Hunter? Do they have a freezer?"

"Cory's been filling and freezing half gallon jugs of water for a few days for their ice box. Brayden said you guys saw the poachers."

"No way to know if it was them," I said, after rinsing the cooler. "It looked like a tug, pushing a barge toward the northeast."

"None of the islands up there are inhabited, except maybe a few people on Bond's Cay" Kat said, stooping to help me put the fish in the cooler. "At least not until the Abacos."

I dropped the last filet in and looked at Kat. "Why didn't you tell me everything that happened after I, uh...fell asleep last night?"

"Brayden told you about me sitting on your lap?" she said, standing.

I picked up the cooler and nodded.

"Nothing to tell. I was cold, and you were warm. I didn't mean anything by it. Everyone else had someone to keep them warm."

Motioning her forward with my chin, I said, "Stop by my boat. I have some plastic freezer bags we can put some of these in for David and Carmen."

In my galley, we put six filets into two bags and dropped them in my freezer. "That won't last them on a long voyage," I said. "Where are they going?"

"Anguilla," Kat replied. "They have a friend there who owns a little bed and breakfast. They're going to manage it for a few months. We've been stocking them up with supplies for a couple of weeks now."

"All for one and one for all, huh?"

"Something like that," she replied. "We help and take care of each other."

"About last night," I said, walking toward the companionway. "I really never get like that. Did anything else happen that I don't remember?"

"Trust me," she said, taking a step closer. "If anything else *had* happened, you *would* remember."

Taking her shoulders in my hands, I held her at arm's length and looked down into her eyes. "Nothing can happen between us, Kat. I'm way too old."

"Jesse, there's three couples here. The French brothers give me the heebie-jeebies. Then there's you and me."

"They'd already turned in."

"Oh," she said, looking down at her toes for a moment. When she looked back up, she was grinning. "Well, it was just in fun. So, you're older."

"I'll run interference when the Bourgeau brothers are around," I said. "But it feels weird. You're just a kid to me."

"All right," she said, raising her hands to her shoulders, palms out, as she turned and stomped up the steps. "It's not like I'm begging."

While some men might find a younger woman attractive, I think there's a limit. And I think men who have daughters often won't see a younger woman any other way. Well, to a degree. Savannah was younger by about a decade. But at my age, that's a whole helluva lot different than half my life younger.

Following Kat, I caught up to her at the foot of the pier. "I didn't mean to hurt your feelings."

She stopped and faced me. "And I'm sorry if I made you feel uncomfortable."

I stooped and placed the cooler on the sand. "Friends?"

"Can we pretend there's more when the brothers are around?"

"I'll be leaving soon, Kat."

"They plan to leave on Sunday."

"I may be leaving before then."

She looked up at me, her dark brown eyes dancing back and forth, as if searching for something in my own. "Can't you stay the weekend? You already said you know when you want to be in Tortola. There's at least a whole week to spare."

"I'll stay until they leave," I said. "But I'll be gone most of tomorrow."

Kat reached down and grabbed one of the cooler handles. "Gone where?"

I lifted the other side, and we started along the beach toward the fire pit. "I have to call a friend and get the okay, but I may be taking the mailboat to Andros, then going for a helicopter ride."

CHAPTER THIRTEEN

The dinner the previous night was excellent. Cory really had talent when it came to the rusty old grill. The broiled hogfish was delicious, and his wife's fried conch fritters were as good as any Bahamian mobile kitchen's.

Kat had played my guitar and true to my word, I'd let her pretend we were interested in each other; she even sat on my lap to teach me some chords. Once more, the brothers retired early. I drank only a few beers and didn't smoke any of Brayden's pot.

When the brothers left, Kat extricated herself from my chair and sat next to Macie to talk. I got Brayden aside and asked him if he'd go with me to Andros. He agreed, as long as we were back in time to catch the Friday meal. I explained that we'd probably be returning by helicopter.

It was still dark, but I managed to get down from the big bunk without stepping on Finn or breaking my leg. Flicking on a small lamp mounted on the bulkhead, I dressed in jeans and a lightweight, long-sleeved shirt. It would be warm, but at altitude, the temperature drops.

I retrieved my sat-phone and went up on deck, Finn's claws clicking behind me. He trotted off toward shore, while I scrolled through my very short contact list. I clicked on Charity's number and she answered immediately.

"Where are you?" I asked.

"Panama City."

"I thought your passengers didn't want to go to Florida?"

"The other Panama City," she said. "We're stocking up for a long crossing."

"You're going to the South Seas?" I asked in complete dismay.

"Yeah, and maybe a little beyond that. How's *Salty Dog*?"

"I'm on Chub Cay and heading to the Virgin Islands next week."

"The worm has turned, huh? So, what can I do for you?"

"I admit I do enjoy being under sail, and you were right; other cruisers have been more open. Savannah is headed to the BVI late this month." I paused for a moment, unsure of how she'd react to what I wanted. "Can I borrow your Huey?"

"Sure," came her instant reply. "I'll call the FBO at San Andros and tell them. But the Virgin Islands is barely a two-week sail, taking your time. Remember what I told you? The trip is the destination."

I did remember. And even though it was only a short jaunt under canvas, I knew I was hooked.

"That's not what I need it for."

"When do you need it?" she asked. It didn't escape my attention that she hadn't asked what I needed it for.

"This afternoon."

"Consider it done," she said. "I'll call them as soon as I get off with you. Anything else?"

I hadn't been expecting her to be so receptive. Her voice sounded light and cheerful, a far cry from the woman who had sailed *Salty Dog* to my island not all that long ago. Then, she'd been wary, constantly looking over her shoulder.

"You're really taking Moana all the way home?"

"Fiona is coming, too," she said. "But not for a few days. They're both fast learners and we made it here in eight days of straight-through sailing. We have to provision and rest up. Maybe in a week, if the weather's good."

My head reeled. I had no idea how far it was to French Polynesia, but I knew it was a long-damned way. "How long will it take you?"

"Thirty-five to forty days sailing time, plus a stop in the Galapagos Islands for a few days. So at least six weeks."

"I'm seriously jealous," I said. "Fair winds and following seas. And thanks."

"Jesse?"

"Yeah?"

"It's good to hear from a friend," she said hesitantly. I waited. "Would it be okay if I call you now and then?"

It had only been about two weeks since she'd lost Victor. Charity had no family to speak of. Now she was off on a humanitarian mission of sorts. She didn't have many friends, and I was honored that she thought of me as one of them.

"Please do," I said. "Check in with me every week on Friday morning, if you want. And text me your location every day or so. I'd like to keep up with this adventure."

"I will," Charity said, then she ended the call.

Going back down the companionway, I went to the coffeemaker and set it up. Somewhere between here and Tortola, there was a coffeemaker with a timer that had my name all over it.

While I waited, I went to the nav-desk and started rummaging through the charts. I didn't find one showing just the Berry Islands, but Vic had a large scale Northern Bahamas chart that showed some sounding details of the area I was interested in.

Locating the spot where I'd seen the barge, I was amazed to see that it was barely five feet in many places. Most tugs have a very deep draft, mostly due to their massive propeller. So, what I saw must have been a very small tug or maybe not a tug at all. With the right rigging, almost any shoal draft boat could push a barge.

The machine beeped, and I poured a mug while studying the chart. The course the barge had been on was probably the same way Savannah had come here last week. A shallow, meandering one-fathom pass through the banks.

The barge had looked pretty big, probably fifty feet or more. That was something that really couldn't be hidden easily. And to lift large amounts of live rock and keep it alive meant an onboard dredge and a partially flooded hold. But if the live rock and coral were broken up into smaller pieces that could be covered by a foot or two of water, a barge with a four-foot draft could probably handle a couple of tons.

Whoever was operating the tug was either way off course or knew the water better than the charts. Even at high tide, there would be spots with only six feet of water in the area I'd seen the barge.

"Time is it?" Kat asked, nearly stumbling up the steps from the lower salon.

"About six," I replied. "Coffee's on."

She helped herself, then sat down at the dinette. "Why are you up so early?"

"I'm going to Andros," I replied.

"Oh, yeah. But the mailboat won't be here till nine. You said you know a helicopter pilot on Andros or something?"

"I'm going to *borrow* a friend's helicopter and fly out over the Berry Islands to see if I can find that barge."

"You know how to fly one?" she asked, yawning.

I turned toward her and grinned. "No, I figured I'd just learn on the way there. Can't be all that difficult."

She seemed confused for a moment, possibly because of the hour. Then her dark brown eyes sparkled, and she smiled. "You made a joke."

"I'm not completely devoid of humor."

She rose and crossed the deck to where I was sitting. "So, you *do* think it was the poachers."

I looked up from the chart. The bags under her eyes were nearly gone and she no longer looked like a starving waif; perhaps she'd even gained a couple of pounds. She wore a loose-fitting tank top and high-waisted khaki shorts. Altogether, she presented a much healthier appearance than when we'd first met, just two days before.

"No," I said. "It just fits the equipment needs, to do what they did. But a deep-draft tug looks suspicious out there in those shallow waters. What valid reason would there be for a boat like that out there?"

Kat leaned over the chart, one hand on my shoulder. When she pushed her hair behind her left ear, I barely caught the scent of jasmine, one of my favorite flowers.

"Where did you see it?"

I stabbed a finger at the chart. "Somewhere here, between Cockroach and Whale Cays."

"There's another low island in between there," she said, brushing my hand aside. "It's not shown on this chart, because it's barely above sea level at high tide. The only way past it is on the south side, right here."

I looked closer at the spot. There were no lines showing depth.

"The cut's flat and sandy," Kat said. "In the deepest part, I can touch bottom with my toes and still have my eyes and nose above water. So, maybe six feet, max. It's protected on all sides from the wind and waves." She stood and leaned against the bulkhead. "That's catamaran country. What's the draft on a tug?"

"A lot more than six feet," I replied. "I've seen some smaller ones on the hard that would need eight feet or more, because of their big props."

"Maybe it wasn't a tug you saw."

That was the tack my brain was already taking. For some reason it pleased me that Kat thought the same way.

"I only saw it for a second and it was in that area, roughly. We were halfway back from Bird. The barge was on the horizon at five o'clock."

"Wait," she said. "You were back here long before that."

I was confused for a second, then realized I'd confused her. "I meant that the barge was *at* our five o'clock, the bow of Brayden's boat being twelve."

A light seemed to go on in her eyes. She traced her finger from Bird Cay to Chub Cay, stopping in the middle. "You mean they were in this direction?" she asked, moving her finger from that spot toward where the imaginary five o'clock would be.

"Exactly," I replied.

"That's nearly four miles," she said. "Even as tall as you are, the horizon's at least three miles Maybe it was over the horizon and all you saw was the upper part of whatever it was."

"Good point. It was barely a speck in the distance. I was already thinking it might be some other kind of boat, adapted to working in shallow water."

"A power cat, maybe?" She leaned over the chart again. There was little obstructing my view down her top. "Rigged to push a barge?"

"Could be," I said, standing and moving away from her.

Kat was frustrating. She seemed at times to be an innocent girl, and at others an experienced seductress. Whether the latter was intentional or accidental, I didn't want to find out. I went across to the coffeemaker and poured another mug.

"Take me with you," she said, holding her cup out.

I filled it, shaking my head. "I don't think that's a good idea, Kat. Besides, Brayden is going with me."

"Six eyes are better than four," she said. "It's a big ocean."

"It might be dangerous. I don't want to have to be responsible—"

"Nobody is responsible for me, except me," she said, defiantly. "I don't need anyone looking out for me."

"Everyone needs a six," I said.

"Then let me be your six, whatever that is."

I chuckled. "Six o'clock. At your back."

"Behind you," she said. "Watching that way?"

It was just a two-hour boat ride to Andros, then a few hours flying out over the Berries. Even at just five-thousand feet, it could all be seen in a matter of a couple of hours. I knew how Charity maintained her bird, and she'd told me a kid at the FBO took excellent care of it in her absence. So there really wasn't much danger.

"You really don't like Mayhew and Gaston, huh?"

She leaned against the bulkhead, her left hand on her cocked hip and right hand holding it. "It's not really that I don't like them," she said. "I just can't put my finger on it. Usually, I get a quick feeling about people I meet and can pick out the negativity pretty easy. Those guys just give me a sort of yucky feeling that I can't define. Does that make sense?"

I'd certainly met my share of people who gave me a yucky feeling. Far too many. Maybe that was why I felt attracted to this group of ex-pats. They didn't pry or ask too many questions. For the most part, they allowed life to happen on its own terms, reacting to what was right in front of them now, and not worrying about what tomorrow would bring.

Like Kat, I hadn't been able to get much of a read on the Bourgeau brothers. During the day, they'd been gone, off somewhere in their dinghy. At both beach parties, they'd left early. Maybe they weren't much for socializing. They seemed harmless enough, but I wasn't a single woman.

"Okay, you can go," I told her. "But change clothes. It'll be cooler up there."

"Can I use your—"

"I already told you, Kat; make yourself at home. *Mi barca es su barca.* The machines are apartment-sized, so you can do a good-sized load. If you don't mind washing everything together, it'll do three days' worth of clothes in about forty minutes. I have a desalinization unit and solar with a genset. So, don't worry about using anything up. The detergent's in the locker to the left of the laundry closet. Sorry, no bleach."

She stood on her toes and kissed my cheek. "Thanks, Jesse. I promise I won't be in the way."

While she busied herself with her laundry chore, I prepared pancakes, or as Pap called them, flap-jacks. We ate quickly, and I did the dishes while she moved her clothes up to the propane-powered dryer.

In an hour, she was changed into jeans and a lightweight, long-sleeved shirt that looked expensive. They say horizontal stripes make the body look wider, but the blue-and-white stripes looked great on her. With her dark eyes, hair the color of butterscotch, and deep tan, she looked very wholesome. Until I remembered that she had no tan lines.

"Do you have a small bag you can put a change of clothes in?" I asked. "Just in case."

"In case of what?" she asked, somewhat alarmed.

"Coffee spill, grease stain, fall in a puddle..."

"Oh," she said, moving quickly back down to the lower salon.

A moment later, she returned carrying a cloth backpack with simple drawstring closures that doubled as straps.

"All set," she said.

The sun was above the horizon. "We have better than an hour to kill before the mailboat arrives."

"Go for a walk?"

Finn and Bill found us as we walked past the fire pit everyone had congregated around for dinner the last two nights. The dogs trotted out ahead of us, both zig-zagging, noses to the ground.

"They do that every evening?" I asked. "Dinner and a fire on the beach, I mean."

Kat glanced up at me. "Yeah. At least whenever I've been here. Brayden's good at catching fish, lobster, and crabs, and at least one other person in the anchorage will bring something, even if it's just a can of beans or a big bag of chips."

"And it's usually just Brayden supplying the main course?"

"Macie said that David went out with him a few times but wasn't much help. Brayden says you out-dive him."

"I doubt I'd have his stamina," I said, picking up a shell and throwing it into the water. "And he definitely knows the spots."

"He and Macie have been here a couple of years. And he spent a lot of time here when he was a kid. His parents were cruisers."

"That explains it," I said, as we continued walking. "As a kid, I knew every patch reef and limestone ledge within twenty miles of where I grew up."

"You grew up in the Keys?"

"No," I replied, tossing another shell. "I was raised by my grandparents on Florida's southwest coast. Fort Myers."

"I grew up in Tampa, but never been to Fort Myers. Dad rarely took time off from work. Is it nice there?"

"I suppose. I left when I was eighteen, though. Pap was a Marine, and so was my dad. He was killed in Vietnam."

"I'm so sorry," Kat said, taking my arm.

I shrugged. "Anyway, the Corps seemed to be our tradition. I remember before Dad died, he and Pap would argue about the *Old Corps* and the *New Corps*. Pap and I ribbed each other like that in later years, too. But it was all in fun."

"Is he still living?"

I took a few more steps before answering. I'm sort of a private man and don't talk much about my past, especially with people I hardly know.

"Mam and Pap both died before I retired from the Corps nearly a decade ago."

"So, you joined before I was born?"

"I told you I was old," I said with a chuckle. "Yeah, I served twenty years. Anyway, I sold their house and bought a boat in Marathon. Instant home and a job, chartering tourists. What about you?"

"My folks still live in the same house in Tampa, with my little brother. I left when I was eighteen and lived in Palm Beach for a while, waiting tables. Met a guy who sailed, but he was mostly a day sailor. I wanted to see what was across the horizon."

"More horizon," I said, bumping her shoulder.

She smiled. "Then you get to someplace like this. Where time slows down to a crawl."

"I've felt that already," I said. "Time is a misused commodity, anyway. It doesn't really exist. It's always the tomorrows and yesterdays. Plans and regrets."

"Right?" she said. "I live for today. Always in the moment."

"Not a bad way to live, for as long as you can get away with it. Do you stay in touch with your family?"

"I call Mom whenever I get the chance. Which isn't often. Dad's almost always at work, though."

I dug my phone out of my pocket and handed it to her. "Call your mom."

"Satellite time is expensive."

Grinning, I winked at her. "Remember that picture of me and my friends with the treasure? That was only part of what we found that day. Don't worry about satellite time."

Her eyes sparkled as she accepted the phone. We walked, she talked to her mom, and I threw more shells into the ocean, distancing myself to give her privacy. Finn and Bill trotted up and down the beach past us, playing their own game of tag, or whatever it is that dogs do.

Kat finished her call and handed me the phone. "Thanks. It'd been a couple of weeks since we talked."

"Any time," I said, putting the phone back in my pocket. "We'd better get back. I doubt the mailboat skipper will wait."

"It was good to hear her voice," Kat said, falling in beside me. "Dad was already at work, of course."

"What's he do?"

"Mid-level corporate management," she said, as if the words tasted foul. "Don't ask where. He ran at least a dozen small companies before I turned eighteen. So I'm sure there have been a few since then."

"How come he couldn't hold a job?"

"Oh, it's not that," she said. "Every company he left was in better condition than it was when he arrived. He was a fixer—but would never go out on his own. Great security, but zero adventure."

"And you like adventuring."

"Don't you? I bet the military sent you a lot of places in twenty years."

I laughed as we continued walking. "Nothing even close to this."

As we approached the docks, nearly everyone was there, some holding packages or envelopes. Macie was coming out of the marina carrying several small canvas bags, neatly folded.

Brayden took one of the bags from her and opened it. One by one, the others in the group dropped their mail in. It was kind of surprising, in today's modern age.

"No internet," Kat explained, as if reading my mind. "And like I said, satellite time is expensive. Most cruisers rely on regular mail for a lot of things, using a mail forwarding service."

Finally, the mailboat arrived. The captain looked like an old salt, his hair snowy white and deep wrinkles in the skin of his face, which was the same color as the mahogany rails on the old diesel-powered boat.

"Got room for a few passengers to the next stop, Mick?" Brayden called to the skipper as he helped unload several large canvas bags. A young black man, no more than fifteen, handed them over the rail.

"Sure," the old man replied. "Five apiece."

"Five bucks for a ride across the TOTO?" I whispered to Kat. "That's a helluva deal."

"None of which goes to the company that runs the boats. Mick's a cool old guy."

Brayden carried the half-full mailbag and the empties aboard and placed them in a box on the starboard side.

"You'll be back before dark?" Macie asked Brayden, who looked over at me.

"By mid-afternoon," I said. "We're going fishing, right?"

Cory, who had been passing out packages and letters from one of the bags, laughed. "Friday is crab picking."

We said our goodbyes to the others. The Bourgeau brothers were nowhere around. Glancing out toward what I assumed was their Beneteau, I noticed the dinghy wasn't there.

The mailboat was an older vessel, about forty feet, but it looked clean and well maintained. It had a high bow, a fully-enclosed pilothouse, and a cabin that looked like it would have only a head and watch bunk. In another life, it had probably been someone's fishing boat.

The tiny pilothouse was big enough for two people to get out of the weather, and that was about it. On the fore-deck were two large boxes, port and starboard—perhaps fish boxes in another time. Each was marked with the destination the mail bags inside it were bound for: Chub Cay and Fresh Creek.

Brayden dropped the bags he'd brought aboard into the Chub Cay box and stretched out on it, his back against the pilothouse. Kat and I sat across from him on the Fresh Creek box, as the boat idled backward away from the dock.

Mick expertly turned the single engine boat in the small confines of the marina and pointed the bow toward open sea. The younger man then stepped into the pilothouse and Mick joined us on the foredeck.

"Get yuh legs off my box, boy," he ordered Brayden, who quickly stood, grinning.

Brayden and the old man shook hands. "Mick, you remember Kat, don't you?"

As the younger man throttled up to about ten knots, the skipper turned toward us, unaffected by the acceleration or the rocking motion of the slow boat.

"Why yes," he said, bowing slightly, and removing a salt-stained captain's hat. "Dis girl get prettier every time I see her. How are yuh, Miss Kathleen?"

Kat smiled, thanked him, and introduced me. I stood and offered the skipper my hand. "Pleased to meet you, Captain."

He took my hand. Though he was a slight man, probably no more than a buck-fifty in weight, his grip was deep and firm, his forefinger on my wrist.

"Heard about yuh," he said, his ebony eyes seeming to pierce my own. "Word in di islands is yuh were part of dem people dat busted up di druggie business over dere on Cat Island some time back. If yuh be dat mon, yuh have my thanks. If dat wasn't, happy to meet any friend of Kathleen."

"No idea what you're talking about," I said by way of reply.

"Dat so?" he asked, his eyes sparkling. I could tell he was the kind of man who rarely tipped his cards. "Den I am happy to meet you, Cap'n."

While the younger man piloted us out into the ocean, we all took seats on the boxes, Mick next to Brayden.

"I let di boy drive di boat," Mick explained. "He's my grandson's grandson. But di rules say dat I got to do di docking."

"Government rules?" I asked.

"Mick's rules," he replied with a grin, exposing two rows of straight white teeth. "Yuh ain't never seen dis boy try to dock a boat."

I looked back toward the young man at the helm. He seemed quite content to just be on the water. I knew that look.

"Your great-great-grandson?" I asked, dubiously. "How old are you, Mick?"

"I am ninety-two years in 'bout two months," he said, with defiant conviction. And with good reason.

He went on to tell us that he'd been running a mailboat in the islands since America's prohibition, sometimes running rum into Palm Beach. In all those years, he'd never missed a run.

"A lot of folks got rich in dese islands runnin' rum," Mick said. "I was still a boy for most dat time, but I took some barrels to Florida when I was no older dan dat boy at di wheel."

Mick entertained us with stories of the islands as they were in years and decades past. He talked about old boats and old friends, and the occasional odd character or celebrity that rode his mailboat. The crossing took two hours, but it didn't seem so.

When we arrived at the dock in Fresh Creek, Brayden and I helped unload the port box. At eight feet long and three wide, it was packed nearly full of Bahamas Postal Service mail bags.

Mick pulled the driver of the small mail truck aside once he'd loaded the outgoing mail bags, and said something to him.

"Where yuh be goin'?" Mick asked Brayden.

"Gonna catch a cab to the airport, mate."

"Dis man will take you dere," Mick said.

Fishing my money clip from my pocket. I handed Mick a twenty. "Thanks for the ride. And the entertainment."

He pocketed the bill and grinned. "A pleasure, Cap'n." He tipped his hat to Kat. "Miss Kathleen."

The three of us, along with the driver, carried the bags to his truck and tossed them in the back, climbing in and sitting on the sides of the truck's bed.

The ride to the airport took nearly an hour, with a stop at the post office, just a few blocks from the dock. We helped the driver unload and climbed back into the beat-up old truck. I could have called a friend who lived up above Nichol's Town to pick us up, but that would've been several hours out of his day.

When we arrived at the airport just after noon, a young Bahamian man was at the counter. He wore coveralls with a name tag that said he was Derrick.

"My name's Jesse McDermitt," I said, when he looked up. "My friend, Gabriella Fleming, called you?"

"Ah, yes suh, Mister McDermitt," the man said, smiling brightly. "I have Miss Fleming's helicopter out on di tarmac. I checked her over real good and spooled up di turbine for ten minutes dis morning. No problems at all."

"You're a pilot as well as maintenance chief?" I asked. He seemed young, but lately most of the people I'd met had seemed young.

"Yes, suh, rotary and fixed wing," he replied, handing me a set of keys. "Please follow me."

He walked us out through the back of the building. Charity's bird had a new paint job since the last time I'd seen it. It was solid black now, with a logo proclaiming it to belong to *Tropical Luxury Magazine*.

Derrick left us by the bird, and I unlocked and opened the doors, then walked all the way around the chopper, inspecting everything.

"Kat, you ride in back and help me look off our starboard side, and Brayden can watch the port side."

A few minutes later, I had the turbine running and went through the pre-flight checklist. Contacting air traffic control in Nassau, I requested a VFR flight plan, touring the Berry Islands, and stopping for the night at Chub Cay. Once I received clearance, I brought the helo up a few feet off the ground and taxied to the runway.

Minutes later, we flew over my friend Henry's little marina on the northeast shore of Andros, then out over open water. I leveled off at thirty-five hundred feet with a heading of twenty-five degrees. Chub Cay and the turquoise waters around the southern Berry Islands were just visible ahead.

As we crossed the northern edge of the dark blue waters of the TOTO, and the islands became more visible, I turned a little more easterly, heading toward the southernmost of the small island cluster, Whale Cay.

I adjusted my microphone and pointed down at the pale-blue shallow waters to the left. "That's where we saw it yesterday," I said. "It was headed northeast, up there just north of Whale Cay. We'll circle around all the Berries counter-clockwise and have a look at each island."

"Can you go lower?" Brayden asked.

"No," I replied. "We're at the limit now. Once we turn more westerly, we can drop down to twenty-five hundred feet to avoid IFR traffic."

"What traffic?" he asked, looking over at me.

I shrugged. "Rules are rules."

I flew slow, following the string of islands on the east that border deep water. There were quite a few boats, both traveling and at anchor, on the lee side of Bond's Cay.

We continued northward, flying a slow arc toward the west. Off Little Harbor Cay, the chopper's compass showed that we'd turned past magnetic north and I descended to three thousand feet.

Ahead lay Hoffman's Cay, where Charity had said that she and Savannah had dumped the bodies of four would-be robbers into an inshore blue hole. We could see the blue hole, along with several boats anchored just to the west of Hoffman's. I saw people jumping into the water there. They had no idea there were bodies several hundred feet below them.

"Nothing out of the ordinary there," Kat's voice said over the intercom.

If she only knew.

"The heading they were on?" Brayden said. "Do you think a barge could cross the deep to the Abacos?"

"I guess it'd be possible," I said. "It wasn't built here. That's what? Fifty miles?"

"And then some," he replied.

"With a flat-bottomed barge, they'd have to choose a good weather day. But they might have."

Continuing northwestward, we flew along the eastern shore of Great Harbor Cay, seeing nothing out of the ordinary. Reaching the northern tip of the archipelago, I looped the Huey around Stirrup Cay and Coco Cay and lined up due south to maintain our current altitude. Flying a magnetic heading between zero and one hundred seventy-nine degrees, we'd have to climb to thirty-five hundred.

"What's that?" Brayden said, pointing ahead and slightly east.

Climbing slightly, I turned southeast toward what looked like a platform of some sort.

"It's a power cat," I said, as we got closer.

Kat leaned forward in her harness to look out the forward windshield. "Weird looking."

She was right. It had nothing but flat open deck forward of a tall pilothouse where the cockpit would normally be. Power catamarans aren't uncommon in the Bahamas. They have a shallow draft, just like their sailing counterparts, but aside from no sails, the basic layout of the boat is the same: an expansive salon forward of a wide cockpit, with staterooms tucked down inside the twin hulls.

"There's your cat tug," I said, looking back at Kat.

"But where's the barge?" Brayden said.

"There isn't one," I replied, studying the boat. She was lying at anchor in the middle of a vast expanse of light blue, very shallow water. "What I thought was a barge and tug was just the flat foredeck and raised aft pilothouse."

Brayden was looking down at the boat through binoculars. "Uh, Jesse, there are two people watching us through field glasses."

Still half a mile due north of the odd-looking boat, I dropped a location pin on the GPS, then turned southwest, away from it.

"Describe the two men," I said.

"They ain't men, mate," he said lowering the binos and looking over at me. "A coupla Sheilas, one a blonde and the other with dark auburn hair, all big and poofy."

"That's it?" I asked, craning my neck to look back at the boat, now falling away behind us. "You didn't see a man? Tall, with dark hair?"

"Didn't see anyone else. You know who those ladies are?"

"No idea," I lied. *Could it be Yvette Pence and her skank sidekick Rayna Haywood?*

The odds were extremely small. The Bahamas covered more than five thousand square miles of ocean, and that boat only about fifteen hundred square feet. A virtual needle in a haystack.

"Why'd you turn away?" Kat asked from behind.

"I don't like having people watching me when I'm watching them," I said, slowly moving the stick back and forth, hoping my passengers didn't notice the evasive action I was taking. I've been shot at in the past for approaching a boat that I knew was conducting criminal activity. A mile away, I stopped zigging and zagging, and flew a direct course back to Chub.

The barge type catamaran was definitely the boat I'd seen out on the water yesterday, and the way it was set up, it could easily carry a lot of live rock and coral in partially flooded forward compartments. *And* it would still be able to get over the shallows, an important thing in these waters. They were hiding in plain sight in an area where few boaters ever went.

Or maybe not. I had to find out more about the people aboard.

"What's the plan?" Brayden asked.

"Feel like taking your little boat out tonight?"

"You want a closer look, huh?"

"Yeah," I replied. "Your boat's pretty quiet; we can get to within a mile without being noticed."

"Got a pole and a pair of telescoping paddles, too," he said, with a grin. "For sneaking up on bonefish."

"The moon's waxing," I said, thinking aloud. "Nearly full. It'll be directly overhead around midnight."

"I'm with ya," Brayden said. "It's a big boat, easy to spot."

"I have something that'll make that even easier."

"What are you planning to do?" Kat asked.

"I just want to get close and see if we can find out anything," I said. "Those folks might be completely legit, but they might not be."

"Why not just call the police?"

Brayden looked back at Kat. "Our new friend here isn't real popular with the local constabulary."

Two nights ago, when I'd gone in search of tongs to turn the clams, I remembered seeing a high dune with no trees or shrubs, about a quarter mile east of the point. I flew over the area, slowly checking it out, and saw no obstructions. Turning, I brought us in low over the water and into the prevailing wind. The Huey bounced a couple of feet and came to rest on the dune, well above the high water.

The main rotor was nearly stopped when Macie and the McKays came toward us from the beach.

"You're back a lot earlier than we thought," Cory said as they approached. "Wow, that's a beautiful old helicopter. *Tropical Luxury Magazine*, huh?"

"Belongs to a friend," I replied. "She's cruising to the South Seas right now."

"See anything?" Macie asked.

"An odd-looking power cat," Brayden said. "Might be capable of hauling out live rock."

"We went ahead with an early roundup," Lea said.

My expression must have given away my bewilderment. Brayden explained. "Friday is claws night, mate. We catch blue land crabs using a rather ingenious method."

"Do tell," I said, walking with the others back toward the fire pit.

"Simple," Kat said. "We took some old sail cloth and made two fences a foot high and a hundred yards long. It's got short nylon stakes sewn into the cloth that make it stand up in the sand. We stake it out in the shape of a funnel, with a big bucket buried at the end, then make a lot of noise to get them moving into it."

"How many did you catch?" Brayden asked.

"Nearly two hundred," Lea replied. "But half were already missing the big claw."

I'd heard of many people who ate land crabs, but usually the whole thing, just like a blue crab in the water. "You only take the claws?"

"Just the big one," Kat said. "It's the best part and it's renewable. They grow back when they molt."

"So," Cory said, sitting on a log, "what do we do now? About the poachers, I mean."

I took a seat on the log across from him. "You're jumping ahead. We found a boat that looks like it can do what it'd have to do to remove that much live rock and coral from the reefs and still be able to get across the flats." I glanced at both Kat and Brayden. "But let's wait until we have everyone together before we make any kind of plans or call the cops."

"Meet back here just before sunset?" Macie asked.

"Right now," Kat said, looking toward the docks, "I want a shower and to get out of these hot clothes. I thought you said it'd be cold, riding in the helicopter."

"I said it'd be cooler. About ten degrees cooler."

"Seventy-five is still bikini weather in my book."

We left the group then and walked toward the docks, Finn and Bill running toward us. The two dogs never even slowed down. Finn barked once as they passed us, and I waved to him. He'd been cooped up so long on the *Revenge*; I could tell he was happy to get back to doing what dogs do.

Kat looked up at me once we were out of earshot of the others. "I could see your reflection in the windshield, when Brayden said the two women had blond and auburn hair. You know who they are, don't you?"

"I have a pretty good idea," I replied. "But they'd be in the company of a tall, dark-haired man."

"Who are they?"

I wondered just how much I should tell her. The couple whose Hatteras the Pences had most likely taken were probably dead. If it *was* them Brayden had seen on the cat barge, the same was likely true for whoever had been aboard it, whether they were poachers or just innocent cruisers on a weird boat. The trio didn't look dangerous, but I knew for a fact that they were.

I let out a sigh and looked down at Kat. "I was the anonymous tipster that saw the Hatteras heading north last week. The Bahamas Defence Force has a pretty good idea who it was who stole it, another tip I provided. An auburn-haired woman and a younger blonde, in the company of a tall Englishman by the name of Clive Pence. The redhead is his wife, Yvette."

"And you think that was them on the cat? Like, they switched boats or something? And they have Mark and Cindy Mathis as hostages?"

"These aren't the kind of people who kidnap."

Kat stopped at the foot of the pier and grabbed my arm, turning me to face her. "What do you mean, Jesse?"

"All three are wanted for about a dozen robberies and at least one murder, a friend of mine."

Kat's hands went involuntarily to her mouth and she gasped. "Mark and Cindy are dead?"

"We don't know that," I said, putting a hand on her shoulder, and turning her toward the boat. "We don't even know if those women are who I think they might be. Think positive."

Stepping over to *Salty Dog's* cockpit, I unlocked the companionway hatch and we went down to the pilothouse.

"I think I want to get a shower," Kat said, disappearing below.

I went to the coffeemaker and set it up for another run.

"What's with the AstroTurf in the shower?" I heard her call out a couple of minutes later.

Crap! I hurried down the steps to the lower salon. Kat stepped out of the head, wearing only panties. I stopped and spun around.

"Sorry," I said, heading back up. "I meant to tell you. That shower is Finn's bathroom."

"Yu-uck," Kat said. "Um, Jesse, you've seen my boobs before."

I continued up to the pilothouse. "You can use my shower," I said over my shoulder, as I continued up the companionway to the cockpit. "It's in the aft cabin."

Finn came trotting down the pier toward me. I sat down on the end of the finger dock with my feet dangling inches above the water. The sun was heading toward its resting place on the horizon. It really was quiet and peaceful here.

Finn sat next to me and looked out toward the mouth of the small harbor, as if waiting for me to tell him what time meant or something equally profound.

"What the hell are we doing with a girl on the boat?" I asked him.

He didn't answer but did seem genuinely concerned that I'd changed the subject. So I reached over and scratched his neck. "Where's your buddy?"

He looked back toward shore, then stretched out to lay on the dock, with his head resting on his paws. I guess all the running and playing of dog games was catching up to him. Together, we looked out over the water, watching a line of pelicans flying low over the glassy surface, just off the beach.

The sun was still an hour from setting, there wasn't a cloud anywhere, and the wind had died to a light breeze. After ten minutes, Kat emerged from the cabin, her hair wet. She was wearing shorts and a faded *Soggy Dollar* tee-shirt. I knew of the little beachside bar, down in the British Virgin Islands. Many a young woman just like Kat had danced topless on the tables for a free tee-shirt. It was a different me who had urged them on. A much younger me.

"You're kind of a prude, you know that?" Kat said, walking toward us. "I'm done if you want to shower. The water's still warm."

Rising, I turned to face her, looking down into the swirling depths of twin mahogany orbs set in a naturally pretty face. Whoever that Benny character was, he was a full-bore dumbass. It was getting increasingly difficult to see Kat as a kid.

"Being prudish sometimes keeps me out of trouble," I said. "I'll run the genset for a while in the morning. The water heater doesn't work off battery power."

Ten minutes later, I was showered and changed. Kat was waiting in the pilothouse. I carried the guitar again, as she and I walked silently along the beach to the fire pit. Finn trotted ahead of us.

Before we got there, Kat stopped me. "Look, I'm sorry. We see a few things differently, I get that. I really do live in the moment and you're looking for a woman to settle down with forever."

I started to say something, but she stopped me, placing the tip of her finger to my lips. "Sex is fun. It's energetic and therapeutic regardless of age; ask any doctor. Cory will tell you. You're close to fifty; that's far from dead. You're tall, tan, and muscled. In that picture you showed me, you were shaved, a real babe magnet. But right now, I'm worried about what you're planning to do."

She turned and trudged off toward the firepit, leaving me thoroughly scolded and bewildered. How could a girl half my age make me feel like an errant schoolboy?

The grill was closed, and the fire was already lit. In the fire was a big, cast iron pot filled with water. It looked like the water was just starting to come to a low, rolling boil, moving dozens of crab claws around in a frothy cream of spices, bubbling on the surface.

"It'll be ready in about ten minutes," Cory said. "Brayden thought it'd be a good idea to eat a little early. My guess is you and he already have something planned for later."

Besides Cory, only Carmen was there. "Let's wait till everyone's here," I said. "Then we'll talk about what we're going to do or not do."

One by one, the others arrived. Macie and Brayden took their usual log, and David joined Carmen on another. Lea had a large covered bowl, which she placed next to the fire to warm.

"Where's the Bourgeau brothers?" Cory asked, looking off toward the anchorage.

"Their dinghy's still not back," Lea replied. "They're leaving in the morning."

With everyone seated, I laid out the plan Brayden and I had discussed. Macie asked a few questions, but I assured her that we weren't going to get close enough to get into any trouble.

We ate mostly in silence and Kat never opened the guitar case. While there was no danger in what Brayden and I were going to do, I had to keep in mind that my idea of danger was likely a bit different than that of the people I was with. I had no intention of going unprepared for danger.

"I moved my boat over beside yours," Brayden said when we had finished the crab claws and Lea's butter beans. "I guess we ought to get a little sleep?"

"Wouldn't hurt," I said. "We may be out for a few hours."

The others stayed at the fire, while Brayden and I went to our respective boats to rest up. Before going to bed, I set up the coffeemaker and set the alarm function on my phone for twenty-three hundred. Three hours of sleep and a little coffee would allow me to be fully alert until morning, if necessary. But I fully intended to be back and have time for a few more hours of sleep before the night was over. I spent ten minutes getting a few things together that we might need, then turned in.

CHAPTER FOURTEEN

I'm usually a light sleeper, so when my stateroom hatch clicked and slowly began to open, I was instantly awake, coming up from my bunk, Sig in hand and moving to find my target.

The scream was unmistakably feminine. It was Kat.

"What the hell are you doing?" I said, decocking the pistol, and returning it to the top drawer next to my bunk. My old dog tags, hanging on the knob, fell to the deck. "I could have shot you."

"Why do you even have a gun?" she said, her voice breaking.

Kat was standing just inside my cabin door, wearing the thin tee-shirt I'd given her to sleep in. The soft, silvery moonlight, spilling into the pilothouse behind her, silhouetted her body beneath it.

Finn stood off to the side, the hair on his neck standing on end. He recognized the tension, but with his acute sense of smell and hearing, he probably knew who she was before she opened the door.

I went to her, wearing only my skivvies, and put an arm around her shoulder, trying to comfort her. "It's okay," I said. "Nothing happened."

"I've never had a gun pointed at me before," she muttered as I steered her toward the side bench. Her hands were trembling.

"Did something wake you?" I asked, turning toward the hatch.

"No," she said, grabbing my arm. "I—just wanted to be with you."

"Kat," I said, looking into her soft doe-like eyes. "I thought we agreed on this. I'm way too old. It's weird."

"You agreed," she said, looking up at me, her lips trembling. "Age never mattered to me. I like you. You're a nice person."

I took her shoulders in my hands. "No, Kat. I'm not. I'm not a nice person at all. I am loyal, though. Even if it's only to an idea. I'm moved, I really am. And if I was twenty years younger—okay, ten years younger—I'd lift you right up onto that bunk."

Her eyes darted to the dresser drawer. "Why do you have a gun? You're not supposed to bring guns into the Bahamas. Is it true then? What you mumbled in your sleep?"

Kat was a relative stranger to violence. I could tell. Her handling of Benny notwithstanding. With her carefree lifestyle, it was a wonder she'd not been seriously hurt before. My guess was that she'd only seen the good side of the world. A loving home and mother, a hard-working dad, beautiful islands, and peaceful people. I had no way of knowing these things, but I could somehow sense it.

Sitting next to her, I let out a sigh. "Yeah, it's true. Kinda true, anyway. Even what Mick said on the mailboat. I sometimes worked with an elite team of government operatives; our mission was to hunt down terrorist threats in the Caribbean and dispose of them."

"So you can kill people with no remorse," she said, standing and looking down at me. "But your high moral character won't allow you to have sex with a grown woman, just because she happens to be a little younger than you?"

I could see the fire in her dark brown eyes, but they were also welling up with tears. She spun on her heel and stormed out of my stateroom, slamming the hatch hard enough to make the hinges rattle. I could hear the main hatch in the companionway slam open and the little double doors rattle as they bounced against the bulkheads.

Mission accomplished, McDermitt. She doesn't want anything to do with your old ass.

And I'd thought Benny was the idiot. How could I not see that rebuffing her advance would be a blow to her ego? Any other straight male would be bouncing around in the sack with her.

Good ole stick in the mud McDermitt.

A shaft of moonlight was beaming through the hatch above my head, coming to rest on my feet. The angle told me it was late and I'd slept for a few hours. I picked up my sat-phone and checked the time: an hour until midnight. The alarm went off in my hand, so I rose from the bench and dressed quickly in the darkness

I assumed Kat had stormed off to Macie's and Brayden's boat, or perhaps to the marina and her loft; it was livable now. *Why hadn't she gone there after dinner?*

"That's pretty obvious, dipshit," I mumbled.

Finn cocked his head quizzically.

"Doesn't matter," I said, scratching his neck. "But I do need to apologize."

I heard footsteps approaching outside on the dock. "Jesse!" a voice hissed quietly. It was Brayden.

Going up to the pilothouse, I switched on a light and started the coffeemaker.

"Come aboard, Brayden," I called up through the open hatch.

The boat rocked slightly, but he didn't come down right away. After a moment, his feet appeared in front of the hatch.

"Come on down," I said to his feet.

"You remember what I said about if you hurt Kat? If I come down there, it's to kick your ass."

"We both know that's not gonna happen," I said, stepping back. "Come on down and hear me out."

He took a tentative step down, hesitated, then swung all the way to the deck, holding onto the hatch cover. When he landed, he was in a fighting stance.

I had to hand it to him, he had strong convictions. Even if he didn't know my background, just bowing up to a man who's a head taller and a good seventy-five pounds heavier was gutsy.

"Back off, Brayden," I warned. "There's nothing in this but pain for you. I hurt her feelings, and for that I'm sorry. But I'm not going to fight you about it."

His overhand right was telegraphed well in advance of his move. I stepped into it and caught his fist in mid-swing, throwing him off balance. I shoved his arm up and back, then forced him downward in an awkward stumble. He landed on his butt next to the galley stove.

"Don't trifle with me," I said in as even a tone as I could muster. "I'm *definitely* not a pacifist. What the hell did she tell you I did?"

"Brayden!" Macie said from outside.

"Oh, for cryin' out loud," I muttered, stepping past Brayden. "Come on in, Macie. Join the party."

Unlike her boyfriend, Macie didn't hesitate. Nor did she come to take a poke at me. She came swiftly down the steps and looked from me to Brayden sitting on the deck.

"What the hell do you think you're doing? You stormed off without even waiting for Kat to stop crying. Jesse didn't do anything to hurt her."

"Look, both of you," I said firmly. "Call me old-fashioned, or a prude, or whatever. I don't give a shit. A fifty-year-old man doesn't sleep with a twenty-five-year-old girl."

Macie turned toward me, fists on her hips, her blue eyes sparkling as if building to a sudden discharge of lightning bolts. "Is that so? Well, what about a seventy-year-old man and a forty-five-year-old woman? That doesn't sound so tawdry, does it?"

"If I'm still around in twenty years, I'll let you know."

Her features softened. "You hurt her feelings, Jesse. Made her feel ugly and unwanted."

"I know, I know," I said, slumping into the lower helm seat. "But I didn't do anything to prompt her."

"You were nice," Macie said firmly. "There're way too damned few of you guys left."

"How can a girl who looks like her even think she's not pretty?" I said, knowing my defense was weak. I don't deal well with emotions, either.

Brayden got to his feet. "Sorry for taking that swing at ya, mate."

It was almost comical. I couldn't help but grin. "And I'm sorry for knocking you on your ass."

Turning to Macie, I said, "Look, would you tell her I'm sorry? I can't change who I am. But let her know that it was damned near impossible to say no."

"You need to be the one who tells her that."

"I will," I said. "In the morning. Right now, Brayden and I have work to do. Will you just tell her I'll see her in the morning?"

"Okay," Macie conceded. "But don't you do anything to get Brayden hurt, or Kat's not going to be the only woman after you."

Neither Brayden nor I said anything until we heard Macie's footsteps leave the dock.

"You really are a muppet, you know that?" Brayden said, sniffing the air, then walking toward the coffeemaker. "Before she took off with that bogan, Benny, Kat was the hottest chick anywhere around."

He lifted one of the two mugs I'd left out, raising an eyebrow in question.

"Pour me one, too," I said.

He filled both mugs and extended one to me. "When you brought her back, she looked like warmed-over dung, mate. I don't know what he did to her, but if he ever comes around here again, I fully intend to make the bloke cry."

Brayden sipped the coffee. "Mmm, good java. I can tell ya one thing, mate. In the last coupla days, I've noticed more color to her face and a spring in her step when you're around. I told you she was shook on you."

I took a sip. "Is it really that simple, man? Has society changed so much that an old man can take advantage of a young girl?"

Brayden chuckled. "Kat's a long way from being some innocent schoolgirl, mate. And you're hardly a withered oldie."

"I'm not comfortable talking about this with you," I said. "Why don't we just get on with what we planned to do?"

"Okay by me," he said. "But just what is it you plan to do? I know what you said *we* were gonna do. But I'm guessing there's more that you're not letting on."

"*We* are going to get close enough to see the boat," I said. "*I'm* going to get close enough to hear them snore."

CHAPTER FIFTEEN

With a nearly full moon overhead, Brayden piloted his little boat out of the marina and turned northeast into the cut between Chub and Crab Cay. Once clear of the shallows, he brought the little boat up on the step, just above planing speed, and we headed in the general direction of the cat barge.

I took a handheld GPS out of my bag and powered it on. I'd already put the coordinates in; estimating where the boat was from the waypoint I'd dropped on the GPS in the chopper.

"Make your heading zero-four-zero," I said. Checking the distance, I did the math in my head. New Zealanders are more familiar with kilometers than miles. "The boat's thirteen clicks out."

Making a slight course adjustment, Brayden continued at the slower speed. "What else you got in that bag, mate? And what's with the fly rod?"

Taking out a pair of night vision goggles, I switched them on and handed them to him. "Put these on."

"What is it?" he asked, dropping the boat back down to idle speed. He fitted the straps over his head and slid the device into place over his nose. "Grouse, mate! It's like bloody daytime."

"They gather available light, from the moon and stars, and magnify it. A little grainy and two-dimensional, but you can see more detail than moonlight alone."

"I'll say. I just saw a flying fish jump about thirty meters ahead. Take that rod and reel out, and there's likely to be shark steaks this weekend."

"I think we both know that's not a fishing rod."

He looked right at me through the optical tubes mounted in front of his eyes. I pulled the fly rod case over and opened it.

He followed my movements with the goggles. "I'll be stuffed."

"Just for self-defense," I said.

Brayden pulled the goggles off his head. "I ain't no melon, Jesse. What you've got there's a *sniper* rifle."

"It was the tool of my trade for twenty years," I said. "I can guarantee nobody gets close enough to hurt either of us."

"How accurate is it?" he asked, leaning forward for a closer look under the moonlight.

"A well-trained marksman can drive nails at a thousand meters and bring down a man at nearly twice that. It's zeroed at five hundred, where even a novice could kill a squirrel."

He looked down at the bag, open at my feet. "And the Draegor?"

"You know rebreathers?"

"Used one many times, mate. That's how you're going to get close enough to hear them snore?"

"If the people on that boat are who I think they are, they won't be snoring. These are the type of people who sleep past noon and do bad things at night."

"You're going to slip aboard their boat?"

"Not what I'm planning on," I replied, readying my equipment. "Even a plastic boat will transmit sound through the hull."

"And if they *are* asleep?"

"I'll wake them up," I said with a shrug. "Bang on the hull or something to get them talking. What do you think are the odds of an Englishman being on the same boat with a blond hick from Oklahoma and a redheaded California girl?"

"But you can only hear them, mate," Brayden said with a grin, as he pulled the goggles down and brought the skiff up on plane. "What if the Okie is the redhead, and the blonde is an English woman with a deep voice?"

"There is that possibility," I said, raising my voice and turning forward. "Remote, but possible."

Laying my gear out on the deck in front of me, I checked it over carefully in the moonlight. The bright orb was high above us, and there were no clouds or vapor to obscure it in the slightest. Even without night vision, my eyes had grown accustomed to the darkness, and the moon provided plenty enough light for what I was doing. While Brayden was watching where we were going through the tunnel vision of the goggles, I slipped my Sig into a pocket on the Draegor.

Though the water was a warm eighty or so degrees, I'd be submerged for a long time, and hypothermia was a danger. So I put on my thin one-piece neoprene wetsuit to help retain a little body heat—but not too much; I was going to be swimming underwater for almost half a mile each way.

I checked and rechecked the rebreather. Unlike scuba, there was no bulky external air tank. It was a closed loop system, which basically used a filter to absorb the carbon-dioxide from the diver's exhaled breath, returning the mostly unused oxygen in the air back to the diver. Using a sensor, it monitored the oxygen content of the air being rebreathed and added to it from a small oxygen tank in the enclosed rigid container the diver wore.

Checking the GPS, I saw we'd covered five miles and were clipping along at twenty-six knots. Having checked the charts, I knew the area was mostly devoid of patch reefs— just a wide, sandy plain covered with about five to ten feet of water, with sandbars that breached the surface at low tide. The tide was high now, and Brayden's boat probably only needed a foot when on plane.

"Crikey!" Brayden shouted, slamming the tiller toward the port gunwale.

I nearly lost balance, as the boat suddenly lurched to the right, in danger of flipping over. Grabbing both rails, I waited until Brayden brought the boat under control. Slowing, he looked back.

"What was it?" I asked, as Brayden started to turn the boat around.

"Dunno," he said, straining his neck to see over the bow. "Something big, though."

Reaching into my bag, I took out a small night vision spotting scope and turned it on. Scanning the water ahead of us, I saw something, and pointed. "There. Eleven o'clock."

Brayden turned his head, then the boat, and idled toward what I could already see was the smoking remains of a large boat that had burned to the waterline.

"I see it," he said. "It's smoking."

"Burned out hull," I said, as we neared the bulky remains of a wooden boat. It had probably been about a fifty-footer.

When we were close enough to see by moonlight, Brayden pulled off the goggles and steered toward the wreck.

"Slow," I warned. "There's very little water in the hull."

Brayden slowed, knowing just what I meant. There were only inches of the hull's planking above the surface. If our boat's wake sloshed any more water into it, the hull would sink, pulled down by the weight of the two diesel engine blocks just aft of amidships. The sudden turbulence from such a large boat could easily flip his skiff and suck it into the churning mass of debris.

Something struck me clearly, as I gazed at the charred remains of the boat. There hadn't been a massive explosion. The ribs and planks in the hull weren't broken or splintered. That meant the boat had been adrift or at anchor when it burned. And it meant the fuel tanks were probably empty or very close to empty.

Brayden brought us closer, shifting the engine into gear for a second, then gliding for several more. We came alongside the hull, making barely a ripple. We both stood and looked down into the wreck. The decks and cabin roofs had collapsed into the hull and been burned to almost nothing, indicating a very hot fire. There were tangles of bare copper wires, cables and metal objects strewn through the debris. Any plastic coating on them had been melted off.

"Good Lord," Brayden muttered. "Is that what I think it is?"

I looked toward the stern of the smoking hulk. The boat had a large lazarette. The aft deck had collapsed into the large storage area but was still attached to the transom. In the forward part were two bodies, lying on their sides and facing one another. They were bound hand and foot with copper wire, and burned beyond recognition.

"That's Mark and Cindy," Brayden said, sitting down hard on the aft bench seat.

"How can you be sure?"

"Mark lost his left leg below the knee in a car wreck."

Looking down, I knew he was right. The larger of the two corpses had a prosthesis, loosely attached to the left leg, and bound to the right by the wire. The straps that held it on were completely burned off. Two rings on the left ring finger of the smaller body were probably an engagement ring and wedding band. A husband and wife.

Slowly, I sat down on the middle bench, facing aft. Brayden was just staring off toward the horizon, away from the carnage. "I'm sorry," I said softly.

"They were nice people, Jesse. They didn't deserve to die this way."

"I know." I couldn't think of anything more to say.

Brayden turned to face me. "Do we still go to the barge and see if it's them, or call the coppers?"

Not having bargained on finding the bodies of the kidnapped couple, I thought about his question a moment.

"We've come this far," Brayden said, before I could decide. "We can mark this position on your handheld and call it in after we find out if your killers are on the barge."

"Fair dinkum," I replied with a grin.

"You're an odd dag," he said, bumping the engine into gear for a second.

Once clear, Brayden put the engine in gear again, and turned back to our original course, idling slowly.

I marked the location with a pin on my GPS. Once the wind picked up in the morning, some small waves would likely breach the hull and sink it. The fire was probably from earlier in the night, invisible to any island by distance over the horizon. The keel of the old yacht couldn't be more than a foot or two from the bottom now, so it would be easily seen from the air.

Unfortunately, there was no way we could have retrieved the bodies and we both knew it. If one of us were to step over onto the wreck, the whole thing would surely sink immediately. The sudden rush of water into the hull would throw everything around with great force. It would just be too dangerous.

Glancing down at the GPS, I nodded to Brayden. "Three miles, dead ahead. We should be able to see it soon."

He brought the boat up on plane and I turned around on my bench. Brayden kept our speed just high enough to stay on plane with minimal splashing, but not so fast that the little engine was screaming.

Looking through the scope, I watched the odd-looking catamaran slowly rise over the horizon ahead of us. I couldn't see any lights at all in the unusually high, enclosed bridge. As we got closer, I made out a low light from below the bridge, in what I assumed was the salon, or lounge area of the boat.

Brayden slowed, having picked up the light through the goggles. They weren't magnified like my scope, so he couldn't yet pick out as much detail as I could.

The boat was anchored with the stern almost toward us, and the starboard hull slightly visible. Her bow was pointing northeast. Just above the waterline, a bright light emanated from the port hull, shining on the water. That side was slightly away from us, so the source was unknown.

There were no lights at all forward of the tall structure. In fact, the only portholes visible along that side were aft, and both of them were dark. This reinforced my idea that the forward hulls and foredeck might be used for cargo.

A few minutes later, Brayden slowed to an idle. "How close do you want to get, mate?"

"Let's swing around in front of them," I whispered. "If anyone's up, they're aft."

Turning, Brayden moved off to the northeast, around our quarry. He idled slowly, though at this distance, even over water, I doubted they could hear the quiet outboard. We had no lights on at all, so they certainly couldn't see us.

When we reached a spot about half a mile in front of the cat, Brayden killed the engine. "I can pole us a lot closer," he whispered.

Sound travels over water much better than on land. There aren't any trees, shrubs, or even grass to catch and deflect it.

"No closer than half a kilometer," I replied, getting the anchor ready.

It was obvious that Brayden had poled the boat many times, searching for fish. Even with the tunnel vision created by the goggles, he stood easily and dipped his pole to the bottom, while stepping up onto his seat. I didn't hear a drop of water as he stealthily pulled the pole back, keeping the foot in the water, and pushed again.

A few minutes later, I signaled to him that we were close enough and quietly slipped the anchor overboard.

"How long will you be?" Brayden whispered, barely audible, as he pulled the goggles off and placed the device in a small storage box beside him.

"We're closer than I'd planned," I said quietly. "Maybe five hundred meters. It'll take me ten minutes to get there and another ten to get back. So maybe half an hour in all. I'll swim about two feet below the surface until I get close. You should be able to see an occasional swirl in the water from my fins."

"What if you get caught?"

"Not much chance of that," I replied. "Spotted maybe, but not caught. If they spot me, I'll swim on the bottom all the way back. We're far beyond normal eyesight, and with their lights on they won't be able to see you at all out here."

Reaching into my bag, I felt around until I found a small box, which I pulled out and opened. I took one of the tiny communication devices out, turned it on, and handed it to him.

"Stick this in your ear," I said. "Mine's waterproof and has a mic built into the mask."

Brayden grinned in the low moonlight. "You really are a spy."

I shifted over to the port side of the boat, and Brayden countered my weight by moving forward and sitting next to me on the wide center bench. As I turned and swung my legs over the side, he turned and hooked his feet under the seat, leaning back in the opposite direction just enough to keep the boat balanced.

Sliding toward the gunwale, I could tell without looking back that he was matching my moves to keep the boat level, so as to avoid any splashing. When I was in position, I raised my butt over the gunwale and slipped slowly and quietly into the water. My fins met the sandy bottom and I was able to stand with the water just below my armpits. Standing on the seafloor nearly four miles to the nearest dry land, I looked up at Brayden and nodded.

"Good luck," he whispered, extending my weight-belt to me. The six pounds of lead shot in the pouches would offset the buoyancy of my wetsuit and allow me to hover motionless in the water column.

Slipping the belt around my waist, I pulled it tight and secured the buckle. Then I turned toward the cat and raised my left arm in front of me, a small compass strapped to my wrist. I took a bearing on the boat, then looked back at Brayden and nodded again. Pulling the mask down over my face, I whispered, "Comm check."

Brayden jumped, then looked at me and grinned, giving me a thumbs-up. "Loud and clear," he whispered.

Submerging, I turned and brought the compass up in front of my face, grasping my right elbow with my left hand. I slowly began to swim in the direction of the catamaran, counting my right kicks.

I'd probably made several thousand dives over the last forty years, having started at a very young age. Distance is difficult to measure underwater, especially in minimal visibility. I'd checked my kick rate with every new pair of fins, counting kicks over a known distance. I knew exactly how far I moved with every kick of these fins, whether on scuba or a rebreather. Eight feet with a bulky tank on my back, and nine with the more streamlined Draegor. The catamaran was about a hundred and seventy kicks away.

I felt water seeping into the mask. A full-face mask doesn't seal well over facial hair. It wasn't a flood, but it was enough that it could present a problem. If water covered the microphone, it couldn't pick up my voice. I exhaled hard enough into the mask to displace some of the water, but not hard enough to blow any air out of the seal around the mask. I decided it would have to be a balancing act, as far as pressure inside the mask, but manageable.

Brayden's voice came over the tiny speaker in my ear. "I can see your kicks now and then. You're heading straight toward it."

"Having a little trouble with water getting into the *mask*," I said, popping the last word, to push water out around my beard.

The seal on my forehead and cheeks was good, so the excess pressure would force the water toward the path of least resistance; between the thick hair shafts around my jaw.

"Figured you would," he replied. "I'll let you know if I see you go off course."

Keeping the needle on the compass at two hundred and twenty degrees, I continued counting my kicks. When I reached a hundred, I began glancing left and right, hoping to pick up their anchor rode. I finally spotted the chain on the sandy bottom and turned toward it.

"You're turning away from the boat toward the west," Brayden's voice said over the tiny speaker.

"On their anchor chain now," I replied.

A few minutes of kicking later, and the rode lifted off the bottom and out of the water. The twin hulls became visible, casting a large moon shadow on the bottom. She was riding lower than I'd have thought. Most power cats I'd seen in this size drew about two-and-a-half to three feet. As I slid back toward the starboard keel, I held my depth gauge up and saw that it was well over three feet.

The sea is never a quiet place, not even at night. All around, I could hear the clicks and whispers of sound from whatever crabs and fish were about. Some sounds might even emanate miles away. Listening past those, I could hear the creaks of the catamaran's hull itself. There was also a low hum, maybe a fan or something inside the boat.

Moving slowly along the hull, staying very close to the bottom, I heard a thumping sound. When I reached the halfway point on the starboard hull, I heard the hum start up again, then another thump. They sounded mechanical. Like a hoist raising something and dropping it over and over again.

Diving to the bottom, I was in seven feet of water, with the keel three feet above the bottom. Seas were calm, so I wasn't worried about a wave rocking the boat and crushing me. I quickly swam under the hull to the other side.

Unlike dolphins and whales, humans can't tell which direction sound comes from underwater. In air, sound travels at over seven hundred miles per hour. Water, being denser, allows sound to travel at more than four times that speed. Humans determine the direction of sound by the difference in the time it takes it to reach each of our ears. It's only milliseconds, and we can't even consciously tell there is a difference, but the brain can measure it and tell you where to look. Dolphins and whales evolved under the water, so that part of the brain that deals with hearing is much more developed. Because we're land animals, the time difference is far less than our feeble minds can comprehend, and sound seems to emanate from all around.

Unless you put a fifty-foot-long wall between you and the source of the sound. The thump repeated, quite a bit louder. It was coming from the other hull. I swam toward it.

It was brighter between the hulls. I looked up and saw that a light was shining on the surface. I instinctively froze, until I realized the deck joining the two hulls was above me. There couldn't be anyone up there shining a light down.

The humming noise returned, now sounding more like a buzz, than the hum of a motor. As I neared the port hull, the buzz suddenly ended and there was the thump again.

Rising slowly, and away from the light, I allowed just half my head to break the surface. There was a porthole on the inside of the hull, too. It was about two feet above the waterline and looked to be a watertight hatch. I figured it was to allow whoever was in there to look down and maybe see the bottom. A light was on inside.

Looking around the underside of the dry part of the hull above me, I noticed a brace not far forward of the porthole. I moved slowly toward it and using the tips of my fins against the bottom, I could stand motionless with just my eyes and forehead above the surface.

Very slowly, to keep from sloshing water around, I raised my right hand above the surface. The increased weight of my arm, as it rose out of the water, began to flex my fins and I sank deeper. My hand reached the brace and I grabbed it.

Dangling from the brace with my arm fully extended, I slowly reached up with my other hand and took hold of it.

Now I could pull myself up to eye level with the porthole. What I saw was like something from a cheap porn movie.

Mayhew Bourgeau was lying on a bed, his arms and legs tied to all four corners. He was naked, as far as I could tell. A woman, with her back to me and her hair tied in a ponytail, was kneeling between Mayhew's legs. It was pretty obvious what she was doing.

Then the buzzing started again, and Mayhew's body jerked convulsively. The blonde stood and clapped her hands, as Mayhew arched his back, lifting himself off the bed, for a moment.

The sight startled me, as the buzzing ceased, and Mayhew bounced back down onto the thin mattress with a thump. I lost my grip on the slime-coated brace and fell into the water.

Above my head, I heard a man's voice, with a British accent. "What was that splash?"

Another light came on behind me. I spun around and clearly saw the face of Yvette Pence, staring right at me through another porthole in the starboard hull.

Submerging immediately, I dove for the bottom, flattening my arms at my sides. Tilting my head parallel to the bottom, streamlining my body, I began to take long, powerful kicks toward the bow.

"I was spotted," I said quietly, though it was doubtful anyone on the boat could hear me.

"What do you want me to do?" Brayden's voice came back.

"Hang tight. I'll be back in five minutes."

All around me, I heard stomping feet and a clattering noise, like someone was kicking pots and pans around. I continued, ignoring the noise, knowing that the water accentuated them, and it was probably someone walking softly and dropping a spoon.

"Is it the English bloke and his ladies?" Brayden asked, his voice hushed but excited.

"I heard him, yeah. And I got a good look at his wife's face. It's definitely them."

Exiting the gap between the hulls, I swam a beeline toward where the anchor line dropped into the inky black water ahead of me. Suddenly there were two popping sounds, and twin jets of air bubbles stabbed through the water beside me.

"They're shooting, Jesse!"

Brayden had given up all pretense of stealth, my name, and most likely his position.

There were two more pops, and something tugged at the breathing tube connected to my mask. Suddenly, water flooded in around my face. A bullet had nicked the breathing tube.

Holding my breath, I kicked hard, pulling the mask off. Distance is the friend of the trained rifleman, not the untrained pistol shooter.

When I couldn't go any farther, I rolled onto my back, heading up at an angle, while I exhaled, intending to break the surface for only a second to get a breath of life-giving air. I felt another tug, low on my right side, just as my face breached the surface.

Above me, silhouetted in the moonlight, was Haywood, a gun in her hand and a twisted smile on her face.

I froze.

Time seemed to slow.

I clearly heard Clive Pence shout, "Kill him!"

My right hand was already in the pocket, pulling out my Sig. I brought my other hand up, grasping it in a two-handed grip. Haywood's gun was just coming up again. I had her beat, and my finger began to tighten on the trigger.

There was a sickening thunk, and Haywood's eyes went wide as a fine red mist fell away behind her.

A sudden boom split the night air like a thunderclap.

The pain in my side was still more of an irritation, kind of like a fire ant bite, but I knew that I'd been shot, and the pain would worsen.

Frozen on the surface, I watched her drop the handgun into the water. She stared down at me for a moment, eyes already glassing over in death, then she slowly toppled forward and into the water and the Reaper's cold embrace.

There was a second boom, which I suddenly realized was from my own rifle. Brayden had shot Haywood in the abdomen, probably turning half her internal organs into mush, and killing her instantly.

The second rifle shot was immediately followed by a deafening explosion, and the night suddenly turned into daylight. A bright flame rose up and out from the star-board side of the catamaran, then an even larger explosion smashed the air. It felt like the tail of a blue whale smacking me in the face, pushing me under.

A whoosh of flames and super-heated air plowed from under the belly of the cat and the whole thing lifted out of the water. An underwater concussion wave hit me, floating just below the surface, and my mind went blank.

CHAPTER SIXTEEN

A splash caught Brayden's attention, followed by a man's shout. A moment later he watched in horror as someone ran to the front of the catamaran and began shooting down into the water.

Brayden tore off the night vision goggles and opened Jesse's gun case. He had some experience shooting a rifle, and Jesse had said that his was zeroed for five hundred meters and a novice could hit a squirrel. He shouldered the weapon and peered through the powerful scope.

From five hundred meters, only a portion of the catamaran's pilothouse was visible through the powerful scope. Brayden moved the muzzle around until he found the person who was shooting down at Jesse. It looked like a woman. He kept the scope on her as best he could as his boat moved slightly.

The woman fired twice more before Brayden could center the crosshairs. He moved them to the center of her body and held his breath. He'd never shot a human and had never intentionally harmed a woman in any way. But he couldn't let her shoot his friend. Her head jerked to the right slightly, then she looked down and smiled.

Across the water, Brayden clearly heard the voice of a man shout, "Kill him!"

The woman's smile wasn't one of mirth. Brayden fully believed he was looking at the face of a demon. And the man's shout meant Jesse was still alive.

The woman raised the pistol again. It was obvious that Jesse had surfaced for some reason and now she was about to kill him. Brayden squeezed the trigger and the big rifle kicked him like a rabid 'roo.

When he looked through the scope again, the woman was gone. But someone else was running forward on the deck. A man with what looked like a shotgun.

When Brayden fired the second shot from the rifle, instead of the man going down, there was a small flash behind him. The bullet had missed the man but hit a propane tank mounted to the side rail. The boat exploded with two blasts, less than a second apart.

Brayden dropped the rifle to the deck and quickly untied the anchor line, before moving back to the rear seat to start the engine. Looking at the giant fireball in horror, he figured that anyone on board was now either dead or dying. With any luck, Jesse would be alive, shielded from the explosion by the water, at least to some degree.

Racing toward the burning boat, he spotted two people floating just ahead of it. He slowed his boat, angling toward the first one, while scanning the burning wreckage for any sign of danger.

Shifting to neutral, Brayden scrambled forward as his boat came alongside the first body. He could now see that it was Jesse, floating face up in the water.

He glanced over at the woman he'd shot, and froze. She was floating just beyond Jesse's inert body, much closer to the now-burning wreck. Her tank top was bunched up around her shoulders, the flames blistering the exposed skin there. Just below the surface he could see a jagged exit wound in her back. Bits of flesh hung from around it by threads. The hole in her back was bigger than a tennis ball. Even in the darkness, Brayden could see blood swirling in the water around the woman, and he retched.

Tearing his eyes from the corpse, Brayden knelt to grab Jesse. The man moaned as Brayden tried to pull him aboard—but he was too big, and his equipment, snagging the rail, was too bulky. Thinking quickly, Brayden felt around and released the straps holding the weight belt and rebreather in place and let them drop away.

The boat was burning furiously now, and Brayden had to work quickly. It was no time to be gentle. He turned Jesse so that he was facing away from the boat, then squatted low and reached under his arms, clasping his hands around the man's chest. Heaving with all his might, Brayden used his legs to propel them both up and back.

Jesse landed on top of him in the boat, and Brayden had to push him off. The big man grunted as he toppled onto the deck, and Brayden scrambled for the tiller.

Reversing the engine, he powered his little boat backward, away from the inferno, then clicked it into forward and threw the tiller over, spinning the boat around, and accelerating away.

Once clear of the debris, Brayden slowed and took the engine out of gear. Scrambling over the middle bench, he found Jesse not only alive but awake, struggling to get upright.

"Lie still, mate."

Jesse looked up at him for a moment, eyes blinking in confusion. Then they glassed over, and he collapsed back onto the deck.

Brayden checked him over, at least as much as he could do with the wetsuit on. He was still breathing. If he'd been shot, it would probably be a good idea to keep the tight-fitting neoprene suit in place. Propping a fender behind Jesse's head, Brayden turned him slightly and made him as comfortable as he could.

Moving back to his spot, Brayden put the night vision goggles on, adjusted them, and pointed the boat's bow on a reverse course of two hundred and twenty degrees. He started to twist the throttle, but stopped, remembering the wrecked hull of Mark's and Cindy's boat, which they'd nearly hit.

Reaching over the middle bench seat, he found Jesse's GPS and quickly pulled up the waypoint he'd added, showing the location of the wreck.

In seconds, the boat was planing at full speed, Brayden leaning low and holding onto the starboard rail, as he drove.

The ride was smooth, but it still took more than fifteen precious minutes. When he arrived at the marina, Brayden pointed his boat straight toward *Eastwind*, Cory and Lea's trawler yacht.

Any boat moving at full speed past the marina and through the mooring field would draw attention. And everyone knew that he and Jesse were out on the water. Lights started coming on.

Cory came out of *Eastwind's* side pilothouse hatch as Brayden finally slowed the boat.

"Jesse's hurt!" Brayden shouted.

Cory moved quickly aft. "Bring him to the swim platform. What happened?"

Brayden turned the boat, then killed the engine once he was sure it was moving toward *Eastwind's* stern. "I think he mighta been shot."

Cory turned, flung the aft hatch open, and yelled inside. "Lea! Bring my bag up."

Moving to the transom door, Cory opened it and stepped out onto the wide swim platform, just as Brayden's boat bumped it.

"Grab his shoulders," Brayden said, bending to lift Jesse's legs at the knees.

Together they managed to get Jesse onto the platform, then they lifted the big man, and carried him through the transom door.

Lea arrived, tossing a black bag onto a chair. She turned and swept everything off the small dinette table with a clatter.

Brayden and Cory lifted Jesse onto the table and Cory went to work, pulling a stethoscope from the pocket of the bag lying next to him.

"Get me some lights, Lea," Cory said, pulling the zipper down the front of Jesse's wetsuit.

He listened for a heartbeat, as Brayden helplessly stood aside and waited.

"Heartbeat's slow." Cory moved the stethoscope lower and listened to his breathing. "Respiration is clear, but shallow. I think he's in shock."

The bright cockpit lights came on, and Cory immediately saw the entry wound, high on Jesse's hip. Blood was pulsing from it.

"Brayden," Cory said, "there's pouches of QuikClot in my bag, get two and tear them open. Be ready when I cut away his wetsuit."

As Brayden searched through the bag, he heard a boat engine start. He found the pouches and tore the first one open with his teeth.

Cory used a pair of scissors to cut Jesse's wetsuit from the zippered top, toward where he'd been shot. With each snip of the scissors, the wetsuit peeled open, and the bleeding became more intense.

"It's a good thing you didn't try to get his wetsuit off," Cory said, as his scissors reached the wound. Blood now pulsed out of it.

Cory continued cutting past the bullet hole, then ripped the neoprene open, exposing the small puncture in Jesse's side. The blood was flowing freely now. Cory took the pouch from Brayden and dumped it over and into the wound. The bleeding stopped almost instantly.

Gently, Cory rolled Jesse onto his side, checking his back for an exit wound. The grisly image of the huge hole in the woman's back came quickly to Brayden's mind.

"No exit," Cory said, rolling him back. "We have to get him to shore, so I can get the bullet out and try to fix any damage done on the inside."

"We can use one of the paddle boards for a litter," Lea said, scrambling up the ladder to the flybridge.

David and Carmen arrived on their dinghy, and Carmen jumped to the swim platform, holding the inflatable so David could step over.

"Holy shit," David said, upon seeing Jesse stretched out on the table.

Carmen handed David the lines and moved quickly through the transom door. "I'm an LPN, Cory," she said, coming quickly to the doctor's side, "but I only worked for a few months in a retirement home."

"Thanks, I'll need you," Cory said, reaching up to get the paddle board his wife was handing down. "But we have to get him on solid ground. He has a bullet in his abdomen and I'll have to go in."

Positioning the board next to Jesse, David and Brayden gently rolled him onto his side, so Cory could slide it under. Rolling him back, they shifted him onto the center.

"We'll lay him across David's dinghy," Lea said. "Brayden, your boat has drifted away."

Brayden ignored his boat until they had the make-shift litter on the dinghy, with Cory and David aboard. As David's little motor sputtered away, Brayden dove head-long into the water and swam to his boat. He returned to *Eastwind* to pick up Lea and Carmen, then he chased after the dinghy, now almost to the beach beside the marina.

Macie and Kat were waiting on the sand, Bill and Finn standing beside them, and helped pull Brayden's boat up onto shore.

"What happened?" Macie asked, going to Brayden.

"Jesse was shot."

"Oh my God!" Kat cried out, as she rushed toward where the dinghy was approaching the shore.

The men pulled the inflatable up. "Bring him to the store," Cory ordered, grabbing his medical bag, and racing ahead. "I need to scrub."

Kat ran alongside the men as they hurriedly carried Jesse toward the building. "What happened?" she asked.

"It was the people Jesse thought it was," Brayden said. "He got close, underwater, and positively IDed them."

"You weren't gonna get close," Kat said, tears already running down her cheeks. "You both said!"

"We also found Mark's and Cindy's boat," Brayden said, as he and David carried Jesse up the steps. "It was burned to the waterline. Their bodies are still aboard."

"Oh no," Kat said, stopping at the door.

Carmen pushed past her and Finn, then turned. "Wait here." She then closed the door behind her.

Finn nudged Kat's hand, whining softly.

An hour later, Carmen and Cory came out and the others gathered around them. "He's stable," Cory said. "But he's lost quite a bit of blood. He really needs to get to a hospital."

"Can't someone give him a transfusion here?" Macie asked.

"No microscope," Cory said. "No way of knowing his blood type."

"Would that be on his military dog tags?" Kat asked.

Cory turned to her and nodded, "Yeah, it should be."

"Give me the keys to his boat," she said. "His dog tags fell on the floor earlier tonight. I know exactly where they are."

Cory went inside and returned a moment later, handing Kat the keys. She took them and ran for the docks, Finn chasing after her as if he knew his master needed their help. They returned a moment later, and Kat handed Cory a long chain with a pair of military dog tags, each in a black rubber case.

Cory examined the tags. "Okay, he's B-positive. That's kind of rare. I'm A-positive, not a match. Anyone know their blood type?"

"I'm A-positive, too," Carmen said.

Looking around the group, everyone shook their head, some muttering that they had no idea what type blood they were.

"It has to be the same?" Kat asked.

"No," Carmen replied. "Any B type or O type can be used."

"I'm O-positive," Kat said. "I know because I used to give blood all the time."

Cory reached for the door. "He needs you, Kat. Come on, let's get started."

CHAPTER SEVENTEEN

A sense of movement woke me. Or perhaps I was dreaming. Or I was dead. The last thing I remembered was seeing Haywood's guts exploding out from her back and the catamaran exploding.

My eyes slowly opened. It was dark. As my eyes focused, I recognized the overhead and trim work of my cabin. To my right were the three portholes in *Salty Dog's* stern. Through them, I could see the moon near the horizon. It was nearly dawn. And I was alive.

When I felt the sheet over me move, my eyes darted to my left. Kat was lowering herself onto the bunk beside me. She was naked. I tried to move, but she stopped me.

"Be quiet and rest," she whispered. "You lost blood and need to be kept warm."

"What happened?"

"Don't talk," she said, aligning her body with mine and wrapping an arm and leg around me. "Just rest. Cory said you'll be okay."

I tried to raise myself up, but pain tore through my right abdomen and I dropped back onto the pillow.

Everything went black again.

Whether it was hours or days later, I woke again. I felt stiff, but a little stronger. I was still in my cabin, and it was warm. The sky outside the aft portholes was bright blue, but I couldn't see the sun. It was close to noon, I guessed. Remembering that I'd hurt my side, I slowly eased myself up against the bulkhead.

"Kat," I called out weakly.

She appeared in the hatchway, wearing cargo pants and a yellow bikini top. The color made her skin appear much darker. Most of her hair was pulled back in a ponytail, but a few strands hung down on either side of her face.

"Don't get up," she ordered, coming toward me. "I'm making breakfast, if you feel like you can eat. Cory said you need to eat."

"Coffee?"

She gently placed a hand on my bare chest and smiled. "Yeah, I'll get it. But you stay put."

When she turned to walk away, I lifted the sheet and looked down. There was a large bandage on the right side of my belly, wrapped around my side. Other than that, I was naked.

Kat returned carrying my large Force Recon coffee mug. She placed it on the dresser and helped me to a higher sitting position, propping another pillow behind my head and shoulders. She handed me the mug.

"Thanks," I said, taking a slow sip.

"Cory said you need to rest for a couple of days. You were shot. Brayden brought you back."

"How bad?" I asked, reaching a hand tentatively behind my back. No bandage there.

"Brayden said you were underwater when you got shot. What the hell were you doing that close?"

I gave a half-hearted shrug. "It's just something I do."

"Cory said that the bullet got slowed down by the water and it missed everything except an artery, but you'll be sore for a few days."

"An artery?"

"You lost a lot of blood and had to have a transfusion."

"Cory keeps blood on hand?"

"Of course not," she replied, looking down at me. "You now have a little bit of Weber blood flowing through your veins."

"Weber blood?"

She put her hand on my arm and grinned wickedly. "Since we've now slept together, I guess you should know my name. Hi, I'm Kathleen Weber."

I grinned. "Pleased to meet you, Miss Weber. Hope I didn't disappoint you, I really don't remember much."

She lightly punched my shoulder. "Nothing happened."

"Who took off my clothes?"

"Cory had to cut off your wetsuit," she replied, turning toward the hatch. She stopped and turned around. "When we got you aboard, he told me you'd been in the water too long and to make sure you stayed warm, so I took off your shorts and slept next to you."

She turned and went to the hatch. "I made pancakes and sausage. Be right back."

The flapjacks were good, and I was hungry. When I finished, I felt strong enough to get up. I'd been several feet underwater when Haywood shot me, so the bullet hadn't penetrated very deeply. Pain is a tolerable thing. It's merely a warning that something is wrong.

"Would you mind?" I said, inching toward the edge of the bunk, with the sheet over my lap. "I want to get dressed."

Stepping away from the bunk, Kat crossed her arms and smiled brightly. "Oh no. Cory said you gotta stay in bed. Besides, your body's no secret to me anymore. I examined every inch of you while you were sleeping. Just in case there were other injuries. You have a lot of scars."

She looked at me defiantly, and I felt my face flush. She certainly didn't look like a girl.

Throwing off the sheet, I swung my legs over the edge and stepped down to the deck. The pain in my side radiated outward like lava. My head began swimming and my knees started to buckle. Kat caught me under one arm and helped me back to the bunk.

"I couldn't give you all my blood," she said, rolling me onto the mattress. "Cory said you'd be light-headed for a day or two."

Groaning, I conceded the win and flopped onto my back.

"Maybe you'd better wait a bit longer, Captain Courageous," she said, pushing me over and pulling the sheet back up over me.

For just an instant, my mind went back in time. Four years ago, my late wife had often used such names for me. In my mind, Kat's face morphed into Alex's. Other women's faces came and went. Women who I'd loved or who'd loved me. It wasn't always mutual.

"Ahoy," a woman's voice called from outside, bringing me back to the present. My eyes focused on Kat's face.

"That's Macie," she said. "You stay in bed."

A moment later I could hear the two women talking up on deck but couldn't quite make out what they were saying. Then Kat came back into my stateroom, Macie right behind her.

"Feeling a little better?" Macie asked.

Did Brayden tell her about shooting Haywood? I wondered.

"I've seen better days," I replied, placing my empty mug on the dresser.

"Want more?" Kat asked, hurrying to pick it up.

"Yeah, thanks."

When she left, Macie approached my bunk. "The Bourgeau brothers never returned last night."

"They won't," I said. "I saw Mayhew on the catamaran."

Macie looked down at the deck. "You mumbled that, when we were bringing you aboard last night," she replied. "David went aboard their boat this morning. He found the turtle shells."

"They were the poachers?" I asked, as Kat returned.

Kat nodded and handed me the mug. "I knew I had a bad feeling about them. We think the killers came across their catamaran and took over somehow."

"Did Brayden say what happened after they discovered me?"

Macie sat on the bench. "He did. He said he had no choice. She was about to shoot you again. Brayden's not a violent man, Jesse. He's taking it pretty hard. But we're a community and we take care of one another. Brayden did what any of us would have done to protect one of our own."

One of their own, I thought. I'd come here under subterfuge, disguising myself to get information. In just a few days, I'd changed. Whether it was the people, the slower pace, or the surroundings, I wasn't sure. Maybe all of that rolled together.

Brayden had taken another person's life to protect me. Had he waited just half a second more, I would have killed Haywood, and he wouldn't be shouldering that burden. I decided that was something I needed to keep to myself. He did what he felt he had to do at the time. He had no way of knowing I had the drop on Haywood and she would have been just as dead had he not fired.

"She was an evil person," I said. "All of them were. Where's Brayden now?"

"He and David went out to try to find Mark and Cindy's wrecked boat."

"What for?" I asked. "Did anyone call the authorities?"

"No," Macie replied, looking down at her feet. "We don't want to get you into trouble."

"They're going to recover their bodies," Kat said. "And bring them here."

Macie left then. I could see that something was weighing heavily on her mind. And I had a good idea what it was. I'd brought violence to their little island community. Maybe it would have come without my being here, but that was the way Macie saw it.

"You need to get more rest," Kat said. "I'll wake you when they get back, okay?"

She wasn't going to take no for an answer, and I knew it. I *was* tired. I slid down under the sheet and closed my eyes. Within minutes, I was asleep. But it wasn't a restful sleep. The spirits and ghosts of my past visited me. I hadn't had those dreams in years.

Waking in a sweat, I could see the sun through the port-hole. It was just touching the horizon. Over on the beach, I could see the fire burning. It was much larger than I remembered it being the last few nights.

I watched as the sun slowly disappeared, closing my eyes to make the same wish I'd made for years. When I reopened them, the sun slipped silently below the horizon without fanfare. There were no conch horns.

When I tried to sit up, the pain in my side reminded me to move slowly. Easing my feet down, I stood and shuffled toward the dresser at the speed of rock, where I dug out a pair of skivvies and cargo shorts.

Finn raised his head and whined softly, as if he was concerned about my getting out of bed.

"I'll be fine," I told him.

I was bending to put my skivvies on, when I heard bare feet slapping on the deck. They came lightly down the companionway, then Kat appeared at the hatch. She was barefoot, wearing a black dress. She had tears in her eyes. She took one look at me and rushed into my arms, sobbing. Looking up, she kissed my lips—softly at first, then with more insistence. I returned the kiss and it became more sensual, as the rising force of her passion overwhelmed both of us, and she urgently pulled me toward the bunk.

CHAPTER EIGHTEEN

I t was early morning when I woke again; not yet light outside. Only half of the moon was visible; the other half was swallowed up by the sea, just beyond the point. A rippling reflection pointed straight at me, as if blaming me for all the world's sorrows. It would be daylight soon.

Across the spit, the bonfire from the previous night was still burning earnestly. A solitary figure moved around it, adding more wood to the hungry flames.

Kat lay next to me, her head on my shoulder and her left arm draped across my chest. She'd told me last night that the bonfire was a funeral pyre for Mark and Cindy Mathis. They had no children, nor any immediate family. The mourners were their adopted cruising family. A coded message had gone out on the net and would be spread to other mourners. As she'd told me about the couple, I'd found myself wishing that I'd met them. They really seemed like nice people.

Slowly, and with some pain, I managed to extricate myself from the bunk without waking Kat. I looked down at her sweet face in the remnants of the silvery moonlight. Her color was back, and she no longer looked as if she were on the verge of starvation. Nor did she look like a little girl. Maybe age really didn't matter in the simple act of giving affection and support.

However, the realist part of my mind harbored no illusions about attempting to build a relationship that spanned generations. On that, I knew Kat agreed. Neither of us was looking for anything more than a permanently temporary sharing of affection, and we both knew it.

I dressed and made my way up to the pilothouse, set up the coffeemaker, and turned it on. Then I went down to the lower salon, to the guest head. There, I turned on a light and slowly peeled back the bandage, while looking in the mirror.

Cory had made a diagonal, three-inch incision across the bullet wound, following the lines of the oblique abdominal muscles. The incision looked clean and his sutures nice and straight. I'd add another scar, but this one looked like it was fast on the way to healing.

Looking up, I studied my face in the mirror. Kat's blood coursed through my veins and I could see her face in my eyes. She'd given me life and for that, I'd forever be in her debt.

I was in dire need of a haircut, and the beard was frightening-looking. I kept a pair of shears under the sink for Finn. Like me, he was collecting scars. I'd had to shave off some fur more than a few times, to bandage a cut or barb.

Opening the box, I clicked the little battery-powered shears on. It hummed quietly. Switching it off, I looked at my reflection in the mirror again. Seeing the same face over and over, a person doesn't notice the subtle changes. My brown hair had turned kind of a sand color at some point in the last ten years.

I lifted the hair at my temple. There were some grays, but they mingled with the dark blond of the surrounding hair shafts after an inch and were nearly invisible. If I trimmed my hair to how I wore it as an active duty Marine, what we called a high-and-tight, the gray would show a lot more. But those days were long ago.

The gray hair didn't bother me. I was getting older. It's the reward a man gets for not dying young. Still, I was only in my late forties, with plenty of miles left.

Deep lines extended from the corners of my eyes. A lifetime spent outdoors, squinting into the sun. My skin was dark and starting to get a bit leathery-looking. I wondered what I'd look like in twenty years. Would I be completely gray, weathered, and wrinkled, like an old cane cutter?

Right now, my beard was a darker shade of brown than my hair. The gray hairs there were a lot more visible, mostly on either side of my chin, as if my mustache was dripping silver paint.

I flicked on the clippers and proceeded to remove the man hair. I didn't have a razor, so a millimeter of stubble was as close to clean shaven as I would get.

Finished, I went aft to the nav station and powered up the chart plotter and laptop, laying in a course for Tortola. It was eight hundred and fifty nautical miles. At an average five knots, sailing straight through, it would take a hundred and seventy hours, or a full week of non-stop sailing. Even if I didn't have eleven stitches in my side, I figured that was a bit too much. Autopilots and warning alarms are great, but a solo sailor would only be able to sleep in short fitful naps.

Stretching the course more southerly and following the string of Bahamian islands down to Turks and Caicos, Hispaniola, and Puerto Rico, would make it nearly a thousand nautical miles. Anchoring at night, I might make seventy miles a day, taking two weeks to reach the British Virgin Islands. I had twenty days; a six-day buffer, sailing easy.

"What are you doing up?" Kat asked, startling me.

I turned and closed the laptop. "Restless," I replied. "I'm not used to being cooped up."

She stopped in the middle of the pilothouse. She was wearing another of my tee-shirts. "You shaved."

"Not really," I said. "Just trimmed it to almost nothing with the shears I use to shave Finn whenever he runs through saw palmetto or something.

"How's your side?" she asked, going to the galley and pouring two mugs of coffee.

I accepted the offered mug and took a sip. "I checked it in the mirror. Cory did nice work, it's healing pretty good."

Kat reached up and touched my jaw. "I knew there was a babe magnet under there somewhere." She sat at the dinette and studied my face. "You're leaving, aren't you?"

"Yes, I am."

"When?"

"Today, if Cory thinks I'm able." Which meant tomorrow if she balked for even a second.

She sipped at her coffee, looking at me over the brim. "I doubt Cory telling you to rest for a week would change anything."

Rising, I walked over and sat across from her. "I have to go."

"I know," she said. "And I'm not gonna try to talk you out of it." She paused and took another sip. "We'll see each other again one of these days. I'd offer to help crew, but—"

"That'd hardly be appropriate," I blurted out, without thinking.

Kat smiled. "Baby steps, Jesse. You'll enter the twenty-first century sooner or later."

I started to say something, but she reached across and put a finger to my lips. "I checked the weather right after you got up," she said. "There's nothing in the weekly forecast between here and Tortola."

An hour later, after Kat and I had shared a hearty breakfast of steak and eggs, Brayden arrived. Kat and I were saying goodbye on the dock while Finn was rollicking on the beach with Bill for the last time.

"You're leaving?" he asked.

Kat said she had something to take care of, lifted herself up on her toes, and kissed me on the cheek. "Fair winds and following seas," she whispered. "Look me up next time you're in port, sailor."

She walked off toward the end of the dock and out of my life.

"I still say you're nuts, mate."

"You're probably right," I said, extending my hand. "I want to thank you for the other night."

"No worries," he said, taking my hand. "We look out for one another. Even after you leave, you'll still be a part of our little Chub Cay community of misfits."

"How are you handling it?"

He met my gaze and I could see it. Something was missing. "Never done anything like that before," he said reservedly. "I don't rightly know how I'm supposed to feel."

"You saved my life, Brayden," I lied. If he had to know he took another person's life, he had to feel that it was the last resort. "I'm forever in your debt."

He looked down at his feet. I could tell he was unaccustomed to someone being obligated to him.

Finally, he looked up and grinned. "Make it one worth saving, mate."

"I will."

"Sorry about your Draegor," he said, clearing his throat. "I put all your other toys back in their boxes and stashed them down in your engine room. You might wanna put them in their proper places, eh?"

"Thanks again," I said.

He extended his hand and I took it, pulling him in for a quick hug.

"What's gonna happen with the whirly-bird?"

"I'll contact a friend in the states to come and take it back to its home base," I replied.

"Gotta say, mate. Gonna be bloody boring without you around. Come back again one of these days, eh?"

"I will," I said, then called Finn.

Brayden helped me throw off the lines and I idled *Salty Dog* out toward the cut, the sun just peeking over the horizon. As I rounded the point, I could see that it was Macie who was tending to the fire. A huge pile of driftwood lay beside it.

The community would keep that funeral pyre going day and night until only the Mathis's dust remained to mix with the sand and be washed out to sea on the tide. Then the stones would be moved to a different spot on the beach and the little community would move on.

Macie waved as I pointed the bow to the right of the rising sun and set the autopilot. I waved back, looped the main halyard around a winch, and hoisted away. When the mainsail was halfway up, I inserted the winch handle and raised it the rest of the way.

I could feel the burn in my side but chose to ignore it. If the stitches didn't pull out, it would heal nicely. I'd just have to resist using that part of my body to exert force for a while. And sometimes a little pain can make you feel alive.

Moving slowly, I killed the engine and raised the mizzen sail, then unfurled the jib for a beam reach. The big boat increased speed slowly, as if sensing I was in no hurry. She heeled over slightly and soon reached seven knots in the strong morning air.

I had plenty of supplies on board, so I had no intention of stopping in Nassau. So, for right now, living in this moment, it was just me, Finn, and *Salty Dog*. The name was starting to grow on me.

Cat Island lay about a hundred and sixty miles ahead, and I could reprovision there. Rose Island, just east of Nassau, was a good anchorage and start-off point for crossing the shallow banks to Exuma Sound in daylight. Once in the sound, I planned to sail straight through the rest of the day and tomorrow night to make Cat Island before the second nightfall. I hoped I wouldn't have to, but Nassau and Exuma were there, forty and a hundred miles away, if I needed to stop in an emergency. I'd rested, my body was healing, and I wanted to sail through the night.

Nearing Nassau at noon, I turned more easterly to keep wide of the tourist island and its busy shipping lanes. In the distance, I could just make out a powerboat heading my way. As it got closer, I recognized it. Recognizing it, I lowered the sails and waited.

Detective Bingham hailed me with a bullhorn, as his patrol boat slowed. "*Salty Dog*, heave to and prepare to be boarded."

I was already adrift, so I simply sat there at the helm seat and waited.

"Cap'n McDermitt," Bingham said, standing at the gunwale of his patrol boat as a uniformed officer held it away. "I was coming to Chub Cay to talk to yuh."

"I'm not there anymore," I replied, however needlessly. "On my way to the BVI. What did you want to see me about?"

"Yuh shaved off di beard," he said, studying my face closer.

"You were coming to Chub Cay to comment on my grooming?"

"Have yuh heard anyting else about di Pence couple or dat Haywood woman?"

I didn't know what Brayden planned to do about the wreck of the catamaran, or the bodies that were aboard it. Way out on the flats, it might go undiscovered for weeks. By then, the only evidence left would be the burned-out boat itself. The sea has a way of reclaiming anything that dies.

"Nope," I lied, reaching into a small cooler and lifting out a cold beer. "Haven't seen or heard anything about them."

I offered the beer to Bingham, but he declined. "And di poachers?"

"I'm pretty sure they've moved on," I replied, opening the beer and taking a long pull as the wind tugged at my hair. "No problem in days."

"I see," he said, studying my face. He stepped back and nodded to the helmsman. "Well den, I won't keep yuh, Cap'n."

Pushing the patrol boat away from *Salty Dog*, the uniformed cop went to the helm and the boat roared away. Once clear, he turned the boat back toward Nassau Harbour.

I took a long pull on the cold Kalik as the *Dog* wallowed in the wake and small waves. I knew I wasn't a convincing liar. Had he read the lie on my face? If so, had he not followed up on it out of a sense that justice had already been served, or out of some mistaken notion of who I was? I decided it didn't matter and stuck the bottle in a drink holder. Once more, I set sail for Tortola.

CHAPTER NINETEEN

The run to the BVI took two weeks. Several days the wind had let up to the point that I'd had to start the engine to maintain headway. The boat and all her systems worked flawlessly. I'd spent most of my nights in small, out-of-the-way coves, dropping anchor just before sunset whenever I could. I avoided the crowded tourist islands as much as possible.

The experience of sailing slowly across the sea, with only the wind and my wits to get me where I wanted to go, was one I'd not soon forget. Aboard *Gaspar's Revenge*, a thousand miles could be accomplished in two days, just at cruising speed, with a ten-hour overnight stop for fuel and rest. It took several days to become accustomed to the much slower pace of sail. Then I remembered what both Kat and Charity had said, about the voyage being the destination.

The days had been long and some of the nights even longer. Since leaving Chub Cay, I'd watched thirteen beautiful sunsets, each different, yet still the same. The days of sailing, unaided by the autopilot, coupled with the utter beauty and tranquility of the tropical sunsets, soon lulled me into a very laid-back state of mind, as Jimmy would say.

On my third day out, Deuce sent me a message. He and Tom Broderick had gone to Chub Cay and returned Charity's chopper to Andros. Tom had been a rotor pilot in the Corps, but, being deaf, he couldn't get a civilian license. Of course, there wasn't anyone on Chub Cay to check it, so they had no trouble.

Deuce said he only rode along to warn Tom if a warning buzzer came on. Reading that, I chuckled, knowing that the buzzer would have been accompanied by a flashing light on the dash. Deuce just wanted the seat time.

My injury healed quickly. I'd checked in at Aguadilla, Puerto Rico and sailed the leeward side to Ponce, then on to St. Thomas in the US Virgin Islands.

I decided the incision had healed enough to remove the stitches. The constant itching when the tiny threads snagged on my shirt had been a constant irritant. So while watching the sun go down over the bay, a bottle of rum at my side, I snipped and pulled each stitch out. Without the stitches to snag on my clothes, the itchiness was a lot more tolerable.

Anchoring in Cane Garden Bay the following evening, I planned to stay aboard. It was a Monday, and if she was on time, Savannah was still six days out. While I couldn't be sure exactly when she'd get here or why she was coming, at least from what Macie told me, I knew that she wanted to be here on the first.

Cane Garden Bay was a popular, well-protected anchorage with a consistent sandy bottom. A beautiful, white-sand beach arced around the eastern part of the small bay. There, you could find just about anything a cruiser might want.

Salty Dog's bow was pointed toward the beach, her stern to the west. I quickly readied her for the night, then Finn and I sat on the aft deck to watch the sun go down. There'd be no green flash; Jost Van Dyke was barely four miles away. We watched the winter sun slip quietly into the bosom of Jost's eastern peaks. Picking up the old conch shell, I joined in the chorus of farewell horns.

"That was a good one," I said, reaching down to lightly rub Finn's neck and shoulder. His tail thumped his agreement on the deck.

With the sun gone and it still early, I switched on the spreader lights and went below to prepare something for dinner. I'd used a trolling lure during much of the crossing and had a good supply of mahi filets.

I turned on the stereo in the lower salon, and brought the old Silvertone out to the cockpit, along with two filets. The filets went on the small gas grill I'd picked up in Puerto Rico, along with a new coffeemaker. One filet well-seasoned for me, and the other with just a little black pepper for Finn. While the fish broiled slowly on a low heat, I strummed the guitar.

Sitting in the cockpit, the music turned up just loud enough for me to hear, I tried to strum along, just practicing the chord changes. Over the last several days at sea, listening to the stereo and remembering the chords Kat showed me, I'd grown to recognize and anticipate them in the songs.

After a few minutes, I put the guitar aside and flipped the filets. Finn monitored my every move. He'd grown accustomed to this new life. In secluded anchorages, he could come and go from the boat as he pleased, launching himself into the water and climbing back up the ladder.

Cane Garden Bay was different. There were more than twenty other boats at anchor around us. None were close; the nearest was more than a hundred yards away. But that was still too close for Finn to run around alone. There were just too many people around for him to go exploring. I never worried that Finn would hurt someone; he was a gentle giant. But his size frightened some people. I worried more that someone might hurt him, mistaking his exuberant play as aggression.

While the fish cooked, I sat back down and absently strummed along with the music playing on the stereo. I'd always preferred jazz, but this new tropical island music was growing on me. Maybe the ambiance had a little to do with it.

"Ahoy *Salty Dog*," a voice called out from behind me. As I set the guitar aside, my hand instinctively went to the small cabinet on the side of the table and its hiding spot.

When I turned, I saw a man in blue baggies standing on a paddle board. He was tall and thin, with a dark tan. His unruly blond hair was to his shoulders and gray stubble covered most of his chin.

"Hello," I said, rising to face the man.

Finn joined me in watching the stranger, his attention momentarily diverted away from the grill.

"Was just heading over to Myett's to see him play," the man said.

"Hear who play?" I asked.

"Eric Stone's playing tonight at Myett's. I saw you come in, and heard you playing his songs, so I thought maybe you didn't know."

"Thanks," I said, lifting a beer. "We might head in after supper."

The man's paddle dipped, and he leaned into it. "See ya there."

Finn and I ate our mahi. I also had an ear of corn, one of the last on the boat.

"Wanna go ashore and see what's happening?" I asked, leaning from the side deck and rinsing our dinnerware in the water.

Finn cocked his head questioningly, his amber eyes bright and sparkling with mischief.

"I don't know if they have clams here," I replied to the look I'd come to recognize. "You're a bottomless pit."

Going down to the galley, I quickly washed everything and put it all away. Then I went down to my stateroom, showered, and got dressed for a night on the town: cargo shorts and a faded *Rusty Anchor* tee-shirt.

With my appetite sated, I got in the little dinghy and started the engine. Finn paced the deck, as if he thought I was going to go off and leave him. He'd gotten pretty good at climbing up *Salty Dog's* boarding ladder, but he couldn't climb down. We'd learned that him simply jumping into the water from the boat and then climbing into the inflatable Zodiac wasn't a smart idea.

Turning, I pulled the little boat alongside and planted my feet firmly in the middle, calling Finn closer. He grudgingly obeyed. When he was in the right position, I quickly wrapped my arms around all four of his legs and lifted him down into the boat. He was close to a hundred pounds and most certainly not dead weight; it was always a gamble whether we would both end up in the drink.

I don't know if dogs are capable of the emotion, but he always looked embarrassed when I had to lift him into the little boat.

Minutes later, I slowed as we neared the beach. There were nearly as many dinghies pulled up on the sand as there were boats at anchor on the bay. To my right, a couple dozen beach chairs were lined up in regimented rows. I imagined most of the chairs were probably still warm from the people who'd occupied them to watch the sun go down. Beyond the chairs was a beach volleyball net.

The sound of music spilled from an open, two-story structure built on huge dock pilings. It had porch rails all around the front and sides of both floors, with tables arranged inside. The building seemed to be a part of the landscape, surrounded by palm trees, orchids, and other tropical foliage.

"You stay close," I reminded Finn as we climbed out of the dinghy.

He immediately bolted toward the first palm tree he could find. He used his fake-grass head when he had to, but there's something in the dog's nature that requires him to pee on a tree every chance he gets.

I didn't worry. I knew he'd be at my side before I reached the steps up to the entrance of the open-air bar and restaurant.

Inside, I made my way toward the bar, Finn right at my heels. The stage seemed to be the main focal point. It was festooned with decorations and posters and had dozens of lights mounted on bars above the front of the stage, pointing down at it. The music wasn't live but was coming through the speakers on either side of the stage.

I spotted a table for two in the corner and we weaved our way toward it. There were about fifty people scattered at the tables, but it wasn't anywhere near packed. The mixture of people was about evenly split between locals and cruisers.

I pulled out a chair on the far side of the small table and sat down. Finn circled the table, looking for a suitable place, and finally dropped himself onto the wood floor next to me.

After a moment, a man came over to take my order. I asked for a bottle of Carib and a bowl of water. He didn't blink at what would be an unusual request in most bars back in the States. A moment later, he returned with a dripping cold bottle for me and a scarred wooden bowl for Finn. He asked if I wanted to start a tab and I declined, paying him with American dollars. A tab meant waiting around to settle up, and I preferred to be able to move quickly.

Finn looked up at me, then down to his bowl.

"You behave and later I might add a little beer, okay?"

He licked his chops with a slurp.

The beer was cold. I looked around at the people in the bar. Many were eating—some just munching on bar food, while others had full dinners served. Though we'd already eaten, the aromas were enticing.

A familiar-looking man with long hair was moving among the people at the tables, saying hello, and occasionally handing something to someone from a small box under his arm. He was about six-foot, with big shoulders, carrying an oversized plastic cup with a straw.

"Here ya go," the man said, as he approached my table. He handed me an insulated beer holder. "Don't let that get warm."

I thanked him and took it, looking down at the logo on the side: *The Eric Stone Band.* He started to turn but stopped and looked back. "Don't I know you from somewhere?"

"Marathon," I replied. "You were playing at a friend's place; the *Rusty Anchor.*

He snapped his fingers and pointed at me. "Jesse, right? Rusty's silent partner."

I nodded, though I didn't really consider myself a partner in Rusty's business. He'd needed a stake some time ago and cut me in for a percentage. We'd argued the amount, him wanting to give me a higher cut and me wanting it lower.

"Dude, Rusty saved our asses there," he said, spinning the other chair around and straddling it. "I had a two-week gig all set up at *Dockside,* just so we could make enough money for this trip. Then they closed up, and we were short on funds to get here."

"You probably saved his ass, too. I've been telling him for years, he needs to get better entertainment."

"Thanks! Anyway, my wife's a yogi and brought her classes to that big back yard Rusty has. The ladies really loved it. That's where Rusty met Sidney."

"A yoga class at the *Anchor?*"

"It went over well," he said. "And Sidney is helping Rusty look at better shows to book."

I couldn't recall meeting anyone named Sidney. *A new bartender or bouncer?* I wondered.

"Who's Sidney?"

"Rusty's new lady-friend," Eric said, with a grin.

I nearly choked on my beer. "Rusty? A girlfriend?"

Rusty and I had known each other for nearly thirty years. I was his daughter's godfather, and I'd flown down when his wife died bringing Julie into the world. That had been more than twenty-five years ago, and as far as I knew, he'd never had a girlfriend since then. My first wife left me not long after that, and I didn't make room for anyone serious in my own life for over a decade. To me, that was a long time.

"Yeah," Eric replied. "Sidney Thomas."

"Sidney Thomas?" I said, still confused.

Eric's eyebrows did a little dance. "She used to be a Playboy bunny back in the eighties."

Now I was sure the man was off his rocker. "How is Rusty dating a centerfold?"

"Oh, I don't think she was ever a centerfold model," he said, grinning. "But she did appear in the magazine back then. She drives a beer truck now."

I knew the guy who delivered beer to the bar. I'd met him dozens of times. He was an older guy named Hank, who'd visited Marathon on vacation about a million years ago and never left.

Maybe Hank retired, I thought.

"Well, good for him," I said, scratching my chin, still wondering. "That's another thing I've been telling him he needed to get."

"He's a bit hard-headed, isn't he?"

I laughed. "Now that's an understatement."

Eric tipped his big cup. "But he'd give you the shirt off his back if you needed it."

"This is also true," I said, raising and tilting my beer in salute.

"Sidney knows every guitar picker up and down the Keys, and a bunch more on the mainland. She got Scott Kirby to play the weekend we were leaving. And I heard she was trying to get the Boat Drunks to come down from up island."

Rusty had almost always hired out-of-work fisherman who knew how to play a guitar, but occasionally he brought in others with a following. Eric was probably the best-known act he'd hired. To get names like that takes money, and Rusty is kind of a tightwad.

"Hey, I gotta get on stage. You be around for a while?"

"Yeah," I replied. "For a few beers, probably."

"Cool. Always good to have a familiar face in the audience." He handed me a business card. "If you gotta leave before my break, that's cool. But give me a call tomorrow; I'm playing a party on a friend's yacht in the evening, and we're doing some diving before that. Always room for more." He reached over and rubbed Finn's neck, then stood and walked away.

Finn cocked his head, looking up at me.

"It's a mystery to me, Bubba."

The lights on the stage came up as Eric stepped up to the mic. He took up his acoustic guitar, throwing the strap over his shoulder, and the people in the bar began clapping. He checked his tuning, then launched into a slow ballad that I immediately recognized and had even been able to strum along with.

"You know Eric?" a middle-aged blonde asked from the next table. She was sitting with another woman and two men.

"We know each other from Marathon," I replied.

"Bring your pooch over and join us," the man sitting next to the blonde said. "We're big fans."

CHAPTER TWENTY

The following morning, I woke up with a dry mouth and my head hurt. It wasn't a throbbing hangover, just a dull ache in the back of my neck and head. I'd only planned on a few beers but ended up watching Eric play three full sets while talking with two couples cruising together.

After the first set, Eric brought his wife over and introduced her. She also mentioned how Rusty and I had saved their plans to sail to the BVI, which further ingratiated me with my tablemates.

At some point during the evening, Eric asked what had brought me to Tortola and I'd let it slip that I was looking for someone.

Rising from my bunk, I decided to call Rusty and find out firsthand if what Eric had said was true. Taking my sat-phone up to the cockpit, I pulled up Rusty's number and stabbed the *Talk* button.

"Where the hell are you?" my old friend said, instead of the usual polite *hello*.

"Watching the sun come up over Myett's from the middle of Cane Garden Bay," I replied. "The weather is here, wish you were beautiful."

"Hardy-har," Rusty said. "You looked in the mirror lately?"

"Ran into Eric Stone last night," I said. "He told me some interesting news."

"He did, huh?"

"Yeah," I said. "Some BS about you settling down."

"Well, I don't know if I'd go that far."

"Who is she?"

Rusty laughed. "You take off outta here and gone six weeks, and the only time ya call me is to ask about my sex life?"

Rusty isn't one to squirm, but he was wiggling now. "Not all the sordid details," I replied. "Just curious how she lost her sight."

"She's a nice lady, bro. You'll like her." He sighed again. "A lot of folks here worried about your ugly mug. The BVI is a long-ass way from Marathon. When ya comin' home?"

Looking off to my left, I saw a stately-looking trawler moving slowly through the anchorage. I watched as the Grand Banks stopped and dropped anchor a hundred yards away, then reversed and payed out the anchor chain.

"Jesse?" Rusty's voice came over the phone, now a few inches from my ear. "You still there?"

In the bow of the Grand Banks, a blond girl's head and shoulders appeared. She waved up to the bridge and the chain rode tightened. The big trawler backed down on the anchor, pushing the flukes deep into the sandy bottom.

"Hello?"

I put the phone back to my ear. "She's here," I said.

"Who's there?"

"Savannah," I replied, watching her step out of the side hatch. "She just dropped anchor a hundred yards away. Gotta go."

Ending the call, I felt suddenly nervous. How was she going to react, seeing me here? I stood and was about to call out to her when I noticed a center-console tender heading toward her boat. It was polished white, about twenty feet, with a blue Bimini top, and gleaming white outboard. Not your typical small sailboat dinghy. A man in a long-sleeved white shirt and khaki cargo pants sat at the helm. Looking back in the direction the tender had come from, I saw a large motoryacht on the north side of the bay, easily eighty feet long, glossy white with smoked windows.

Looking back, I saw Savannah, with Florence at her side, something blue in her hand. They were standing at *Sea Biscuit's* side rail and Savannah was waving toward the tender. Her big, black Rottweiler was standing on the aft cabin roof, watching the approaching boat intently. Mother and daughter wore matching blue and white sundresses.

The tender came alongside, and the man held the two boats apart as Savannah stepped down first. Florence placed what I could now see was a water bottle on the deck. Savannah helped her down.

The man took Savannah's hands, holding them up and out as they both smiled and spoke. I could hear their voices but couldn't make out their words. He stepped into her arms and they held each other close, looking into one another's faces. Then they kissed.

I fell back against the combing, dropping my phone. It felt like I'd been gut-punched. The tender turned and continued toward a sailboat just beyond Savannah's trawler. Breathing became difficult. My mind was swirling in all directions. I'd dreamt of this day for months. I'd even decided I'd give up my island and we'd sail off together. The time we had, so many years ago, had been special. And finding her again, I'd felt that she'd known it also.

But that was years ago. I'd moved on, remarried, and become a widower. I'd been with other women since then, hurting some and being hurt, but that special feeling had never been there.

I knew that Savannah had returned to her husband, then left him again, and had a child. I didn't know anything about the ensuing years. We'd only run into each other a couple of months ago, when her sister was killed. I'd assumed from her body language, and the things I thought she'd wanted to say but didn't, that she wanted me. That she wanted me to be Florence's father.

Had I read the signs all wrong again? Of course I had. I always did. Savannah had a life for the last eight years and I wasn't in it.

The tender slowed as it approached the sailboat, a center-cockpit Morgan. At this distance, I couldn't make out the people on the sailboat. Absently, I opened the side hatch on the helm console and raised a pair of binoculars to my eyes.

Forcing my attention away from the tender, I found the sailboat. Eric and Kim Stone were waving to the approaching boat, a guitar case at his side. After a moment, Savannah's tender came alongside, and the couple stepped down into it. The man at the helm, with Savannah on his arm, greeted the Stones, then turned the tender back the way he'd come.

Setting the binoculars aside, I picked up the phone, lying on the deck. I fished the card from my pocket and dialed Eric's number. I could just hear his voice over the buffeting wind from his end.

"Eric," I said loudly. "It's Jesse, but don't say my name."

"Hey, I was hoping you'd call," he replied.

"I have to leave suddenly," I said. My voice breaking a little. He probably couldn't tell over the wind, wave, and engine noises, as the tender sped away. "Do me a favor, man. Don't say anything about me being here to Savannah."

"Huh?"

"Don't mention my name to Savannah or Florence." I had tears in my eyes. "Please, man, I made a mistake."

His voice changed. "Oh, um, yeah, dude. Don't worry about that. I'll make sure Kim knows, too."

The call ended. A moment later, the tender slowed and approached the stern of the sleek-looking yacht. They were much too far away to see, but I figured there were a lot of smiling, happy faces.

I sat there a moment, still somewhat dazed. A feeling started to rise from the pit of my stomach. An urge to get moving came over me. It was a sudden, overpowering need be somewhere else. Anywhere. I couldn't take the chance of running into Savannah on Tortola. She'd know why I'd come here, why I'd crossed some twelve hundred miles of ocean.

Reaching for the binoculars to put them away, I glanced over at Savannah's boat, and something caught my eye. Raising the binos to my eyes, I scanned the boat. The big dog was trotting along the side deck. He stopped and sniffed at the nearly empty water bottle Florence had left, knocking it overboard.

Thinking of the girl, I again wondered. Savannah maintained that she didn't know who the father was. At least that's what she'd told both Rusty and Charity, and what they'd told me. I'd never asked, and she'd never volunteered that her ex might not be the father.

I went to my dinghy and stepped down into it, telling Finn to stay put. He paced the deck as I motored slowly away, trying not to attract any attention.

Finn's tail was thumping against the gunwale when I returned a few minutes later. I tied the dinghy off securely to a stern cleat and climbed aboard. A moment later, *Salty Dog's* engine was purring, and I engaged both it and the windlass, pulling the anchor rode up in short order. I pointed the bow toward Jost Van Dyke, just a few miles beyond the bay, activated the autopilot, and went forward to secure the anchor.

With the anchor locked in place, I paused at the bow, and looked toward the island four miles in the distance. My ketch was moving toward a spot on the south shore. I could motor over in just forty minutes or so, make the Soggy Dollar by happy hour, and drown myself with cheap rum. Or...

Going below, I got a freezer bag from the galley and returned to the cockpit. Finn jumped up onto the windward bench seat and lay with his head on his paws, his sad eyes looking up at me. He knew something was wrong.

"Let's go see what's on the other side of that horizon," I told him, scratching the top of his head. I dropped Florence's water bottle into the zippered bag, threw a loop around the winch and hoisted the main.

The End

RISING CHARITY PREVIEW

Coming in early 2019

CHAPTER
ONE

Monterey, California, fourteen months
after Jesse's disappearance

On a nearly barren promontory, jutting out into Monterey Bay, stands the oldest active lighthouse on the west coast. Point Pinos Lighthouse rises above the rocky shoreline at the southern end of the bay and has been guiding mariners to safe harbor for more than a hundred and fifty years.

Unlike many lighthouses, it barely rose above the roof of the tender's home, built around it. The land itself lifts the lighthouse above the Pacific and the bay to allow its piercing light to be seen for miles.

Inland just a couple hundred yards are the artificially green fields of Pacific Grove Golf Links and El Carmelo Cemetery.

Two men had been watching from the observation deck of the lighthouse since the sun had made its first appearance over the rugged landscape. One man was tall and ruggedly built. The other, slight and balding, looked like he'd be more at home in an office cubicle.

The early morning golfers were on the course, and occasionally a car would turn into the cemetery.

"How sure are you that she will be here?"

"I'm not," the taller man replied, his voice gravelly. "You asked where I thought she might be, and this is my best guess."

"And you haven't had contact with her in over a year?"

The tall man shifted his weight, as he watched through powerful binoculars. "Correct."

"So, how do you know she'll be here?"

Lowering the binos, he looked down at the smaller man. "Like I said, I don't know. But I do know human nature, Bremmer. She was an only child, abandoned by her mother when she was very young and orphaned before reaching adulthood. I know she sailed into the Pacific a year ago last January. She could be in Hong Kong. Or she could be standing right behind me. Do *not* take this woman's abilities lightly."

"I've read her jacket."

Travis Stockwell raised his binos again, peering toward the cemetery. "Not all her training was included."

The smaller man, wearing a gray business suit, sans the tie, looked out toward the links. "You keep alluding to that but never mention specifics. Our agency wants to know more."

"Not from me, you don't. She won't want to be a part of your organization." Stockwell lowered his glasses and looked at the balding man. "By the way, your organization could use a better name."

"Yeah, well, that's not for me to decide," Charlie Bremmer replied, looking up at the former Army Airborne Officer. "We're counting on you and the others to persuade her, Colonel. All of you have said she's the only person who can find McDermitt."

Stockwell grunted. "There's another one who doesn't want to be found. What do you want with him, anyway?"

"It's not just you and Livingston who have said that he's the absolute best at infiltration."

"Yeah," Stockwell said. "There's that. He could be standing behind her, standing behind me, and neither of us would know it. But last I heard, he slipped off the deep end."

"And nobody's heard from him in over a year?"

"Have you ever been to old South Florida, Bremmer?"

"I *am* the AIC in our Miami office."

"Fishermen settled the Keys more than a hundred years before anyone even *thought* about draining the swamps to build a trading post called Miami. The people of the Keys are tough and resilient; that's why they're called Conchs. And they look after one another. He's been back there now and again, I'm sure. But nobody on those bony rocks will say anything about it to an outsider. He's one of them."

"We want him to be one of us," Bremmer said, looking through the binos once more.

"None of us have agreed," Stockwell said. "And those two? It'll take a helluva lot more than money to win them over."

"We're working on that," Bremmer said. He paused, leaning forward until his binoculars almost touched the glass surrounding the lighthouse's observation deck. "Is that her?"

Stockwell had already seen her. She'd arrived on a small scooter, wearing jeans, a blue flannel shirt, and boots, a small pack on her back. She'd parked a hundred feet from where he knew her father was buried.

The woman got off her scooter and stood, looking all around. She was tall and lean. Her hair was piled beneath a faded blue cap, but a few blond locks fell on either side of her face.

"She's beautiful," Bremmer said.

"She's also a cold-blooded killer. If you screw this up, neither of us might ever leave here. You shut up and let me do the talking."

"This is—"

"It's my meet," Stockwell said, lowering his glasses and glaring at the man. "She was my asset. And I think a part of her saw me as a friend. Now let's go."

Exiting the front of the lightkeeper's house, the two men got into a white Suburban with dark tinted glass. Though the cemetery was only two hundred yards from the lighthouse, the landscape made it faster to take the road around the point.

Bremmer pulled into a parking spot just past the cemetery entrance, and shut off the engine. He started to reach for the door, but Stockwell stopped him.

A narrow lane turned off the entrance road and ran parallel to the main road. Stockwell could see the scooter, leaning on its stand, but the woman was nowhere in sight.

"Sit tight," Stockwell said, his hands on his knees. "Roll down the windows and keep your hands on the wheel."

"What—"

"Just do it, Bremmer. She was expecting us."

"I don't see her."

"Me neither," Stockwell said. "I haven't had any contact with her in a year. And at that time, she suspected I might be trying to kill her. So not seeing her has me a little on edge. Best thing to do is sit tight and let her make the next move."

For ten minutes, the two men sat in the car, looking beyond the weathered picket fence in the direction of the scooter. The only movement either man saw was occasional crows flying from one tree to another, cawing at one another.

There was the slightest sound of crunching stone outside his window, but before Stockwell could shift his eyes to the passenger side mirror, the long barrel of a suppressed pistol was placed against the side of his head.

"What do you want?" Charity Styles asked, her voice calm and deadly serious.

Stockwell didn't flinch. He kept both hands on his knees, and prayed Bremmer kept his on the wheel.

"Jesse's missing."

"No, he knows exactly where he is. But you don't."

"We're just here to talk," Bremmer said. Stockwell winced slightly.

"Shut up, whoever you are," Charity hissed. "Or the next thing you *won't* feel is a nine-millimeter jacketed round exiting Stockwell's head and entering yours."

Neither man said anything.

"I asked you what you want."

"We want you to find Jesse."

"Why?"

"So the man beside me can ask him for his help."

"Unlock the back door."

Bremmer moved his left hand very slowly and pushed the button. The doors unlocked.

"Both of you," Charity ordered. "Left hand only; disarm and toss them in the back."

"I'm unarmed," Bremmer said.

Slowly, Stockwell pulled his jacket open with his left hand. Even more slowly, he lifted his Colt with two fingers and moved it over his head, releasing it to fall to the floor behind him.

In an instant, Charity opened the back door and slid in. Stockwell didn't have to see that she'd picked up his gun, he heard the hammer cock.

"You won't be offended if I don't take you at your word," she said, reaching over Bremmer's shoulder, and holding Stockwell's pistol against the man's chest.

Stockwell noticed that his Colt needed only change a few degrees of angle to be pointing at him. Charity used her right hand to search under Bremmer's jacket and all around his waistband. He knew that she was equally adept at offhand shooting and was more than familiar with a Colt 1911.

Satisfied, Charity sat back in the middle of the backseat. "How did you know where I was?"

"Your father died ten years ago," Stockwell said, quietly. "He was all you had."

"You got a lot of balls interrupting me. I saw you in the lighthouse."

"We were just going to wait," Stockwell said. "We really do need your help. You know the man's true worth better than anyone. Even Deuce."

"Who's this guy?"

"Agent Charlie Bremmer," Stockwell replied. "He can tell you who he works for."

"Well?" Charity asked, bumping the back of the other man's seat.

"I'm the Associate-In-Charge in the Miami recruiting office for Tactical Homeland Research, Logistics, Linguistics, Intercession and Enforcement Division,"

"Do *what*?" Charity asked. Travis grinned slightly.

"The Tactical—"

"I heard you the first time. Quite a mouthful."

"I get that a lot," Bremmer said. "We're working on it."

"And just what does this word vomit organization want with Jesse McDermitt?"

"I can only talk to him about it," Bremmer said, with a gulp.

"So call him," Charity said. "It's what I do."

"We don't know how to reach Captain McDermitt."

Charity leaned forward and glared at Stockwell. "And how is this different than what we did before?"

"For one thing," Travis began, "It seems to be privately funded. No government oversight."

"And nobody gets killed," Bremmer added.

"Seems to be?" Charity asked.

"A few others have been approached, besides me. But none of us have been given very much information. I was asked to find you, so you could help find Jesse."

Charity sat back in her seat. Stockwell and Bremmer slowly turned their heads. Though she looked relaxed, it hadn't escaped Stockwell's attention that both the suppressed weapon and his Colt were leveled at the middle of their backs.

"All I'm allowed to say right now," Bremmer began, "is that our organization is on the good side. We're well funded. And our intent is to thwart evil without hurting anyone."

"You think I care about money, Bremmer? I have more than I can spend in two lifetimes."

"No, I don't," he replied confidently. "That's part of the reason most of you were chosen. That and your individual skills."

"What individual skills would that be?"

"In your case," Bremmer said. "Your notoriety as one of the best Olympic swimmers of modern times. In Captain McDermitt's case, his reputation as a commercial boat captain."

"You're tipping your hand," Charity said. "Anyone who knows Jesse knows he never really liked chartering tourists."

"Yet he was once very successful at it," Bremmer said. "We're looking for a crew to operate, and supply logistics to, a small fleet of remarkable research vessels."

"Research?"

"The full scope of our plans will be unveiled to very few, very closely vetted, former operatives, who believe in justice and self-determination."

"Big words," Charity said. "But that's not enough to get me back into the fold. Jesse, too, considering his current state."

Stockwell turned in his seat. "What current state?"

"Mostly drinking," she replied honestly. "And hanging around with the wrong people."

Bremmer's finger tapped the wheel as he studied Charity in the mirror. "I can tell you one more thing," he said. "Our goal is to collapse the plans of those who would oppose liberty in such a way that they won't be taken seriously by anyone again."

"Collapse the plans?"

"Outsmart them and make them look like fools," Stockwell said. "I asked the same question."

"The meeting will be at the sundial at Coral Castle," Bremmer said. "At the time of the vernal equinox."

If you'd like to receive my newsletter for specials, book recommendations, and updates on coming books, please sign up on my website:

WWW.WAYNESTINNETT.COM

THE CHARITY STYLES CARIBBEAN THRILLER SERIES
Merciless Charity
Ruthless Charity
Reckless Charity
Enduring Charity

THE JESSE MCDERMITT
CARIBBEAN ADVENTURE SERIES

Fallen Out
Fallen Palm
Fallen Hunter
Fallen Pride
Fallen Mangrove
Fallen King
Fallen Honor
Fallen Tide
Fallen Angel
Fallen Hero
Rising Storm
Rising Fury
Rising Force

The Gaspar's Revenge Ship's Store is now open. There you can purchase all kinds of swag related to my books.
WWW.GASPARS-REVENGE.COM